HEY DIDDLE DIDDLE, THE RUNAWAY RIDDLE

A RETIRED SLEUTH AND DOG HISTORICAL
COZY MYSTERY

ONE MAN AND HIS DOG COZY MYSTERIES

P. C. JAMES

A One Man and His Dog Cozy Mystery Copyright © 2023 by P.C. James

All rights reserved.

No part of this book may be reproduced in any form or by any electronic or mechanical means, including information storage and retrieval systems, without written permission from the author, except for the use of brief quotations in a book review.

This is a work of fiction. Names, places, characters, and incidents are either the product of the author's imagination or are used fictitiously, and any resemblance to any actual persons, living or dead, organizations, events, or locales is entirely coincidental.

For more information:

email: pcjames@pcjamesauthor.com

Facebook: https://www.facebook.com/pauljamesauthor

Author website: https://pcjamesauthor.com

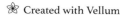 Created with Vellum

1

NORTHERN ENGLAND, AUGUST 1964

AFTER AN HOUR or two in gloomy contemplation of his retired future life, staring at the walls or weeding the herbaceous borders of his tiny garden in Newcastle-upon-Tyne, Tom Ramsay gave himself a shake and said to his dog, "Bracken, we're going to brush off the city dust and head for the mountains of the Lake District. We'll climb every high peak before summer ends."

Bracken, who was bored of his friend's moping, sat up and took notice. He understood very few words, his name being the most important, but 'climb' was one he'd heard before and always before they set out on a walk. When Ramsay showed no sign of moving from the armchair where he'd made this pronouncement, Bracken, disappointed, lay back down and waited.

"Tomorrow, we'll climb Cheviot to get us in shape. We can't not do that. Meanwhile, I'll find us somewhere to stay in the Lakes."

At the word 'climb' Bracken sat up again eagerly. Once again, he was disappointed, for Ramsay didn't move. And when he did, it was to go to the telephone on a small side table in the cramped hallway. Bracken followed and waited patiently as Ramsay went through the Lake District hotels in the phone book, receiving a negative answer at each one. All were full in these last weeks of summer.

Finally, Ramsay said, "I'll try some more in the morning, and we'll go out for a walk now. You'll run off your fidgets, and I will soothe away the melancholy of the last hour in the bosom of Mother Nature." He took his hat and Bracken's leash from the coat hooks by the door, and they set out.

Walking in the nearby park, the closest he could get to nature without driving out of town, he mused on the past few weeks where he'd once again worked with his friend Miss Riddell on a missing pets' case. With that case wrapped up, he'd bade farewell to Miss Riddell and her young sister, Jane, and driven back home to Newcastle, which had given Ramsay five hours of quiet to decide his own next steps.

His thoughts were all about recent events and what he could learn from them. *Miss Riddell was settling into her new daytime job in Manchester, her flighty (in Ramsay's view) sister Jane was off to London and a new life, while he was wandering home with nothing in mind. Life was opening up for them and closing in for him. As retired Detective Inspector Ramsay, he'd enjoyed working on the pets' case as an 'amateur sleuth.' The challenge of bringing criminals to justice without the team of detectives he was used to having under him had been exhilarating.* In truth, he realized, he was growing impatient to be doing something more fulfilling than managing annual plants in a garden.

FIDEL THORNTON, successful Hollywood and Pinewood movie producer, wandered the rooms of his shooting estate manse on the moors below the summit of Skiddaw, one of the tallest fells in England's Lake District. It was a slate stone manor house, built in the 1700s and extended with additional wings over the centuries, one of which was now his office, and other necessaries of the times. The stables were now garages, the Orangery was now a Conservatory, and the gatekeeper's Lodge was now guest rooms. Everything recently renovated by Fidel and his wife, Catherine, called Cat by family and friends, in the latest ideas of a 1950s and now 60s fashionable home.

All these expensive Swedish furniture and American furnishings couldn't, however, alter the house's location. Set behind the twin towering peaks of Skiddaw, it remained a chilly, isolated place and no favorite of Fidel, Cat, or his three children; Sophia, by his now deceased first wife, and Rupert and Jeremy by his present wife. They much preferred London and holidayed here only in the warmest of summer months.

After failing to find his daughter in any of the rooms, Fidel returned to the drawing room where Cat was flicking through a pile of magazines glamorizing the coming revolutions in fashion, furnishings, society, and sexual morality.

"Have you seen Sophia?" Fidel asked. "I've looked everywhere."

"She went out earlier," Catherine replied, without looking up from her magazine. "Up on the hills, I think."

"She's never out this long," Fidel said. "I thought she would be back. I was going to ask if she wanted to drive into Keswick with me. I have some business, and I thought she might like to do some shopping." Keswick was the nearby town, set just off the head of a large lake, Derwentwater, and a bustling place at this time of the year when visitors came from all over northern England. Boat trips on the lake, sailing, paddling, and swimming in the lake, or hiking from the town up Catbells or Latrigg if they were young and energetic, brought thousands of people every day. Although the town had ancient roots, it was a bustling modern town rather than a picturesque Lakeland village, and a place for farm suppliers rather than poets and painters.

Cat didn't reply.

"Well, I'll go," Fidel said, used to his wife pretending he wasn't there. "I may see her on the road out." He left the room, crossed the entrance hall, picked up his jacket and the Land-Rover's car keys, before leaving the house. The Land-Rover was standing outside the door, so it was only a minute later that he was heading down the long drive connecting the manse with the world.

He couldn't see Sophia on the open hillsides on either side of the half mile drive to the narrow rural lane that would take him into town.

With his business concluded, Fidel also indulged himself in some summer vacation activities beginning out on the water with a sailboat and the pleasure of his own company. It was five o'clock in the afternoon before he arrived home to find Sophia was still not returned.

"She may be injured," Fidel said to Catherine, when she said she still hadn't seen the girl. "I'll get some of the men and we'll start a search."

By nine o'clock, with the sun setting and shadows deepening among the hills, Fidel called off the search and returned home, hoping Sophia would be there.

"I'm worried, Catherine," he said, when he found she wasn't. "Something must have happened."

"She's putting some space between herself and you," Cat replied, "after that long rant this morning about her marrying Alastair."

"Girls don't run away because their father recommends a perfectly respectable, likeable young man as a prospective husband," Fidel scoffed.

"When the father pushes his recommendation too hard and too often," Cat said, "they might."

"I don't believe it. I'll phone round our neighbors and see if she's there." He left the drawing room and sat himself down heavily at the phone in the hall. By the time he'd spoken to their few neighbors, it was dark outside. He once more picked up the phone handset and dialed 9-9-9. The operator asked which service and he answered 'police.' It was a scene he'd directed in films on more than one occasion but doing it for real and for a family member was unsettling.

He explained to the police his concern and what steps he'd taken to be sure Sophia was missing.

"You say she's seventeen, sir?" the officer asked.

"Yes, what of it?"

"If she's twenty-one, an adult, we must wait a full day before taking up the case because she might have left the house and, as an adult, she wouldn't need to tell you where she's gone. If she's seventeen, however, we can start right away."

"She's seventeen," Fidel repeated, anger overcoming his concern.

"It's too dark now for a search," the officer said, "but we'll get word out to nearby police stations right away and organize a search for tomorrow morning. Now, can you give me details of your location?"

With the call made, Fidel felt better but still wanted the support of a large whisky and water. In the drawing room, Cat was listening to the radio while reading a book. Her lack of concern irritated Fidel, but he was used to that too.

Sophia was only a stepdaughter, and Catherine had two sons to fuss over.

"I've told the police she's missing," Fidel said.

"You'll look foolish when she comes home tomorrow and asks if you've now understood how much she hates your matchmaking," Cat replied.

"If she does, I'll put her across my knee," Fidel said, angrily, "even if she is seventeen. I'm worried sick."

"You've spoilt her for too long to suddenly become the stern parent," Cat replied. "It was always going to end badly; I told you so many times."

"Maybe, if you'd shown her a bit more affection," Fidel retorted.

"We've discussed this before as well," Cat said, bored by his fidgeting. "I tried. She resented me for replacing her mother. I stopped trying. We were both the happier for it."

"You were the adult—" Fidel began, but Cat's raised hand stopped him.

"I had two children of my own to look after, remember? I thought she'd come round, but she didn't. Not my fault, not Sophia's either, just life. Maybe if you'd been home more...." Her smile at this old barb was as cruel as she meant it to be.

"I did my best. Moviemaking took me away a lot, I know. It was my job," Fidel responded with all the same replies he'd made over the years. "I can't believe her disappearance today has anything to do with all that."

"Can't we just wait for Sophia to realize that her and Alastair getting married is what's best for her?" Cat asked, jumping ahead of the conversation.

"We can't," Fidel said, grimly. "I can't sell the place and we can't afford to keep it."

"Can you mortgage it?"

"I've already done that, but the money's gone. Your

gambling debts took most of it. We really need something to tide us over until she comes of age or marries," Fidel responded. "It would just be better if she married rather than we wait four more years."

"My gambling debts? What about yours?" Cat said, in a voice that declared her bored with the entire conversation. "Still, I'm sure you know best."

"I do and what's best is she marries Alastair Elliott and soon!"

"As I said," Catherine replied, "too much forceful matchmaking at breakfast. It curdles the oatmeal."

"Sophia didn't have porridge," Fidel said.

"I did and it curdled mine," Cat replied, meaningfully.

2

FOUR DAYS LATER

SOPHIA THORNTON LISTENED INTENTLY, hoping to hear something of what they were saying. She couldn't. It was just the usual low mumbling of men's voices through the solid walls and door of the cellar room she was being held in.

She'd been brought here four days ago. She knew this because she was marking scratches on the wall with her keys, which they'd left in her bag. The cellar was dark, but not wholly so. A small window, high above her head, no doubt at ground level, let in a shaft of sunlight that lit the farther wall in a bright square and the room with a pale, eerie light.

The room was bare beyond one broken, but still serviceable, chair and the camp bed with a mattress they'd placed in the room for her to sleep on. There were no rats or mice, thank heavens, at least not yet. The door was solid oak by the look of it and had clearly been fitted for the sole purpose of imprisoning her. It was the only new thing to be seen.

There were two men, she knew, and they weren't local. She may not be able to hear exactly what they said but she could hear their accents. Northeast England certainly, probably Durham or maybe Northumberland. When they brought her food, they didn't speak. Not even when she asked them why they'd taken and imprisoned her. At first, she'd feared what people used to call 'a fate worse than death,' but they hadn't laid a finger on her that way. Sophia decided that meant they were ransoming her. Her father was a wealthy man, and she had no doubt, despite their many differences of opinion, he would do his utmost to get her back. But that was four days ago, and here she still was. Was daddy being difficult? Were they asking too much, and it was taking time to raise the money? All this flashed through her head as she knelt on the flagstone floor vainly listening at the keyhole for some clue to what was happening.

There was silence again, and she rose to her feet. Momentarily, the light from the window was obscured, and she realized what she'd seen. One of the men had walked past it, his legs blocking the light. She thought she heard a car door slam and an engine start. This hadn't happened before. Were the men growing anxious at the time passing, as she was? If so, it didn't bode well for her. She shivered. She had to escape and there were only two ways out of the cellar, through the door or through that window.

She'd examined the window more than once, but now things were growing serious. Sophia pulled her bed over to below the window, stood on it, reached up, and measured its width with her hand. With her fingers splayed, the frame was just over two hand widths, say fourteen inches. She measured herself across her shoulders, fifteen inches. She did the same with her hips and found the distance to be much the same. Climbing back on the bed, she measured the window diagonally, corner to corner, about seventeen inches. In theory, if there was no glass left in the frame, she could get out through there, if she went out diagonally. In practice, there was no way she could break the glass, remove all the pieces, and then climb up and out without being caught. It had to be the door, which meant overpowering whichever one of the men brought her next meal and stealing the keys after locking him in the cellar. But there were two men.

After her initial terror at being grabbed, a hood thrown over her head, and being flung into the back of a vehicle, and after it became clear they weren't going to molest her, she'd settled down and become almost calm about her predicament. Dad would pay and she'd be released. Now, without any sign of release, and one of the men leaving, her stomach was again in turmoil. Was the one left behind going to kill her? Is that why the other left? Her watch said another hour until they fed her again. Would the food be poisoned? If she didn't eat, she wouldn't be strong enough to escape when the time came, if 'the time' wasn't today, of course.

The hour passed slowly, while she planned how she'd attack him. If the other kidnapper wasn't back by feeding time, she had her opportunity to escape and must seize it. They'd left her key ring and keys, and they were the nearest thing she had to a weapon. She practiced ways of holding them in her fist to be effective. When she finally had them comfortably in her grip with the keys protruding between her fingers, Sophia sat down to wait.

THE DOOR OPENED and the taller one of her two captors entered the room. He held a tray and the door key in his hands. With his foot, he pushed the door closed behind him. As always, a knitted balaclava covered his face leaving only his eyes seen.

"What's going on?" Sophia demanded.

He didn't reply, just offered the tray to her.

"I won't eat it," Sophia cried. "It's likely poisoned. Where is your friend?"

He offered the tray again, and Sophia put her hands behind her back.

"Not until you tell me what's going on," she said.

His eyes showed puzzlement, but he tried again.

"I've told you. I won't eat until you tell me why I'm being held here and what is happening."

This time he shrugged and backed to the door.

"Hey," Sophia cried, "talk to me. If it's money you want my dad will give it to you." It had to be money for there was nothing else about her, except the obvious, that was desirable. And they'd had four days to demonstrate it wasn't 'that' they were after.

She was still pushing herself to attack him when, using his foot, he swung the door open and stepped quickly through, swinging it swiftly closed. The bang when it shut startled Sophia into action. She raced to the door, but the key was already turning in the lock, and she was back to being alone for another twelve hours.

RAMSAY HAD FOUND it hard to get accommodation in the Lakes. Summertime was the busy season. In the end, he'd booked into a hotel that he'd never even have approached but thanks to the generous reward Magic Mal had given him for the safe return of Mittens and the substantially larger sum that was his share of the reward Tosh had provided for the return of Mimi, he could now afford. The cost still shocked him when he thought about it, and it explained why the room was vacant, even at the height of the season. Still, he opined, he was a man of means and he'd never spent a penny on himself his whole life and this was his reward.

He found he even enjoyed sitting in the bar on an evening after his day on the fells, with Bracken at his side. Posh hotels, it seemed, understood about their guests and their pets better than the places he was more familiar with. He'd started his mission to hike as many peaks as he could in his stay. So far, they'd done Catbells ridge, then High Spy, then Latrigg Fell, then Gummer's How, all small fells among those who knew, and now he felt he was ready for the big ones.

One disturbing undercurrent that had nothing to do with his hiking and everything to do with his former career bothered him. The radio in the bar played pleasant music that was broken by snippets of mainly local news, and it was that he found disturbing. A young woman was missing, a girl, really, seventeen, just home from school. Her parents and the police were anxious to hear from her; if she would phone home to confirm she was well, they could talk.

Ramsay knew these cases well. At first, they all assumed she'd run away then, as time went by, they feared the worst, and sometimes it was the worst. Often it was just youngsters acting up, angry with their parents, torturing their parents by silence. He hoped this was one of those cases, but it bothered him.

"I'm like one of them Pavlovian dogs," Ramsay said to Bracken, whose ears perked up at the sound of 'dog' and then drooped when he realized it was another false alarm.

For Ramsay, the alarm was still ringing. He'd heard the

call and felt he should do something. It was nonsense, of course. He was no longer in the police, and it was someone else's worry now. As he thought that, he smiled.

"You know, Bracken," he said, after a sip of Glenfiddich, "I'm over it. I'm cured. We're living life for pleasure now and no more horrors for me."

Bracken lay down. He'd become excited again at the sound of his name but saw now there was no walk in the offing.

The sounds of waltz music filled the bar, emanating from the ballroom just the other side of the wall and linking double doors. If he'd chosen to look through those doors, Ramsay would have seen couples in evening dress dancing across the polished ballroom floor. He didn't choose to look. It wasn't that he disliked people enjoying themselves, it was just he felt it a world away from the real world, the one he'd inhabited so long it felt like home. Ramsay finished his drink and placed the glass on the bar, wished the barman goodnight and said, "Come on, Bracken, we may have walked all day but there's still another mile in me."

Bracken leapt to his feet and followed Ramsay out into the dimly lit secluded grounds of the hotel. Perhaps, in the darkness, the real world was preparing a new future for him.

3

THE GREAT ESCAPE

MORNING CAME and Sophia sat up in bed. There were hurried sounds outside and her heart leapt. She was going to be rescued. Trousered legs rushed past the window; a door opened and closed. Once again, she could hear muffled voices but not what they said. The newcomer, if it was a newcomer and not just the other returning, had arrived in a hurry and his words were hurried too. Something was up, but what?

She heard someone approaching the cellar door and grabbed her keys again. The lock was opened and then the door. This time both men were here. Her heart sank. Never quite finding the 'right moment' last time had doomed her. She was here to the end. And was this it? Apparently not, for the second man was carrying a breakfast tray with an unopened cereal packet and an unopened bottle of milk on it. He offered it to her.

Could they have poisoned the food through the packages? They could, but they seemed to be genuinely concerned about her health. Maybe dad was just struggling to come up with the money they'd asked for.

She took the tray.

The first man took up the bucket she used for a toilet and took it away. The second watched her as she sat on the bed, placed the tray on her knee, and broke open the packet of cereal. When she poured milk onto the cereal in the bowl and placed the bottle on the floor beside her, he carefully stooped, watching her the whole time, and took the bottle from her.

"Hey," Sophia said. "I want that to drink."

He poured the rest of the bottle into the metal mug on her tray and retreated to the door with the bottle.

"Why won't you tell me what's going on?" Sophia asked. "Are you afraid I might recognize your voices?"

His grey eyes, she'd noticed them particularly when he'd picked up the bottle, seemed to smile.

"You're afraid if you're caught and I'm asked to identify you, then I'll recognize your voices. That's it, isn't it?"

He probably didn't hear all of that because he was out, and the door was shut before she'd finished the sentence.

She ate the cereal gratefully. Missing last night's meal had left her ravenous and taught her she wouldn't hold out long if they ever did decide to poison her food.

Sophia sighed. "I always did have a healthy appetite," she said to herself. "Everybody says so."

She finished eating and placed the tray on the floor, storing the rest of the cereal for later when the window was again darkened by legs passing by.

"Both of them?" Sophia thought.

Again, a vehicle started up and she heard its engine rumbling unevenly until it was out of hearing. She watched the window intently. No one came back. She moved to the door, not taking her eyes off the window, and listened.

Minutes passed. Thirty minutes passed before she decided she was alone.

Sophia had seen this in a movie once and lifted her bed up so its legs were leaning against the wall below the window. Gingerly, she climbed up with the breakfast spoon in her hand. Grasping its handle in her clenched fist, she smashed the spoon's round nose against the glass. Nothing happened. She tried again, aiming dead center and this time, the glass cracked, a long snaking crack that reached a corner of the frame. She hit the glass again and was lucky to catch herself before her hand went right through and a sharp edge slit her wrist.

Climbing down the bed, Sophia picked up her jacket, and wrapped it around her hand and forearm before climbing back up and knocking out all the rest of the windowpane. There were still jagged edges, and she spent many precious minutes breaking them off until there was no glass protruding from the frame.

Sophia laid her jacket over the frame and up the sides before pushing her head out to see she was unobserved. Seeing no one, she carefully wriggled her way through the window and, after what felt like a lifetime, found herself on a cobbled yard of a tumbledown, abandoned farm. Looking around, she could see why it had been chosen for her prison. It had no neighbors as far as she could see, which wasn't too far, for it was situated in a hollow between rounded grassy hills. An overgrown track led out from the yard, heading toward what looked like a pass between two of the surrounding hills.

Throwing her jacket over her shoulder, Sophia began walking quickly away down the track. She'd only gone a quarter of a mile when she heard a vehicle, and she dived off into a thicket of broom bushes. It was them alright.

While she'd never seen their faces before, she'd recognize them anywhere. The taller man was fair-haired, and pale skinned. She remembered his hands and wrists had been almost translucent, they were so white. The shorter man was darker haired. She was surprised to see how ordinary they looked without the balaclavas.

When the van was past her, Sophia stepped out, crossed the road, and ran to a small track she'd seen on the opposite hillside while she was waiting. It was only a sheep trail; one they'd used to come and drink at the stream that she now saw ran alongside the road. The sheep would return to their own farm for anything beyond that. She would follow the trail they'd made and find the farm it led to.

RAMSAY SAT on a rounded boulder that seemed to invite such acts. Its surface looked polished by all the backsides that had rested on it. Bracken chased imaginary rabbits through the swaying ferns. Ramsay wished he smoked a pipe; it would be particularly satisfying at this moment, he thought.

"It's like our first walk together, Bracken," Ramsay said.

Bracken stopped in his chase and looked at his friend. Did he want something?

"You were so tiny, you could barely make your way through the bracken stalks that day," Ramsay continued. "You've grown."

Bracken returned to Ramsay's side and sat, looking at him. He wasn't disappointed. Ramsay gave him a dog biscuit from his jacket pocket.

"You deserve a treat," Ramsay said, "and so do I. Our first big one is behind us, literally behind us. We've walked right over Skiddaw and now we just need a moment's rest before heading back around it to the hotel." He gave Bracken another biscuit.

Ramsay's eyes narrowed and focused on a small figure running up the trail toward them. Bracken saw Ramsay's attention shift and quickly turned to see what had alerted his friend.

What they both saw was a young woman running up the path toward them.

"She's crazy, Bracken. Young or not, that's a steep climb to run up."

As he was speaking, they heard voices, male, harsh, and angry. Then a dog, a big dog, barking.

Bracken leapt to his feet, growling, his hackles raised. His affectionate nature had led to an unhappy incident with an Alsatian only days before.

"It's another German Shepherd," Ramsay said, "and it seems as angry as the last one we met." That time, if Ramsay hadn't acted promptly, Bracken would have been badly mauled.

Bracken growled louder this time. This time he wouldn't be caught unawares.

"She's being chased," Ramsay said, the realization dawning on him. "She's running and there are men and a dog after her."

She was still two hundred yards or more from him, and the pursuers were still out of sight. Ramsay was no country boy, but he'd read books and watched films. *The Thirty-Nine Steps* came immediately to mind, and he assessed the surrounding countryside for a hideout.

Between him and the girl was a stream flowing down the hillside through a narrow gully filled with broom and gorse bushes. Below the track, which bridged the stream by large slabs of rock, the stream ran openly down to the narrow valley floor. It might work to send the pursuers off the scent.

Behind the boulder where he'd been sitting, an ancient holly bush spread its prickly leaves across a wide area. Provided the pursuers didn't round the hillside before she reached the stream and he pushed her into the prickly bush, like Brer Rabbit, he thought grimly, it would work.

He strode quickly to the bridge over the stream and blocked the way.

"Help me!" she cried as she saw him blocking the path.

"Get on my back," Ramsay said. "Quickly," He added, when she hung back. "You can't leave a scent past this stream." She nodded and he took her up in a piggyback as he remembered doing with his sons all those years ago. He ran as well as he could to the holly bush and dropped her in it, all the while watching the track where the voices and barking were growing louder.

She cried out as the thorns scratched her skin.

"Quiet," Ramsay commanded. "Hide."

She understood and by the time he was back on the trail with Bracken at his side, she was invisible.

The men and dog were soon in sight, and Ramsay took up his seat on the boulder again. All three looked like ugly customers, and Ramsay knew that if his story didn't persuade them, he and Bracken were in for an unpleasant time of it.

After stopping at the bridge over the stream, where the dog searched for a continuing scent, they came upon Ramsay quickly. "Did you see her?" the taller man demanded.

Ramsay looked at them. They were soaked in sweat and furious. The dog strained at its leash, impatient for action and not caring what that action might be.

"What's going on?" Ramsay asked.

"None of—" the shorter man began but was silenced by the other.

"The girl isn't right in the head," the man said. "She's escaped from the home; we have to get her back."

"Is she dangerous?" Ramsay asked.

"Only to children and animals," the man said.

"Just as well she didn't reach my dog then," Ramsay said. "Quiet, Bracken." Bracken was answering the German Shepherd's increasingly vocal challenges with his own. Ramsay had him on a leash but with the leash extended to keep the men's dog at a distance. As it was, Ramsay suspected the dog was catching a trace of the girl's scent. He'd removed his jacket where she'd pressed against him and folded it with the outside in and sat on it as a precaution.

"She turned off?" the man said, looking down the hill where no one could be seen.

"Up that stream into the bushes in the gully," Ramsay said, pointing back to the stream, the way they'd come. "Your dog was trying to tell you."

The man's face creased up in disgust. "You sure?" he asked, suspiciously.

Ramsay nodded. "Yes. I thought it was me and Bracken she was frightened of. It seemed extreme, but with you after her, I now see why she took such a desperate step."

The men looked at the line of bushes snaking up the steep hillside and disappearing around a shoulder of the land.

"She can't have gone far in that lot," the smaller man said. He sounded hopeful rather than sure.

The taller man nodded, and without another word, retraced his steps to the bridge. His partner followed, then stopped and turned to stare at Ramsay. "Are you sure this is where she went?"

Ramsay gazed back at him with a steady gaze. "Well," he said, "she isn't anywhere else, is she?" He swept his gaze and arm across the bare hillside and empty track.

The man nodded. "Okay," he said, "but if we find out you've lied to us, it will go hard on you. The authorities don't like people helping dangerous lunatics escape." He turned and followed the gaze of his partner and dog standing on the bridge considering their options.

Ramsay found himself holding his breath. Were they going to follow his misdirection or return and beat the truth out of him?

4

SOPHIA BECOMES ASTRID

RAMSAY WATCHED the men as they eyed up the slope and the stream. They spoke briefly. Ramsay couldn't make out what they were saying before they began climbing, one on either side of the stream and its bushes. It was slow going and Ramsay feared they might give up before they were out of sight. They didn't and finally the three disappeared around a fold in the hillside. He waited another ten minutes in case the gully ran out just around the bend and their quarry, being nowhere in sight, returned to the track and Ramsay.

"Let's go," Ramsay called softly, and the girl climbed out of the holly and returned to the path.

As quickly as they could, Ramsay wasn't quite fit enough yet for running up hills, they made their way up and out of the narrow valley and then down the other side of the rise to where the trail was surrounded by shrubs and bushes. Here they took the opportunity to walk and recover their breath.

"Are you the missing girl?" Ramsay asked when he could manage to speak coherently.

"I'm Sophia Thornton," she replied. "I don't know if I'm the missing girl you're talking about."

"Your parents and the police have been appealing for you to come home," Ramsay replied. "I assume those men are why you couldn't?"

"They kidnapped me."

"You're unharmed?"

She nodded. "I assume it was money they were after."

Ramsay considered this. There'd been no mention of kidnap or ransom in the appeals. Just a request for a runaway to phone home. *Is that the latest police policy? To hide that she was abducted. Why?*

"We should get you home as fast as we can," Ramsay said as they set off on a slow jog to keep a distance between them and the pursuers.

"I'm not going home," Sophia said. "My parents want me to marry Alastair Elliott and I won't."

Ramsay laughed. "This is 1964 not 1864," he said. "They can't make you marry anyone you don't want to."

"Oh, can't they," Sophia replied, grimly. "You don't know my father. And my stepmother's the same."

The trail was leading them to a farm where Ramsay could see a man working in the yard. He was about to point this out when Sophia stopped. Ramsay and Bracken stopped and turned back to her.

"What is it?"

"That farmer is one of my father's tenants," Sophia said, moving slowly to get out of his line-of-sight among the trees.

"We can't stand here until he leaves," Ramsay said.

Sophia looked about wildly and saw he was right. "What have you in your backpack to disguise me?"

"A light rain jacket, a towel, and my empty flask," Ramsay said.

"Does the jacket have a hood? Just covering my hair would be a start."

Ramsay nodded. All the police appeals had commented on her shoulder-length blonde hair. He retrieved the jacket.

"It isn't long enough to hide my skirt," Sophia grumbled.

The appeals had mentioned her blue denim skirt as well. Ramsay frowned, then brightened. "Wrap the towel around your waist. It will look like a white cotton skirt."

"Do you think he might wonder about the hood when it isn't raining?" Sophia asked.

"Maybe, but as far as I can tell, here it's always raining or just stopped or just about to start raining. Can you tie your hair back? It still shows at the front." He fumbled in his pocket and found the string he knew was there, one of the odds-and-ends he carried for emergencies.

With that done, they set off again, trying to look like weary ramblers as they passed the farm. Once past, and with a brief glance back to see they weren't watched, they again picked up their pace.

It was evening before they reached Keswick and Ramsay's hotel, armed now with new clothes, hair dye, and a lot of make-up purchased at a local beauty shop by an excruciatingly embarrassed Ramsay.

"You can't stay here," Ramsay said, when Sophia emerged from the bathroom, bathed, brunette, her pale English skin now suitably 'suntanned,' and wearing a serviceable but not fashionable skirt and blouse.

"I can't wander the streets," Sophia replied. "The police will want to know why I'm there."

"There's a Youth Hostel in town," Ramsay said. "That will do for tonight. We'll find somewhere for tomorrow."

"I'm starving," Sophia said.

"We'll go out to eat. The hotel's restaurant will be certain to have a customer or customers who know you."

"I've never eaten here," Sophia said. She frowned, then

added, "Maybe some of daddy's friends might though, it looks expensive enough."

In her newly bought duffel coat, Sophia looked like most of the young people wandering the streets, Ramsay was happy to note. So far, he'd guessed well for her disguise. They ate at a noisy café packed with holidaymakers and hikers, and they didn't look out of place. A hiking dad and his daughter, perhaps.

Ramsay had packed his backpack with her toiletries and his towel. He handed her this when they reached the hostel before she went inside and booked her place. With that confirmed, they arranged their meeting the following morning and parted for the night.

Ramsay walked back to his hotel deep in thought. He didn't like what he was doing; her unwillingness to go home, her desire to avoid the farmer, all seemed strange behavior for someone who was kidnapped. But unless he wanted her to run away from him as well, he needed to discover what was behind her strange belief that her parents were forcing her into an arranged marriage and, also, her abduction. Were these connected?

Sophia woke after a disturbed night's sleep. Part of the unrest was caused by her fellow guests at the hostel who seemed more inclined to talk, sing to a guitar strumming, and laugh the night away, and part was due to a recurring nightmare that she was back in the cellar and the hubbub all around her were the voices outside she could never quite understand.

She looked at her watch and saw it was hours too early

for her meeting with Ramsay. She didn't know if that was his first name or family name. She also didn't know anything about him other than he'd taken a terrible risk saving her so he couldn't be all bad.

By the time she had washed and made herself presentable enough to be seen on the streets of town, it was nearly time for him to be outside. She looked out of the window. All around, hikers were preparing to leave the hostel or, having left it, milling around in the street discussing whatever it was hikers talked about when they weren't actually hiking. It took a moment for her to find Ramsay's middle-aged figure standing at the farther side of the street surveying the young people with a stern eye, presumably looking for her.

She stepped outside. He saw her, pointed down the street into town, and they met away from the crowd who were heading out to the hills.

"Good morning," Ramsay said.

"Good morning," Sophia replied, smiling at his old-fashioned formality. "I'm Astrid, by the way."

"Astrid?" he asked.

"My mother's name," Sophia said. "She's where my blonde hair comes from. I thought it best to not be Sophia for the next few days."

"Very wise," Ramsay said, "and what's your new family name?"

"Jackson," Sophia replied. "I have relatives called Jackson," she added by way of an explanation.

"That sounds a perfectly good alias," Ramsay said. "I'm Tom Ramsay, a retired Police Inspector, which isn't an alias. Now, first things first, we eat and then we buy you walking shoes."

"Why?"

"Because the less time we spend in town the less likelihood of any of your family's friends spotting you," Ramsay replied, "and we can talk without being overheard."

"Couldn't we just go somewhere quiet?" Sophia said. "I'm not a great walker."

"Another day," Ramsay said. "Today, those two thugs who held you will be out looking, and they'll have help. Whoever they were working for, and from what you said, I assume they weren't the people in charge, will have more people to call on. That's what I want us to talk about. See if we can't find some clues in your background."

They entered a small café that was in the act of opening. As they ate, Ramsay talked of their walk today and what they might see. Sophia occasionally suggested the promised treats weren't what she considered a good time.

Ramsay was pleased with her general lack of enthusiasm and didn't contradict her. He felt it gave credence to the father-daughter trip he was hoping others would imagine when they saw Ramsay and Sophia together. After they'd finished eating, he bought sandwiches to carry for lunch and they made their way to a hiking store he'd seen earlier. Hiking boots were also not to Sophia's taste, which made him chuckle.

"Now where?" Sophia asked as they left the shop with her old shoes in a bag and her feet encased in what felt like lead to her.

"We'll drop your shoes at my hotel room and take the car to the south lakes, away from here," Ramsay replied. "They'll assume you're on foot and staying hidden somewhere nearby, if you haven't made it home, which you can be sure they'll be watching."

"I'm not going home, so they'll have a long wait," Sophia replied.

Once they were in the car heading south, Ramsay asked, "Who would want to kidnap you? Is your family very rich?"

"You don't know?" Sophia said, surprised.

Ramsay shook his head. "I don't know you from Eve. Tell me about you, your family, and their friends. Why does someone think you're worth kidnapping?"

"Dad makes a lot of money in films," Sophia said. "When he became rich enough, he bought the estate up here for mum. It's where mum was from."

"Was?"

"She died before I was two," Sophia said. "I never really knew her, though I have some small presents she bought me, and photos."

"I'm sorry to hear that," Ramsay said. "From what you've said, your father married again."

"Have you never heard of him, Fidel Thornton?" Sophia asked, puzzled.

"I don't go to the cinema anymore, I'm afraid."

Sophia found this strange, but continued, "Daddy did marry again, it was all over the news, you must remember?"

When Ramsay shook his head ruefully, she added, "He married another wealthy woman, Catherine. We all call her Cat. She's American," Sophia added, as if that explained the name.

"Your mum was well off, then?"

Sophia nodded. "It's the circles you move in, isn't it? With daddy making money, he met only other rich people."

"I suppose that's true," Ramsay agreed, "though I have no personal experience on that."

"Of course, you have," Sophia said as though speaking to a rather slow child. "You don't meet rich women because you don't get invited to their social events. Your experience is the same as everyone's. Become rich, and you'll see."

Ramsay laughed. In her reply, he could hear himself speaking. "You're right. I do only move in my own social circles. So, your father has plenty of money, and that's why you were abducted."

"Well, it wasn't for my body," Sophia said. "They avoided even touching me once they had me in that cell."

"You may not believe it right now but that was a lucky escape."

"A fate worse than death, you mean?"

"No. Generally when the motive is sexual, the woman is killed after."

"Oh. I never thought of that," Sophia said. "Somehow, I thought it would be the other way around. They'd kill me if daddy didn't pay."

"You were held four days," Ramsay mused. "Would your father struggle to raise a large sum, do you think?"

Sophia shrugged. "Everyone struggles with money nowadays, don't they? I don't have money so I've no idea how long it might take a bank or a broker to come up with the money."

"Your mother didn't leave you anything?"

Sophia shook her head. "She didn't know she was going to die, and my guess would be her will was the one she and dad made when they married, each leaving everything to the survivor. That's the usual way, I understand."

"You're right. The most likely reason you were abducted is for money," Ramsay said. "But could there be another reason? Is there something important you had to do, or attend, that they might have stopped you from doing?"

Sophia shook her head. "There's nothing. I've just left school, I'm not important enough that I could affect anything."

"That was an example," Ramsay added. "I'm asking you

to think beyond ransom."

"Still nothing," Sophia said as Ramsay pulled the car over and parked on the verge at the side of the road.

"We're here," Ramsay said, pointing at a gate in the drystone wall and a signpost pointing to a path leading through trees and, undoubtedly to the high fell behind them. Even on this summer day, what Ramsay thought was the top seemed ready for snow.

"Hey, I can't climb up that," Sophia cried.

"We'll go as far as we can," Ramsay said soothingly, as he opened the door and climbed out while Bracken sprang out, happy to be on the move again.

Reluctantly, Sophia also got out, still glaring at him.

"There's no one on the path," Ramsay said, pointing to the trail they could see above the trees. "We can talk safely there."

"We can talk safely in the car," Sophia grumbled, but closed the car door and followed him through the gate and into the trees.

"Did you ever hear them mention ransom?" Ramsay asked.

"I could never hear what they were saying," Sophia replied. "But it had to be, didn't it?"

Ramsay frowned. The family and police appeals were all about a 'missing girl.' The police would never have done that if there'd been a ransom demand. The kidnappers would have reacted badly to the abduction being made public.

"You're not happy with this, are you?" Sophia asked. "Why?"

Ramsay hesitated but decided she was old enough to hear his thoughts. He explained about the appeals. *Would she understand what their words suggested to an ex-copper?*

5

NO REASON WHY

"You don't think they'd demanded a ransom?" Sophia asked, slowly.

"Which is why I was asking if there was another reason you needed to be kept out of the way."

"Then dad wouldn't even be trying to raise money?"

"Not if he didn't know you were kidnapped and not just missing," Ramsay replied.

Sophia frowned. "But there *is* nothing else. Could it just be they hadn't yet approached my family with their demands?"

"I don't have a lot of experience with kidnappings," Ramsay said. "It isn't a very British crime. So, it's possible. Maybe the way they're doing it is to wait until the family is terrified and are more likely to settle quickly without the police."

Sophia's face brightened. "Yes, that's it. Poor daddy. I should call him and let him know I'm safe."

Ramsay shook his head. "Right now, we should assume the kidnappers are looking for you and may have connections in your family home. You stay as Astrid Jackson and in disguise. In fact, I'll call you Astrid from now on. Even when we're alone."

"Can't we let dad know somehow?" Sophia asked. "I feel bad about letting him suffer when it isn't necessary."

"Who knew you were walking on the fells that morning and where you'd likely be?" Ramsay demanded.

Sarah was taken aback. "Dad, Mum, anyone in the house, I suppose," she answered slowly. "I see what you're saying. The kidnappers were tipped off by someone in the house."

"It has to be," Ramsay replied. "I'm not picking on your parents because anyone can listen in to phone conversations in a big house with lots of extensions, or just listen at doors. We can't risk it."

"I suppose not," Sophia said, sadly. "How awful. Knowing someone in the house set those men on me, I mean."

"Are there any new servants in the house?"

Sophia at first shook her head but then added, "Actually, now you ask, we always have new servants. Only the house-keeper and her husband, the gardener, are there all the time; they manage the house all year. Every summer, the housekeeper hires temporary staff to help her while the family is here."

Ramsay frowned. This wasn't good news. "Are any of them regulars?"

"Oh, yes," Sophia replied. "Women and girls from nearby farms mostly, so they're often the same each year."

"I don't like the sound of that 'mostly.' The two men who were after you wouldn't likely have contacts among the senior staff and regulars but maids and kitchen workers, they might. What about the outside staff?"

"Her husband also has extra help, but I don't know anything about them. They don't come indoors, you see."

"None of them?" Ramsay asked. Sophia's understanding of the staff in the house was so small, he wasn't prepared to let this settle.

"Well, our Steward has extra help too, of course, and they come inside to the gunroom and the cold cellar."

Ramsay sighed. As he'd thought, there were plenty of possible suspects in the house. "We'll find out what this is about quickly," he said. "Then we'll hand the evidence over to the police and that will be the end of it."

"How will we do that?" Sophia asked.

"Tomorrow, we'll walk back to where you were held. If the kidnappers are still there, you might recognize them. If not, we'll see what they left behind and what that tells us."

"I saw them drive by in their van when I escaped, and I didn't recognize them at all. And what if there's nothing at the farm that helps?"

"Then we'll find another way," Ramsay said. "I'm a retired police officer and have experience in this sort of thing, you know. You don't hand in your brains when you retire."

"I suppose," Sophia said and stopped as they left the trees. "What is this?" she demanded, staring at the track making its way up what looked like a vertical face.

"Don't you know?" Ramsay asked, taking her arm and restarting her walk. "It's Helvellyn."

"How would I know that?"

"You live here," Ramsay replied.

"I live in London," Sophia said, sharply. "I told you. Daddy only bought the estate when he married my mother. We only come up here for the shooting in summer."

"But you've been coming for how many years?"

"Sixteen, I think," Sophia replied, frowning in concentration. "But we stay around the estate and have guests and parties. We don't climb mountains."

"Fells," Ramsay corrected her. "Did your mum have family here? Does that suggest possibilities?"

"Her family are mainly old or dead and, no, it doesn't suggest possibilities."

"You and they get along well?" Ramsay asked, as they slowly continued climbing.

"I think so," Sophia said, her words slightly shaky because she was gasping for breath. "Look, when can we go back to the car?"

"When we've seen something of the view," Ramsay said. "Do you have relations who might benefit from you being out of the way?"

"My step mum has two sons, my half-brothers. They're eight and nine. I babysit them sometimes when I'm home from school."

Ramsay continued, "There's no one in the neighborhood visiting from London who might have a grudge?"

"No one that I know of. There was a cousin, Rupert, staying with us last week but he's gone now."

"What about this young man your family wants you to marry?"

"Oh, Alastair is all right," Sophia said. "He agrees with me, but his parents are big on the alliance too."

"Why is that?"

"Land," Sophia said, flopping down on the grass. "His family's estate is right next to ours. Joining them would make it a huge family property. It's like living in a Victorian novel up here in the North. His father is right out of the Middle Ages."

Ramsay bit his tongue on her slighting the northern

counties and continued his questions. "You're sure Alastair isn't agreeing with you to win your confidence? This kidnapping couldn't be him?"

Sophia laughed. "Alastair hasn't a wild spirit in him. He's one of nature's gentlemen."

"What about his parents?"

"Why would they?" Sophia said, climbing to her feet and starting out again. "They can't imagine holding me in a cellar for days would make me want to marry into their family, would they?"

"I can't see it myself," he agreed, "but someone did and there has to be a reason. In what way 'the Middle Ages?'"

"Oh, you know," Sophia said, "head of the household, word is law, the gentry and aristocracy should rule, the more land you have the higher up you should be. All that old-fashioned stuff."

"Is Alastair's family aristocracy?"

Sophia laughed. "They were no more than gentry when Alastair's dad took over the farm from his father." She paused, "To do him justice, he has built up a sizeable land-holding and, if we were in the Middle Ages, he might be looking to enter the ranks of the aristocracy with a favorable marriage for his son."

"Then he might think a marriage settlement with you that gave the Elliotts your father's estate is something to be desired," Ramsay mused.

"I know it is, and that's why he's so pushy about it," Sophia replied. "It drives Alastair as mad as my father pushing the marriage drives *me* mad."

"I see why Mr. Elliott may have a desire for your father's land but not why your father wants you married?"

"I think it's his wife, my 'beloved' stepmother, who wants

me out of the way, so she has the family all to herself," Sophia replied.

"And if he is out of work," Ramsay mused aloud, "maybe getting rid of an estate that only brings his new wife memories of his previous wife would help the family circumstances all around, less friction and less expense. An old-fashioned marriage deal, I mean, if people still do that." He frowned. "But why not just sell?"

"Maybe," Sophia said, "but I don't care. I'm too hot and hungry. Can I have my sandwich now?"

"We're not even close to lunch time," Ramsay said.

Sophia shook her head. "It doesn't matter. I'm not climbing another step. We can see the view from here."

This was disappointing to Ramsay. He'd set his heart on reaching the top, but he could see she was serious. He opened the backpack and handed her the sandwich she'd ordered from the café and the flask of water he'd brought for her use.

"Bracken and I will go on a little farther," Ramsay said. "Stay here until I get back. And hide if you see any suspicious people coming."

"Hide where?" Sophia asked, looking around the bare hillside.

"As you eat your sandwich, you can look for a place."

"Well, it won't be another thorn bush," Sophia said, smiling. "I'm still scratched to death from the last time."

"There are ravines, gullies, dips in the land, tall tussocks of heather. Find something and stay until I return."

Ramsay had hoped he'd been looking at the top of the fell as he and Bracken climbed but, ten minutes later, standing on where he'd imagined the summit to be, he saw it was just a ridge. The summit was miles ahead and beginning to be shrouded in ominously dark clouds, which suggested rain was on its way. Reluctantly, he turned and retraced his steps back to where he'd left Sophia. She was nowhere to be seen. He couldn't let Bracken off the leash to find her for there were sheep all around and Bracken would start herding them.

"Come out, come out, wherever you are," he called.

"You said to hide when I saw suspicious characters," he heard her reply from somewhere nearby.

"I meant other suspicious characters," Ramsay said, smiling. "By the way, I was wondering, why is your father called Fidel? It's an unusual name for an Englishman."

"His father, my grandfather, went off to fight in the Spanish Civil War," Sophia replied, rising out of the dip in the land where she'd hidden. "He came back with a Spanish bride, my grandmother. It was all very romantic."

"I should have guessed," Ramsay said.

"It's why I'm Sophia, also not a very English name, but I like it because I like grandmama," Sophia said. "Her name is Sofia."

"Very international, your family," Ramsay said as they reached the car and jumped in.

"It wasn't until grandfather met grandmama and then daddy became a film producer. Since then, we only mingle with the Jet Set, really, which is why Daddy wanting me to marry Alastair is so peculiar. Even if we married and joined the two estates, Alastair can't help Daddy at all. He hasn't the right connections."

Ramsay drove back toward Keswick considering her words, until Sophia suddenly said, "We should go right now to that farmhouse where I was held."

"We'll do that," Ramsay replied, looking out for signs to Skiddaw while his mind raced on. *Who in that house tipped off the kidnappers? No man would hurt or hold his own child in a place like a remote cellar, Ramsay was sure of that so not her father or her stepmother, no matter what nursery stories told us about them. The Estate Manager's new hires were where he should start, or maybe the maids. Women could be very unpleasant toward other women in better circumstances than their own. Were they this time?*

6

THE CRIME SCENE

THANKS to the short time they'd spent on their abortive morning hike, there was still plenty of daylight left for investigating, so Ramsay was happy when he saw a sideroad leading off for the farther side of Skiddaw.

He parked close to the point where they'd passed the farm and farmer during their escape and once again, they set out on foot; this time returning to the scene of the crime. Just thinking of that made Ramsay's heart leap.

The abandoned farm, settled in the valley's hollow with the rising land behind it, looked vacant of life, but Ramsay insisted they watch and wait before searching it.

"Police work must be very boring," Sophia grumbled, as the hot afternoon sun shone down on them. There was little shade on the mountainside.

"Most of the time, it is," Ramsay said. "But there are moments when you wished it was still boring."

"Can we go now?"

"Soon," Ramsay said. Apart from the birdsong and the sheep bleating, the whole small valley was almost silent, but he knew from experience, appearances could be deceptive.

There was the farm they'd passed near the start of the valley and there was certainly a farmer there. Maybe today, he was nearby tending to an injured sheep or whatever it was farmers did on their land.

After five more minutes of Sophia fidgeting beside him, swatting the innumerable flies that considered them lunch, Ramsay nodded, and they rose from their hideout and covered the last quarter mile to the farm in a rush.

"What are we looking for?" Sophia asked as they stepped through the partly open door into what had once been the living room. The roof was gone. Slates from it lay all around the crumbling stone walls, only the beams and joists that had once supported it remained.

"Everything that looks like it has been here only a few days," Ramsay said, stooping and picking up a cigarette end. "Like this. Someone who smokes Players has been here lately."

"The tall one smelled of tobacco," Sophia said. "Here's another one." She handed it to Ramsay who placed them both in the bag that had earlier held his sandwich.

"Apart from the dishes in the sink, they cleaned the place pretty thoroughly," Ramsay said as he looked at the plates and cutlery coated with congealing bacon fat.

"Here's an oily rag," Sophia said. "Does this count?"

"Possibly, but possibly not," Ramsay said. "We know they had a van, but the oil could have come from anywhere. I'll go down and look in the cellar if you stand guard."

"I'll go," Sophia replied. "You stand guard. My bag may still be in there. I couldn't get it and me through the window."

Her bag wasn't in the room. Nothing was, other than the bed without its covers, and now back on the floor. After staring intently at the broken window where she'd climbed out, and shivering at the memory, Sophia returned to the door where Ramsay was studying its lock and hinges. They were new, and he thought they might provide a clue, but it would need police work to find where they came from. *Somewhere local, a shopkeeper would remember a man buying two heavy hinges and a gate sized bolt. He'd phone his old colleague Jimmy Logan tonight and he could point the local police in this direction.*

"What now?" Sophia asked, seeing Ramsay puzzling out the next steps.

"We search outside where they parked the van. Same with the outhouses. There's always something."

"If we have no motive, no suspects, and no evidence," Sophia said, "can I phone my dad and say I'm alive?"

"We haven't finished searching," Ramsay responded, but he was afraid he wouldn't be able to stop her for much longer and he still felt it would be unwise to let the Thornton household know where she was.

Their search widened until they came to the shed where it was clear the van had been kept. The shed still had its walls and roof intact, though its doors lay on the ground alongside the walls.

Immediately, Sophia cried, "That's my bag."

She darted forward and was about to pick it up when Ramsay called, "Stop. There may be fingerprints," he explained when Sophia looked at him in surprise.

"On the leather?"

"If the man had oily hands, maybe," Ramsay said. "But even if he didn't, on the metal catch is a good place to find them."

He picked up the bag using a stick under its strap and placed it in the bag Sophia's sandwich had been in.

"All the police will get from our evidence is what we had for lunch," she said, laughing.

He smiled and shook his head. "They can see beyond that, trust me."

"Can't we at least look inside?"

Ramsay used the stick to lift the flap and another stick to open the bag for inspection. They both peered inside, but it was empty.

"Will your parents recognize this?" Ramsay asked, indicating the bag.

"Cat, my step mum, might," Sophia said, hesitantly.

"You stay hidden again tonight, and I'll take this to Keswick police station saying where I found it," Ramsay said. "They can take it from there."

"I'd rather just head home to London," Sophia grumbled. "Lend me the money, and I'll get the night train."

"They may be watching your London home as well," Ramsay said. "Until we know what is behind all this, you should stay local and hidden."

"What can we do?"

"The van must be local, it couldn't have come far, not the state it was in, we'll find that," Ramsay said.

Sophia laughed. "It's true, it sounded like it was about to die, even from the cellar."

"And there was oil on the floor of the shed where it had leaked. They aren't wealthy kidnappers; whatever else they are."

"Where do we start?" Sophia asked.

"It starts with me calling in some help from my old colleagues again," Ramsay said. "There can't be too many old, white vans in this neighborhood."

"I see fishmonger, greengrocer, butcher, and baker vans all the time," Sophia said, "and many of them are white."

"And that's the other way we might see it," Ramsay said as they headed back down the lane to Ramsay's car. "Keeping our eyes open in town. After all, they may not realize we saw the van."

"Sounds pretty amateurish to me," Sophia said. "I'd prefer to go home and forget all about this."

"Whatever 'this' is," Ramsay replied, "isn't going to forget about you. You were kidnapped for a reason and that reason, whatever it is, probably still exists."

By this time, they were entering Keswick and driving through its narrow streets with the gray stone buildings pressing in.

"There's the cop shop," Sophia said, pointing. "You might want to go and get your old colleagues started."

Ramsay smiled. "These aren't my old colleagues. I worked in Newcastle all my life, but you're right about getting them started. You and Bracken wander the streets, and I'll find you when I'm done."

The local police were skeptical about the bag and cigarette ends when Ramsay handed them over, and he was forced to provide his now-retired credentials before they'd take him seriously. His suggestion that an old, white van may be involved was greeted with equally non-committal thanks. After telling them where he'd found the bag and seen the van, he left the station feeling there would be little urgency given to his help.

As soon as she saw Ramsay enter the police station, Sophia had set off quickly to the pawnshop she'd seen in their earlier walk. There, after some initial haggling, she exchanged her watch and bracelet for enough cash to buy a ticket and food for a day's travel.

It wasn't long after leaving the shop; she saw Ramsay exiting the police station. She stepped quickly into a door-way, tugging Bracken with her, and peered around the frame. Ramsay was heading along the street and away from where she was hiding. Grinning, Sophia stepped out into the street and followed the direction Ramsay had taken.

She saw him turn and she immediately stopped to examine a shop window. From the corner of her eye, she saw him approaching. Ramsay arrived as Sophia and Bracken stared into a butcher's window. Bracken was window-shopping, and Sophia was pretending to surrepti-tiously watch the street for white vans.

"Did they like our evidence?" Sophia asked, still watching the street and being rewarded by the butcher's van turning into the narrow entrance beside the shop. "You see? Every business has a van here in the country."

"That van's not white," Ramsay replied, "and it's not old."

"I've seen two others, and they were white, but also too new."

"We don't really know for sure the van and men are from Keswick," Ramsay said. "Now, we have an hour before we should eat. Let's take a stroll around the place and peek into the back streets."

"More walking," Sophia grumbled but set off with him, while Bracken trotted happily alongside.

The narrow streets were busier now that hikers were returning from the fells as the afternoon was sliding into evening. No one took any notice of an elderly man, young woman and dog, which pleased Ramsay. People could still see Sophia's face, even with the changed hair color and eyebrows, and he feared she may yet be recognized. He knew it was irrational. None of the hikers had seen Sophia before and had nothing to compare to. The appeals described the 'missing girl,' but none provided photos.

"Do you think they could have abducted the wrong girl?" Sophia asked in a quiet moment. "After all, people here hardly know me. Maybe it was another rich family daughter they were after?"

"What makes you think that?"

"The way one of them left the farm the evening before I escaped. I wondered if they'd just found out I wasn't who they were told to abduct, and they were going for new orders?"

"It's possible, I suppose," Ramsay said, "but I think it unlikely."

"But what I'm saying would explain why my family didn't get a ransom demand, which was what you suggested."

"It would," Ramsay agreed. "We have plenty of questions right now. Tonight, I'll phone an old colleague and get him doing some background checks."

"Inspector," Sophia whispered, "over the street behind that group of hikers. Isn't that the taller one?"

7

THE SEARCH MOVES SOUTH

WITHOUT STARING, Ramsay picked out the face that stood above the knot of people. "Your eyes are better than mine, but it does look like him. We'll watch carefully where he goes and follow at a safe distance." This would be a lucky break if it was true. He had no doubt the two men were working for someone, and it was that 'someone' they needed to find.

When the man had turned away, they crossed the street and gave chase, stopping when they came to the place Ramsay estimated the man had been standing.

"Player's cigarettes again," Ramsay said, pointing with his toe to the crushed cigarette end. "Sadly, they're one of the most popular brands in the country, so not a great help." He encouraged Bracken to sniff the remains, and they set off once again in pursuit.

Unfortunately, Bracken had interpreted his instructions as finding every Players cigarette end on the street and he dutifully performed that service until they hauled him away. By then the man had disappeared down a side street and, after peering around the corner, they followed. He wasn't in sight now, but Bracken seemed to have the scent and led them on quickly.

"What will we do if we catch him?" Sophia asked, her complaints about walking forgotten, now that they had a quarry in mind.

"Watch and take note," Ramsay said. "After all, we don't know it is him, and even if we did, there's nothing to physically link him to your abduction at this time. It will be days before the police lab has answers to the items we gave them."

"Can they get anything from the cigarette ends?"

Ramsay laughed. "Only if he wears lipstick. We don't have a way of identifying people from their saliva. Fingerprints and blood are what the labs can identify, there's little else."

"Then I don't know why we collected them," Sophia grumbled. She was jerked by Bracken to a pair of high doors in a wall. "Even Bracken can do better than that."

They studied the doors as if they would answer their questions.

Ramsay noted the number, adding it to the street name he'd seen as they rounded the corner. "Now we see who lives here and what they do for a living. Let's look around the front."

The front of the house was unremarkable; it was a normal Victorian terrace house with a cream-colored paint wash on the walls. A little shabby but so were most on the street. On the wall beside the door was a shiny sign announcing this was the offices of Lakeland Lorries. It was information, Ramsay thought, but there was no indication that the people working there were in the habit of abducting young women.

"What do we do now?" Sophia asked.

"We look in the local council rolls for who owns the company and the building," Ramsay replied, "but as the council offices will be closed, we'll find somewhere to eat and decide about your accommodation for the night."

The cafés and restaurants were full of hikers, all boasting about the miles they'd walked and the peaks they'd conquered, while consuming large plates of Cumberland sausage or steak and kidney pie, chips, and huge pots of tea.

"We'll sort out accommodation first," Ramsay said. "You might have to spend another night in the Youth Hostel."

"Why can't I stay in your room?" Sophia grumbled.

"You know very well why," Ramsay said. "The hotel will assume the worst, and we'll be thrown out or, worse, they'll alert the police."

"Nobody cares about that stuff anymore, not in London, anyway," Sophia said, shaking her head in despair at the backwardness of the outer reaches of the country.

"This isn't London," Ramsay said, shortly, "and I hope it never will be. Maybe the answer is to buy you a tent and be a real hiker."

Sophia's expression told him this wasn't an acceptable answer, and he grinned. All the guest houses they passed had 'no vacancies' signs displayed, and it soon became apparent Sophia needed to get into the Hostel before it too filled up. They signed in there and returned to town to find an evening meal.

"We could go into a pub," Sophia suggested. "They don't know I'm underage."

"If they hazarded a guess, it would bring attention to you. We can't have that happen. You must be invisible to those around you."

"I hardly know anyone up here," Sophia complained. "The chances are tiny of someone recognizing me."

"Tiny or not, it could happen. We stick with the plan for now." Ramsay saw a restaurant that was upmarket for the hiker crowd and certainly down market for the likes of Sophia's parents. They crossed the street to investigate. Inside, Ramsay noted, the customers were better dressed than they were but not outrageously so and not enough to arouse notice or comment. "This one shouldn't include any of your family's friends, and they'll probably let us in."

Sophia studied the clientele carefully before agreeing. Inside, a waiter escorted them to a table and brought menus. Orchestral music of the kind the BBC Light Program played, provided enough background noise for them to talk openly.

"After we find out who owns the building," Sophia said. "What else can we do tomorrow?"

"To some extent, that depends on what we learn from the council rolls," Ramsay replied. He was about to continue when the radio announced six o'clock and the national and local news. "We need to listen to this so quiet, please."

The national news was the same as it always was. Ramsay had long ago concluded the news was always the same: wars, crimes, and international duplicity they called diplomacy; only the names and places changed. His interest lay in the local news. This was where they would hear an update to the appeals for information about the 'missing girl.'

He didn't have long to wait. Sophia's disappearance was still high on the local media's list of events. What was a surprise was the announcer saying, 'A local lorry driver has come forward to the police saying he took a young woman down to Manchester three nights ago. Police are appealing to anyone in Manchester who might have seen a young woman around five feet four inches, with long blonde hair, wearing...' He went on to describe Sophia's clothes that were now folded in her rucksack.

"What does that mean?" Sophia asked.

"That means the kidnappers are sending the search for you down southwards," Ramsay said. "That was the night one of the two was gone from the farm, remember?"

"He was laying the trail, you mean?"

Ramsay nodded. "I presume he has something that resembles a truck and he drove it south, being sure to be seen at service stations and at some place in Manchester."

"You think all the local appeals had too many people noticing and they were scared of a search?"

"I do," Ramsay said. "Abandoned buildings were always one of the next places we looked at, in cases of missing people."

Sophia considered a moment before suggesting, "Maybe, I don't need to hide so much anymore, if the search has moved to Manchester."

Ramsay laughed. "Your parents' and the police's search may move to Manchester, but the two villains who kidnapped you will still be looking here."

"We have to do something," Sophia said. "I can't stand that Youth Hostel for very long."

"They're people your age, for the most part," Ramsay reminded her. "Join in with them."

"They're noisy, sweaty, come back from the pub smelling of beer, and then talk about hikes they've done, or worse politics, until the early hours," Sophia said. "And I wouldn't come out of it well if they knew I was from a wealthy family. Their politics are extreme."

"They're young people. They always think they can change the world and right all the world's wrongs. It's just talk." He paused while the waiter delivered their meals.

"I won't stay there tomorrow night," Sophia said firmly, when the waiter was far enough away not to hear.

Ramsay nodded. "Then after we've found out who owns that business, we'll find some accommodation that can take both of us, father and daughter."

"Wait," Sophia said, "if you're my father, your name should be Jackson, or my name should be Ramsay."

"Or I could be divorced, and your mum married again. You have your stepfather's name. This hiking holiday is you learning all about your real father."

"Sounds a bit iffy to me," Sophia said. "I think they'll assume the worst; you're a cradle-snatcher or I'm a gold digger, or both."

Ramsay laughed. "We have all night to find a better story. Now eat up and we'll get you registered at the hostel. After, we can spend the evening down at the lake until the light goes. That way you'll have less time with your fellow hostelers."

AFTER WATCHING the sunset over Catbells Ridge and the stars appearing in the still light sky, Ramsay escorted Sophia to the hostel before heading to his hotel. There was a fish and chip shop somewhere nearby; its distinctive scent on the evening air made him instantly hungry and he set out to find it. However, he hadn't walked far when, along the street, he saw two men who looked like the kidnappers entering a public house. When they'd disappeared inside, Ramsay and Bracken walked to the pub door where they stopped while Ramsay decided whether he should risk going in and being recognized or just note the place for a future visit. Then he heard, coming from inside, an old favorite, *The Skye Boat Song*, being sung by a Scot, or at least someone with what

sounded like a genuine Scottish accent. Intrigued, and
feeling a little homesick for a land he hadn't lived in for
decades, he went carefully inside, eyeing the crowd for
the men.

The bar was packed with hikers singing along with the
chorus, while on a raised dais was the singer, a young man
with ginger hair and beard. The song ended before Ramsay
had pushed his way to the bar, still without seeing the two
men. He was considering leaving, in case they spotted him,
when the singer began *The Mingulay Boat Song*. He was
hooked. He'd listen out the evening, wallowing in nostalgia,
while keeping his eyes open for the men. Ramsay remembered his father singing these songs to him as a very young
child and, ever since, he always heard them with pleasure.

Pint in hand, Ramsay pushed his way to a corner that
was empty because it gave no view of the singer. It was
perfect for him because he didn't need to see the singer. All
he needed was to hear the songs and the Scottish accent. He
sat on a plain high-backed wooden bench, sipped his pint,
Tennents Bitter, of course, and looked around at his neighbors. Young people, enjoying the old songs, was something
he would always approve of.

The song ended and, when the applause died away,
there was a clamor for more, which lasted some minutes
before it too died away. Ramsay peered around the bench's
wooden back to see the singer putting down his own pint
glass and preparing to sing again. Ramsay sat back, rested
his head against the back of the bench—and stiffened. Now
he knew why he hadn't seen them. They too had wanted an
out-of-the-way corner and were sitting right behind him.
From the other side of the partition, he could hear their low
voices and what was said was chilling.

"She has to be offed," were the first words he overheard.

The cheers muffled the reply as the singer began *Westering Home*. And Ramsay was back at home in Glasgow, his dad singing, a coal fire blazing in the hearth, and the family singing along. They'd never had enough money to go to the Hebrides, but the songs made you feel you were there.

Ramsay turned his head and pressed his ear against the wood. The low conversation had moved on.

"You know I never liked the plan," the second voice said. "It's a heck of a risk taking her to London and killing her, even if the hue-and-cry had died down."

"We both agreed to it," the first voice said. "No second thoughts now. She might have heard us talking about it and her."

"Mebbe," the other said. "That last day she thought we were going to poison her."

"We have to find her and quick," the same voice said.

"Easier said than done," the second voice replied.

"If we find that old geezer who sent us off in the wrong direction," the first voice continued, "he'll know."

"He may not still be here," the other replied.

"They'll both be here," the first voice said. "He's on holiday, and she's nowhere else to go."

"Could have gone to London," the second voice replied, "if he gave her the train fare."

"That would be perfect. She can only go to family and friends down there. She'll be even easier to find."

Loud applause told Ramsay the song was over, and it drowned out the next words in the conversation. He took a sip of beer and returned to his eavesdropping while the crowd begged the singer for more. Ramsay prayed the singer would agree, for the conspirators behind him seemed confident they weren't being overheard while the songs were being sung.

The singer began again, *Farewell to Tarwathie* this time. Quieter than the earlier songs, the audience hummed along, and Ramsay heard the conversation again.

"And we'll reward that old man and his dog for their 'help' that day," the first voice was saying.

There was a low, ugly chuckle from the other. "Aye," he said. "It's only fair we reward him when we find him."

8

SOPHIA RUNS AWAY

RAMSAY NOW REALIZED he had a serious problem. He couldn't leave his seat for the door without being seen by the two men. He could return to the door by way of the bar, which was how he came to be here. Only they might see him as he made his way through the crowd. It had never occurred to him that his own life might be in danger for rescuing Sophia. Somehow, he'd assumed her kidnapping was just to stop her from doing or saying something at a particular moment in time. That they'd always meant to kill her had only briefly crossed his mind. After all, why hold her, with all the risks that entailed, only to kill her later? This grew more puzzling the more he dug into it.

"An old man and a border collie won't be hard to find," Ramsay heard, and he looked down at Bracken who was sitting at his feet. This got worse. Whether he liked it or not, he had to get this sorted out before these men caught up with him or Sophia.

Two more songs were sung. Ramsay could hardly take them in now, as he sat hoping the two men would leave. He was certain they wouldn't take their glasses back to the bar.

They didn't sound the sort to do housework, but he couldn't be sure. If they did, they'd pass right by him, and he had to be quick enough to hide his face and Bracken when they did.

Finally, as the singer was saying goodnight, and the barman was calling 'time, please,' he heard the men getting up to leave. Ramsay ducked down to push Bracken under the table, whispering 'shh,' as he did so. Bracken was puzzled at this sudden attention and was inclined to take exception to it. Ramsay's command, however, was urgent enough to silence him.

Fortunately, Ramsay had been right about the men. They made straight for the door, leaving their glasses on the table. He watched them go. They were the two he'd spoken to that day on the trail. Even if he'd considered walking away, he had to get those two men locked up before they got him. At least, for now, he had the advantage of knowing their plans, and they didn't know where he was.

Ramsay phoned his old colleague and fellow Scot, James Logan, from his hotel room after he'd returned from the pub.

"You want something, I suppose," Logan said, resignedly, when Ramsay greeted him.

"I wouldn't be bothering you otherwise, Jimmy," Ramsay said. "I know how you value your privacy."

"Less of the smart aleck blather, Tom," Logan said. "What is it?"

"What can you tell me about Fidel Thornton, his wife Catherine Thornton, and a trucking firm called Lakeland Lorries?"

"Nothing," Logan said. "Never heard of them."

"You're not a cinema goer then," Ramsay said. "I'd never heard of him either. Fidel Thornton is the father of the missing girl you might have heard of."

"Sophia Thornton I've heard of from the police reports," Logan said. "But you know how it is with appeals for missing persons, they're always seen places miles away from where they'll be found."

"But you have been told to look out for her?"

"Of course, why? Shouldn't we be?"

"It's her father, stepmother, and the firm of the driver who says he took her south to Manchester I was asking about. What can you find out about them?"

"You should be able to dig up all you need on the film director," Logan said. "There'll be articles in newspapers and magazines."

"I haven't a way of finding back copies of all that here in Keswick," Ramsay said. "I'll never ask for anything again, Jimmy. Last time, I promise."

Logan laughed. "Tom, it's only a month ago you promised not to bother me again if I provided you with information about cars, impresarios, and gangsters. You've not got good form in the promising line."

Ramsay grinned. "Aye, right enough. But this time I almost mean it."

"Call again tomorrow night," Logan said. "I'll see what we can do. Now, tell me why I'm doing this."

Ramsay recounted how he'd found a woman's handbag at an abandoned farm. The bag had since been identified as possibly belonging to Sophia and there were also signs she'd been held against her will. The local police were working on it. When he heard on the news she may have been seen heading for Manchester, he'd called on his old friend for help.

"Help?"

"I might just be taking an interest in this," Ramsay said. "When you're walking the hills, you have plenty of time to think. I'm not investigating, though, you understand?"

"Be sure you don't, Tom," Logan said. "Real life isn't like books. We don't take kindly to people interfering in our work."

"You don't need to tell me," Ramsay said. After he'd hung up the phone, Ramsay took a bath, a book, and then to bed.

WAKING EARLY, as he always did, Ramsay enjoyed a quiet morning tea in the hotel's dining room before he and Bracken set out to meet Sophia and find breakfast.

At the hostel, he learned Astrid Jackson had already left. He frowned, and asked, "Are you sure?"

The attendant, a bored woman, shrugged. "That's what it says here." She pushed the register toward him.

Ramsay noted the time, which was well before a time Sophia would have expected to meet him and he deduced she'd decided to go home. He knew from her frequent complaints that hosteling and hiking weren't for her, and she probably just decided overnight her dad needed to know she was safe.

Thanking the woman, Ramsay left the hostel. "Well, Bracken," he said, "it's just you and me today. We'll get to the top of Helvellyn and forget all this kidnapping nonsense ever happened. I should tell old Jimmy Logan he doesn't need to do anything. I've finally retired from sleuthing. We're free as birds, Bracken, and we'll stay that way from now on."

Bracken's expression was quizzical, and it struck a chord with Ramsay.

"You think we can't walk away because those two thugs are after me," Ramsay said, "and you may be right. Still, if we moved to another hotel, in the south Lakes maybe, we should be safe enough."

Bracken's expression suggested Ramsay was being ridiculously optimistic. He lay down to await the signal for a walk or, better still, breakfast.

After their breakfast, Ramsay and Bracken set out once again for the fells, and Helvellyn.

SOPHIA LOUNGED in the corner of the carriage, a little unhappy at the decision she'd made. She should have bought a First-Class ticket but had chosen to economize and have more money for food and maybe even lodgings when she got to London. Her parent's home may be watched and not immediately available to her, had been her thinking. Now, she regretted it. Three soldiers with kit bags, and seemingly worse for drink, even at this early hour, had entered the carriage at Preston and they were attempting to engage her in conversation. She hoped someone would take the remaining carriage seats at the next stop because she wasn't sure how they'd react if she took her bag and left for a different carriage.

Fortunately, the train was soon in Manchester and the soldiers left to make their connection back to camp, as they told her. Sophia didn't care where they went so long as they left. Their place was taken by two businessmen, complete with briefcases, bowler hats, and umbrellas. Sophia felt she'd entered a television comedy sketch; they were so true to type. They, however, were more interested in planning their strategy for the meeting they were to attend and barely spoke to her after a brief 'good morning.'

Sophia watched the countryside roll past the carriage window as the train made its way south to London. She wished she'd at least left Ramsay a note thanking him for his concern for her and explaining she didn't want to be part of any investigation. Once in London, far away from her captors, she was sure she'd be safe. Still, she'd heed Ramsay's warning and be sure her parent's house wasn't being watched for her arrival.

Sophia took a taxi to her home, being careful to have the driver stop farther down the street. The taxi had been an indulgence, but the memory of the soldiers and their too obvious attempts to engage her in conversation had curbed her desire to be one of the people and take a bus or tube train. After paying the driver, and he'd driven away, she scanned the street for loiterers near her home. Her heart sank. Two men, not together but both idly lounging, were too near the front door for her comfort. She'd never reach the door and have it opened for her before they would have her.

Picking up her bag, she made her way to a schoolfriend's house nearby. They hadn't really kept in touch, but she was sure Evelyn, and her parents, would be happy to give her a bed for the night. The family, however, she learned from the housekeeper who opened the door, was away and, as the housekeeper didn't know Sophia, she couldn't have a room here.

A boy who'd been a friend in her final school years lived only a mile or so away and she made her way there. Here she was recognized and, though Peter was away, his mother, after hearing of her adventure, took her in. Over tea, Sophia explained further and asked to use the phone because her father and inspector Ramsay should be told where she was and that she was safe.

Sophia phoned her father first and, as she'd guessed, he was overjoyed to hear she was well. He couldn't stop demanding to know who, what, why, where, and most importantly, where she was now. Sophia told him, assuring him of her safety and confirming over and over that only he was to know where she was. By the end, she was glad to put down the phone. She'd never heard her father sound so distraught, and it frightened her a little. He wasn't a man given to great displays of emotion. At least I know he's on my side, she thought.

9

THE INVESTIGATION IS OVER

When Sophia called Inspector Ramsay, he wasn't in his room, and she left a message to say, 'Astrid would call again at nine that evening.'

At nine, she called, and he answered with a brusque question, "Astrid, is that you?"

"Yes. I'm sorry I ran out on you," Sophia said. "I just wanted to get away and forget everything. I'm safe now."

"You haven't told anyone where you are, have you?" Ramsay asked.

"Only my father," Sophia answered.

"I wish you hadn't done that," Ramsay replied. "You don't know who was listening or who he will tell, not knowing of the circumstances of your abduction. Your location may soon be known to the kidnappers."

Sophia laughed. "And they'll drive to London in that old van to abduct me again. Be sensible."

"Remember, one of them has a lorry," Ramsay said. "It may be more than capable of reaching London and back. In fact, I think it very likely. Even if it can't, they can travel by train as you did."

"Dad won't tell anyone, why should he?"

"Relief at knowing you're safe, or because he thinks others will be relieved to know you're safe, or someone nearby overhearing what was being said. There could be many reasons," Ramsay replied.

Sophia frowned. This seemed wildly paranoic. London was more than three hundred miles from Keswick, and the two northern villains who kidnapped her wouldn't have a clue where she was, even if they came to the city.

Before she'd thought of a reply, Ramsay continued, "Only stay there tonight. Tomorrow, find somewhere else and tell no one this time. Not even me."

As he was so vehement in his advice, she assured him she'd move and added, "And please don't do any more investigating. It was nice of you, but the sooner all this is forgotten, the happier I'll be."

"Remember what I said," Ramsay replied. "We have no idea why they took you, but whatever the reason was, it must still exist because they didn't let you go. You escaped."

Tired of this, Sophia said, sharply, "Well they can't find me now so it is over, but I'll do what you ask because I can tell that you are worried and I don't want you to be, any more than I wanted my father to continue in that state."

Ramsay felt he had to explain his concern further and said, "Your father will tell your stepmother and probably the servants in the house too. He will tell the police, and the press will hear of it. Your photo with articles saying 'sources suggest the missing girl is in London' or some such thing will be published. You must vanish from your known associates down there."

"But why would the men follow me? It doesn't make sense. In their minds, I didn't see their faces, and the police will never catch them. They're quite safe."

"They don't know you didn't see their faces," Ramsay said. "In the cellar, you didn't, but as they chased you up the track, you may have looked back. They'll be scared and feel the police may already be closing in on them."

Sophia snorted in a most unbecoming fashion. "What do the police have to go on?"

"From the evidence in that cellar, they'll know you were there. Upstairs, there was an ashtray overflowing with cigarette ends, one lot of Players and one of Woodbines. These are brands favored by working men. The ground at the farm was wet, muddy. The van will have left tracks that the police will measure to get the distance between the wheels. That will narrow the van down to a single manufacturer, maybe even the model."

"Oh," Sophia said. "They could get all that from the farm?"

Ramsay continued, "The wheel tracks will provide the make of the tires, or at least one of them, say the driver's side. So, they will have something like, 'a Bedford van with Dunlop tires on the driver, or passenger side; The van is leaking engine oil of a particular brand, say Castrol, and it's owned by a working man or men or a trades business of such.'"

"Wow," Sophia said. "That does narrow it down quickly, doesn't it?"

"It will," Ramsay replied. "Once the police start questioning Bedford owners in the neighborhood, those two will know you can't be found alive. Kidnapping is a serious offence in this country."

"Not as serious as murder," Sophia retorted.

"No, but with you disappeared for good, they, or a good brief, will wriggle them out of the charges."

"How?"

"The two men parked their van at the farmhouse when they went walking. It rained; they took shelter in the ruined building. They had no idea there was a cellar below and certainly never heard anything to suggest someone was being held there. When the storm passed, they did the hike they'd planned, returned to their van, and drove away."

"You could tell the police about my escape," Sophia said slowly. "Wouldn't that help?"

"It would, if the police have them in custody," Ramsay replied. "My fear is your overjoyed relations and friends will have given the men time to disappear on a trucking trip to London. When they return, the only solid evidence, by which I mean *you*, will have been washed out to sea on a Thames tide."

Dismayed, Sophia thanked him for his advice and returned to the drawing room where Peter's mother was waiting. "Well, dear, what did the inspector say?"

"He thinks I should move out tomorrow to a new location and tell no one where I've gone."

"That means he thinks you're still in danger. You should heed his warning. After all, he has experience from years in the police force to draw on."

"But he also told me he knew nothing about kidnappings because it wasn't a common crime in England," Sophia said, stubbornly. Really, it felt like all the adults were ganging up on her and she was a schoolgirl again.

"But he has experience with criminals and their ways. Sleep here tonight and leave in the morning. I'll give you money. Find a place to stay that none of us know about."

* * *

STANDING ON TOP OF HELVELLYN, with the world laid out below and a strong wind threatening to blow him over the edge, Ramsay patted Bracken's head and said, "This is amazing, isn't it?"

Bracken's expression suggested he'd rather be somewhere warmer, less windy, and closer to ground level. He did his best to show his friend he was in complete agreement with the amazingness of it all, but it didn't quite come off.

"I've been thinking." Ramsay said, crouching down to escape the wind and be more at eye level with his dog. "That farmer, you remember, the one on the road out of that valley from the abandoned farm? He must have seen the van go by at least once."

Bracken began to look more cheerful. This sounded like they were heading down soon. He panted and grinned.

"You agree," Ramsay said, smiling. As he was speaking, he'd been looking at the hikers on the broad flat top. They were all around, lying on the ground eating sandwiches, peering over the edge to see the small lake, Red Tarn, below, or just studying maps to find the way to their next peak. Many, however, were watching him talk to his dog and trying not to laugh.

"I think we might learn something if we were to ask him," Ramsay told Bracken, who could scarcely contain his impatience to be gone. "If we're quick getting back to the car, we might just catch him at milking time, or whatever it is farmers do in the evening."

He rose to his feet, and they set off back the way they'd come. He didn't like the look of the alternate paths, Swirral, or Striding Edge, he just might end up in Red Tarn, at the foot of the fell. "Of course," Ramsay said as they walked, "I'm not really investigating. I'm just satisfying my curiosity about those two men. They didn't look particularly thuggish, not like the ones I've been used to, but they must have some criminal tendencies, or they wouldn't have kidnapped Sophia."

Bracken, pulling on the lead to go faster, didn't even look back to reply.

THE FARMER WAS out in the yard when they drew up near the farm gate. Ramsay quickly jumped out of his car and hailed the man, who looked at Ramsay with a sour expression.

"Did you see a van with two men in it that came, and went, recently to the old farm along there?" Ramsay pointed farther down the valley.

"Who wants to know?" the man replied.

"Chief Inspector Ramsay, though I'm retired now."

"Then what business is it of yours who came and went from the old Leadbetter place?"

"I believe the missing girl was held there and they may know about that," Ramsay replied. "The other day, when I was walking, I took shelter there and discovered a woman's handbag. I gave it to a Sergeant Hardraw of the Keswick police, and they were to follow up."

The man nodded. "The police came, asking questions, and making it sound like I was involved."

Ramsay continued, "Hearing the latest news, I remembered seeing a white van with two men in it that day. I thought you might have seen it too."

"The police asked me that, and I told them," the man said. "You'd best ask them what I said, if you're one of them."

"It would save a lot of time if you just told me," Ramsay replied wearily. "It can't be so secret, surely."

The man frowned, then shrugged. "I saw the van twice,

but only one driver. I couldn't see who it was, and I didn't recognize the van. There. Will that do you?"

Ramsay was disappointed. "Nothing about it was familiar?"

The man shook his head. "Nothing," he said, and turned back to moving the muddy straw he'd been shoveling when Ramsay arrived.

Back in the car, Ramsay said to Bracken, whose expression begged for information, "I don't believe him, Bracken. He must have recognized the van. It's local and a local van and a local farmer's paths must cross sometimes."

Bracken gave him a look that said, 'Are you stupid?'

"You think he was in the plot too?" Ramsay asked. "And I'm a bit slow?"

Bracken's expression changed to one that suggested he agreed with both comments.

"You may be right," Ramsay said, "but that's enough for today. Back to the hotel, a bath and a change of clothes, and we'll have fish and chips from a real chip shop tonight. I've grown tired of expensive food."

Bracken nodded. He too was tired of tiny scraps of food that tasted of nothing and didn't fill you up. Things were looking up, nothing but walks and real food for the days ahead.

10

SOPHIA RETURNS

THE CHIP SHOP was busy with hikers and late staying day trippers, so it was after eight when Ramsay walked from the counter with his neatly newspaper-wrapped, parcel of fish and chips.

"We'll walk to the lakeside park and let these cool down before we eat," Ramsay said to Bracken, whose lust for food was getting the better of him. Keswick's town center was on the road and in a bend of the river Greta, rather than the lake and it would take some minutes to reach the park, long enough to cool their deep-fried meal.

His gaze left Bracken and turned to the path ahead. He stopped dead at the sight before him. Bracken pulled forward.

"What are you doing here?" Ramsay demanded.

"You told me to go into hiding and tell no one where I was," Sophia said. "After trailing around London for the morning and finding I couldn't afford to stay in any of the possible places, I decided to come back here. After all, if everyone thinks I'm in London, this is the safest place."

"Well," Ramsay said, "I'm very pleased to see you and

know you're safe. Down Bracken!" This last was in response to Bracken placing his front paws on Sophia's middle and licking her face.

Sophia laughed. "It seems you both are, though Bracken's pleasure is more evident than yours."

Ignoring this dig at his formality, Ramsay said, "We were on our way to the park at the lake to eat our fish and chips. Have you eaten?"

Sophia shook her head. "I only got off the train ten minutes ago. I was on my way to your hotel to find you."

"There won't be enough here for you, me, and Bracken. Have you the money to buy something?"

Sophia nodded. "I'll get fish and chips and join you in a few minutes."

Ramsay found his description of who would be sharing his meal was inadequate. Ducks and geese also liked fish and chips, it seemed.

Seeing Sophia arriving, he asked, "Have you a place for the night?"

"I'll do the hostel again tonight but make a proper effort to find a room tomorrow," Sophia replied, handing Bracken a piece of cod.

"We'll call in at the newsagents on our way there," Ramsay said. "Maybe the local paper will have an advertisement for a cottage we can take."

Sophia nodded; her mouth too full to speak.

"Are you back in the investigation as well?" Ramsay asked.

"Yes," Sophia said, between bites. "And I want to bring Alastair in to help us."

"I thought you didn't like Alastair?"

"I didn't say that. I said I don't want to marry him. We're good friends, actually."

"Is he local or another Londoner on holiday?"

"That's why I want to bring him in. He's local, lived here all his life and even his school is local, Windermere School. You might have heard of it?"

Ramsay grinned. "The only public schools I've heard of are Eton, Harrow and Rugby. I'm not a fan of boarding schools."

"That's just your reverse snobbery," Sophia said, smiling. "A detective should be wary of his own biases."

"I am, have no fear," Ramsay replied. "How do you plan to speak to Alastair without anyone else finding out about it, and can you be sure he won't talk?"

"He's a big fan of all the adventurous male heroes of books and film," Sophia said. "I'll sell him on the investigation that way. And he won't talk, he's the strong, silent type."

"And contacting him?" Ramsay reminded her of his first question.

"Tomorrow is market day here in Keswick, he'll be here with his father. I'll point him out, and you will bring him to me, well away from anyone who might recognize me."

Ramsay frowned. "There'll be people at the market who will likely recognize you."

"Which is why I won't be there, you will," Sophia said.

"Do public school types go to markets?" Ramsay teased her.

"Windermere isn't Eton," Sophia replied, making a face at him. "They provide a good education for those who need it so, yes, farmers and estate managers and owners' children do go to public schools and markets."

"I'm still hungry," Ramsay said ruefully, looking at the empty wrapper.

"You shouldn't have fed Bracken so much, and those

ducks not at all," Sophia replied loftily, wrapping up her chip wrapper.

"As we're all finished," Ramsay said, "and to get away from these ducks, let's go and get you into the hostel."

Being mid-week, the hostel still had beds and Sophia was once again admitted. "Can I walk with you again this evening to kill time?" she asked Ramsay, eyeing her fellow hostelers with distaste.

Ramsay laughed. "No later than ten," he said. "Bracken and I climbed Helvellyn today and we're puppy dog tired."

"I'm really sorry I missed that," Sophia said, laughing.

"And," Ramsay added, "we all need to get up early enough to have breakfast and be in place to see Alastair arrive and nab him before he gets caught up in the work of the market."

SEVEN O'CLOCK THE following morning saw Ramsay, Bracken, and Sophia watching each Land-Rover that arrived pulling trailers of farm produce. Sophia was growing anxious as the time slipped away, so it was with considerable relief when she could cry, "There. The green Land-Rover pulling the blue trailer."

They watched as the vehicle parked and two men jumped out, a lean middle-aged man and a younger one who looked to be of the same vigorous stock.

"You see him?" Sophia asked.

"Blue windcheater," Ramsay said.

"Go get him and bring him here," Sophia said. "Remember the secret information I told you? I fell out of a tree when I was seven and he was ten. He caught me before I hit the ground."

Ramsay nodded and quickly made his way into the

market. He had to wait as Alastair and his father herded a small flock of sheep out of the trailer and into a pen. That done, and his father in conversation with the two farmers on either side of the pen, Alastair wandered away to look for his friends.

Ramsay was at his side before Alastair had chosen who among the market people he would talk to first.

"Sophia wants to talk to you," Ramsay said.

Surprised at this odd greeting, Alastair asked, "Who are you?"

"I'm a retired police officer, and I'm investigating who brought about Sophia's abduction."

"How do I know this is real?" Alastair asked, looking around to see if there were any other strange men waiting to pounce on him.

"Sophia said to tell you about the time she fell out of a tree," Ramsay replied.

Alastair laughed. "I told her the branches weren't strong enough, but she wouldn't listen."

"But you caught her."

"Of course. She was a nuisance, but you can't help liking her."

"She's waiting not far away, can you come without raising interest in where you are?"

Alastair nodded. "Nothing will happen till the market opens."

As they walked, Ramsay introduced himself and gave Alastair some of the background to Sophia's disappearance. He had high hopes of young Alastair until they arrived where Sophia and Bracken were waiting and Alastair said, "You do look odd, Soph."

"I'm in disguise," Sophia replied. "Do you like it?"

"It may grow on me," Alastair replied, grinning.

"You can't tell anyone you've seen me," Sophia said.

"I see being kidnapped hasn't dulled your bossiness," Alastair replied.

"I'm not bossy, I'm decisive," Sophia stated firmly. This was clearly a discussion they'd had many times.

"Sophia is right, though," Ramsay said. "We're relying on you to say nothing about this meeting if you decide not to join us."

"Join you in sleuthing?" Alastair asked.

"What else, dummy?" Sophia said, scornfully. "It wasn't the pleasure of your company that brought us here, though you can be good company when you try," she added in a more conciliatory tone.

"I'm in," Alastair said, "provided the leader of this band of investigators is Inspector Ramsay and not you, Soph."

"Why not me?" Sophia cried; her spirits aroused at this slight.

"Because you have no process. You'll hop from one clue to the next before anything's finished and we'll get nowhere," Alastair said, a martial look in his eye.

Ramsay stepped in. "I can see you two have a long history of quarrels to be resolved, but for the next few days, I need you both to forget all that and concentrate on the here and now. Can you do that?"

The two smoldering antagonists thought for a moment, then Sophia said, "I can if he can."

"And I will, gladly," Alastair said.

"Good enough," Ramsay said. "How are you going to slip away from your parents for long periods of time, Alastair?"

"I'm often away from the house," Alastair said. "We have a boat on the lake, which I sail whenever I can, and I've friends I often go shooting with. It won't be a problem."

"What about today?"

"I'll tell Dad, I'm off, and then I'm free."

"Do that," Ramsay said, "and meet us back here as soon as you can."

* * *

"WHAT DID THOSE MEN WANT?" Cat asked Fidel when he returned to the room. She'd seen the Lakeland Lorries van drive up to the house and stop at the trades entrance and hadn't liked the look of the two men who exited the van.

"I've hired them to take some of the game birds to Penrith station for the afternoon express to London," Fidel said. "Randall's Restaurant has bought from us again, and I want to be sure the birds are there in good time."

"That's good," Cat said, but her tone spoke of her disinterest.

"Yes, it is good," Fidel responded sharply. "You know how much it costs to keep this place going. If we can't sell the birds we shoot, it eats into our capital."

"Particularly now you're between contracts," Cat said.

"I'll get something soon," Fidel replied, testily. "That last movie should have done well. It was what the public wanted. I may have been a bit over the top with the *avant garde* pacing, but that's no reason for the studio to behave the way they did."

"A failed film eats into *their* capital too, I expect," Cat said, turning the page of her magazine.

"They're rolling in it," Fidel said. "It was that new board member. I could tell he didn't like me from the start."

"Well, as you say, another studio will call soon."

"And in the meantime, we need all our assets to pay their way, particularly this estate."

"That will is a nuisance," Cat said. "If only Sophia had liked Alastair."

Fidel nodded. "She does like Alastair, and he likes her. I'm not wrong about it. They're just at that difficult time where they don't know what's what."

"Pushing too hard will drive them apart," Cat said evenly. "She'll marry someone else out of spite."

"Well, she's safe now and obviously forgiven me enough to let us know where she is so I think it will be all right in the long run."

"I thought you said we couldn't wait for the 'long run?'" Cat replied.

Fidel bit his lip anxiously. "In this case, the 'long run' can't be more than a few weeks."

Cat frowned. "You think if Sophia can be persuaded to marry Alastair soon, his father will pay money for this estate? Won't he think it odd to be asked?"

"He's so hungry for it," Fidel replied, "when I offer to give it as a shared wedding gift, he'll bite. I know he will. Then we'll have working capital and reduced expenses and enough to see off the worst of our creditors."

"Elliott is a businessman, Fidel, not a simpleton. You won't easily part him from his money."

"He'll jump at it, you'll see."

11

NOW THERE ARE THREE SLEUTHS

"I'M BACK," Alastair said.

Ramsay and Sophia had been so engrossed watching the boats on the lake they hadn't heard him arrive.

"About time," Sophia said.

Alastair grinned but ignored this obvious ploy to start another squabble. "Where do we start?"

"We'll start with Lakeland Lorries," Ramsay said, "but first I'm interested in hearing anything you might know about the Thornton estate manager and his assistant.

"Dad will know all about them," Alastair said, grinning. "He watches everything that goes on there like a hawk."

"Charming," Sophia interjected disgustedly.

"Do *you* know anything about them? Alastair," Ramsay persisted before Alastair could respond to Sophia.

"The manager's name's Prescott and he lives over near Cockermouth," Alastair said. "He isn't full-time, and I don't know who his assistant is this year. I could find out if you think it's important."

"I think he or his assistant are the most likely to be the

informants in the house," Ramsay replied, "so, yes, I do think it important."

"Why them?" Alastair asked.

"It's just a hunch," Ramsay said, "but Sophia says the temporary maids are local farming folk. I just don't see them as spies for kidnappers."

Alastair nodded. "You're probably right."

"Then ask your father and find out what you can," Ramsay said quickly. "Now, what do you know about Lakeland Lorries?"

Alastair shrugged. "They're a local company, not very successful, but Dad uses them occasionally if we have things to be transported locally. Why?"

"Do you know what the owners look like?" Sophia demanded.

Alastair shook his head. "Can't say I do. Dad handles all that stuff and, until recently, I've been in school most of the time."

"We'll take a walk to their offices and see if anything strikes you," Ramsay said.

"And if it doesn't?"

"Then you can go in and ask to see the boss because you might have a job for them," Ramsay said.

"Wouldn't that be better coming from you?" Alastair asked. "To them, I'll just look like a kid. They won't believe I have anything to transport."

"But your dad does," Ramsay said. "They'll know you, even if you don't know them."

"What if they phone my home later?"

"You say, quite rightly, you never mentioned your father and your interest was someone to take your belongings to university."

Alastair was thoughtful for a moment. "It might work,"

he said. "Let's go." He paused, before saying, "Hey, you never told me why this place is of interest."

When he saw Sophia preparing a cutting remark, Ramsay jumped in to explain more about the kidnapping, the van, and the two men.

"I see," Alastair said. He grinned. "I'm surprised Soph had to escape, I'd have thought any right-minded man would send her back after one day, let alone four."

Sophia punched his arm, and Alastair's grin grew broader. "But I don't hold with kidnapping so it's time for us to set this straight." He marched off across the road and entered the office door.

"Now you see why I don't want to marry him," Sophia said to Ramsay.

Ramsay smiled but didn't reply.

AFTER ONLY FIVE minutes of watching the Lakeland Lorries office door, Sophia said, "I'm bored. We need to get in there and look about."

Fortunately, that was the moment Alastair left the offices and returned. He quickly explained, "The bosses are out on a job, their receptionist says, and she doesn't know where, but they won't be too long, she thinks."

"A local delivery then," Ramsay said. "We'll come back later and try again."

"What do we do in the meantime?" Sophia asked.

"Do you know the owner of the farm that's in the valley where the old Leadbetter farm was?" Ramsay asked Alastair.

Alastair nodded. "Though he's not one of our tenants. He's a tenant of Soph's dad."

"Could you get him to talk about a white van and its driver going up to the old farmhouse?"

Alastair made a face. "I can try, but Jim Thorogood isn't the most welcoming or communicative of men."

Ramsay smiled. "I noticed."

"How would I do it, though?" Alastair asked. "Introduce it into a conversation, I mean."

"Tell him you heard Sophia was being held there and you're investigating because Sophia means so much to you," Ramsay said.

"Hah!" said Sophia.

"You're kidding," Alastair cried. "He won't believe that."

"Nor should he," Sophia interjected. "You care for nobody but your blasted estate."

"He won't know about the quarrels you have had and, even if he did, he'd put it down to teenage nonsense," Ramsay replied.

Both parties took exception to this, and it was some time before Ramsay could remind them they were investigating a kidnapping and that meant using subterfuge sometimes.

Mollified, the two simply glared at him while he suggested the course of action. "You can drive, I assume," Ramsay said to Alastair.

"Of course, but I don't have a car and Dad has the Land-Rover at the market."

"He won't need it until late afternoon, will he?"

"No, I suppose not," Alastair said. His expression was troubled as he considered ways to persuade his father to hand over the keys without giving away the reason.

"I'll tell him I'm going to sail the boat," he said at last.

"We'll follow behind at a distance," Ramsay told him. "That way Mr. Thorogood doesn't see us. He'd recognize me and my car."

. . .

ALASTAIR HAD no trouble getting the keys and soon he was on the road for Skiddaw with Ramsay, Bracken, and Sophia following.

"Do you think Mr. Thorogood knew what was going on?" Sophia asked, stroking Bracken.

"It's a possibility," Ramsay said. "You'd imagine he'd wonder what was happening."

"They didn't go out much," Sophia remembered, "so there may not have been enough activity to make him suspicious."

Ramsay nodded. "Maybe. And maybe in that old farmhouse of his, he has no radio and doesn't take a newspaper."

"That's quite likely," Sophia said. "Some of the older, more isolated farms are only just getting electricity."

The two vehicles left the paved road and set out along the unpaved track leading into the valley. After a few minutes, Ramsay said, "I'll park here. I think, when we round that corner ahead, we will see Thorogood's farm and that means he'd see this car. We'll walk from here, keeping below the wall so we aren't seen."

"I'm happy staying with the car," Sophia said. "Alastair can look after himself."

"I'm not concerned for Alastair," Ramsay said. "My concern is hearing directly what Thorogood says rather than hearing it interpreted by Alastair."

"You don't trust him?"

"It's not that," Ramsay said. "He hasn't the experience of listening to people, their tone, and the words they use to answer questions." With this, Ramsay set off quickly, stooping low so he couldn't be seen behind the dry-stone wall that bordered the field to his left.

He was breathless by the time he grew near enough to hear Alastair and Thorogood talking.

"It's my business," he heard Alastair say, hotly, "because it was Sophia Thornton being held there."

"Who told you that?"

"A man I met, a retired policeman, he said he'd found evidence she'd been held there," Alastair replied. "And I believe him."

"Bigger fool you," Thorogood said. "That bloke came here asking questions a day or so ago. He's not from round here and shouldn't be poking his nose into other people's business."

"Don't you understand?" Alastair was almost shouting now. "Your landlord's daughter was being held there for heaven knows what reason and you think the policeman should mind his own business?"

"The police were here too," Thorogood said. "They didn't say there was evidence she was held there. They said it was possible, and I'm telling you that's rubbish. I'd have known if something like that was happening."

"Did you see a white van going up this track?" Alastair asked calmly, having taken hold of his emotions.

"Aye, I did," Thorogood said. "Two fellas out walking. That's what they told me."

"Did you recognize them?"

"Nay, visitors most like," Thorogood said.

"The van didn't have Lakeland Lorries on the side, did it?"

"Nay, and the two men weren't the owners of Lakeland Lorries," Thorogood replied. "I know those two. I've used them once or twice to make deliveries for me."

"Could you describe the men?"

"I've told the police this already."

"Well, tell me, please," Alastair said. "I'm going to find Sophia if it kills me."

"She ran away from home, is what I heard," Thorogood said, "or was it you she was running away from?"

"Just describe the men, please." Alastair's voice was now hard, cold.

"One was tall, fair-haired, and the other was shorter, more my height, and thinning brown hair. They were ordinary working blokes, nothing special."

"You didn't see any distinguishing marks?"

"The shorter one had an old scar near his left eye," Thorogood said, "crescent shaped, following the cheekbone."

"Nothing about the tall one?"

"Not that I recall," Thorogood replied. "They both smoked, that I do know. Brown fingers. You can allus tell."

"The van, what do you remember about that?"

"An old white Bedford van with the rear bumper missing," Thorogood said. "You'll see a dozen like it on any day in Keswick."

"And there's nothing else you can add?"

"A decent fella would offer to buy a pint or two for all this information I'm giving you," was Thorogood's answer.

"Tell me," Alastair said, "and I'll buy you a whole night of pints."

"When I see you're serious."

Ramsay could hear Alastair drawing notes from his wallet.

"Five pounds if your additional information is worth it," Alastair said. "Two pounds if it doesn't add anything much to what you've told me already."

Obviously, this was acceptable because Thorogood said, "The two men were Geordies, not from round here. One was called Paddy and the other Ned."

"Thank you," Alastair replied. "There's nothing else?"

"Nothing."

Ramsay began making his way quickly back to the car, so Alastair didn't give his presence away when he saw him. He was halfway back when Alastair, driving the Land-Rover, caught him up.

Leaning out of the vehicle's window, Alastair said, "Need a lift?"

"No and keep going," Ramsay said brusquely.

Alastair continued, passing Ramsay's old Ford Popular and waving to Sophia who waved back.

Ramsay got back into his car and backed it up to a wider part of the track where he could turn around.

"Did you hear anything interesting?" Sophia asked.

"I did," Ramsay replied. "Thorogood says the two men who abducted you aren't the owners of Lakeland Lorries and they're Geordies, so if they've ever been in trouble with the law, my old colleagues back in Newcastle may be able to identify them for us."

"Then why did we see the tall one go into Lakeland Lorries premises?" Sophia asked, puzzled.

"Maybe he'd seen us following him and thought this a good way to shift the investigation to someone else," Ramsay replied. "Or they aren't the owners, but they're relatives of the owners and they're all crooks."

"I think that last idea is the truth," Sophia said as Ramsay pulled out onto the paved road. "I don't think he saw us at all."

"Maybe," Ramsay said. "Alastair is pulling up ahead. Let's see what he has to say." Ramsay pulled into the passing place behind Alastair who was already out of his vehicle, waiting for them to stop.

"Where are we going to talk?" Alastair asked when Ramsay wound down his window.

"Somewhere we can eat and sit apart from others," Ramsay said. "You're the local here, where do you suggest?"

"Follow me," Alastair said. "There's a pub with a lawn down by the lake." He returned to his vehicle and drove off with Ramsay and Sophia close behind.

We need help, Ramsay thought, but will my old colleagues give us any?

12

SEEKING PROFESSIONAL HELP

THEY FOUND a table where they could talk without being overheard, and Alastair went for drinks from the bar. As they waited for Alastair's return, the breeze from the lake and mountains reminded Ramsay and Sophia that summer was almost done.

After sitting, and taking a sip of his pint, Alastair asked, "How much did you hear?"

Ramsay, sipping on his Scotch whisky, told him where in the conversation he'd begun to eavesdrop.

"Thorogood was very cagy before that," Alastair replied. "At first, he claimed he'd seen nothing. When I suggested I'd pay for good information, he began to loosen up. I'm still not sure what he told me is true, though."

"Much of what he said," Sophia interjected, "according to what Inspector Ramsay has told me, fits with what we know."

Ramsay nodded. "I agree. The van is correct, the number of men and their descriptions is correct, so it's likely the rest is true too."

"Does it help?" Alastair asked. "After all, there could be

hundreds of Geordies with those names, even if they told Thorogood the truth about their names."

"It might," Ramsay said. "My old colleagues at Newcastle will have some of those names on file."

"What now?" Sophia asked.

"After we finish lunch, Alastair goes back to Lakeland Lorries and tries to get a sighting of the bosses there," Ramsay said.

AFTER THE MORNING visit's disappointment, this time, they were in luck. Alastair met Evan Williams, a shabby, rotund man, one of the two owners, who gave him some idea of freight rates for delivery to Cambridge. Thanking the man, Alastair left with sheets of prices and weights to examine.

"Well?" Sophia demanded when he returned to the parked vehicles where she and Ramsay were waiting.

"Well, what?" Alastair said, grinning.

"Are they the two I saw?"

"I only saw one, the other is still out on a delivery," Alastair said to Ramsay, mischievously refusing to meet Sophia's eye. "I can't be sure, because I didn't see the two men you saw, but Evan Williams, that's the owner I spoke to, doesn't fit the description you gave me. He's medium height and rather portly. He's also older, I'd say. More like fifty rather than the thirty you both described."

"We should watch him leave," Sophia said to Ramsay. "That's the only way we can be sure."

Ramsay nodded. "We'll take turns, so it isn't too obvious. You and Alastair can be a courting couple over there at that bench under the tree. You'll get a good view from there."

Sophia's expression suggested she might explode. "We are not a courting couple," she said emphatically.

"This is a job," Ramsay said. "You must play a part some-times. You and I can take the next shift, Sophia, because Alastair will have to get the Land-Rover back to the market so he and his father can go home."

"Damn," Alastair cried, looking at his watch. "I'd forgotten about that."

"For the next twenty minutes, you two watch the door," Ramsay said. "I'm going to find a phone box and call my old station as well as some of the rental offices I saw in last night's newspaper."

"All right," Sophia said, "but there'll be none of that courting couple stuff."

Alastair laughed. "I thought it was you who volunteered to be in your school's plays so you could snog the leading man."

"That's different," Sophia said as she marched off to the bench Ramsay had suggested. Alastair followed at a safe distance.

Ramsay was fortunate to find his old colleague, Morri-son, in his office and, after some very small, small talk, explained what he needed.

"Weren't you going to ramble the uplands of England and forget crime and investigating?" Morrison asked.

"I was and after this, I'm sure my plan will unfold as I said it would," Ramsay replied. "I mean, pet thefts and now a kidnapping aren't your run-of-the-mill crimes. There can't be any more of them waiting to pounce on me."

"You could just tell the local bobbies to figure it out themselves and walk on," Morrison reminded him.

"This young woman is in danger," Ramsay said. "I know it. I don't know why, and nor does she, and yet she is." He didn't add that he might also be in danger.

"I'll see what we can do," Morrison replied, sighing. "Phone back tomorrow night."

"Thanks, and I'm sure this will be the last time," Ramsay said and hung up the phone as the end-of-call beeps were beginning. He arrived back at the park where Sophia and Alastair were seated, their gazes focused on the Lakeland Lorries office door.

"Anything?" Ramsay asked them.

They shook their heads in unison. Neither spoke. The air was filled with tension.

"You'd best get off," Ramsay said to Alastair, "and I'll take over the watch."

Alastair wished them farewell and said he'd be back after dinner.

"You don't know what they look like," Ramsay said, as Sophia was still silent.

"True," Alastair said, "but maybe I will if I share an evening shift with you, Inspector." He rose and strode quickly back to his car.

"Nothing happened between you two that shouldn't have while I was away, did it?" Ramsay asked.

"Nothing!"

"You seem very tense for someone to whom nothing happened."

"He just drives me mad," Sophia said. "He gets right under my skin, and he knows he's doing it."

"I see," Ramsay said and then added, "Someone's leaving the office."

They watched eagerly and were deflated when a woman, obviously the receptionist, stepped out and closed the door behind her. She walked out to the road and turned in the direction of a bus stop only two minutes' walk away.

A bus arrived, she got on, and the street was quiet again.

"He could leave from the backdoor," Sophia cried. "The one we saw the tall man enter the other day."

"He could," Ramsay agreed. "I'll wander around there and see if he's still inside."

"I'm going to look odd sitting out here on my own," Sophia objected.

"Here's my car key," Ramsay replied, handing over his keychain. "Sit inside and keep the doors locked."

"Why can't I go around the back of the building, and you stay here?" Sophia asked.

Ramsay sighed. "If you wish, but at the first sign of trouble you come back here quickly."

"Why should there be trouble?"

"Because it will be obvious to him you're watching his premises. There's nowhere to hide in that lane and there's nothing beyond the backs of houses to see, so you aren't there for innocent reasons," Ramsay said.

"Maybe you're right," Sophia replied, after a moment of thinking about what he'd said. "It was a bit of a scruffy street."

"Just sit tight in the car. If he comes out, don't let him see you watching him. I'll be back as soon as I've confirmed he's in there or not."

They walked together to the car, where Sophia got in and Ramsay walked down the street to the alley that led to the back of the buildings.

Ramsay approached the open gates of the yard where they'd seen the taller of the two kidnappers enter days before. He peered around the gatepost to be sure no one was in the yard. It was empty, so he strolled quietly up to the windows of the building. There were lights on inside, but they could just be for security.

He heard someone moving about and stepped to the

side of the window. After a minute, a man appeared, and Ramsay knew at once Alastair had been correct. This man wasn't either of the two kidnappers. When the man left the room, heading back to wherever he'd come from, Ramsay quickly made his way out of the yard and back to his car.

"What did you see?" Sophia asked.

"The man in there isn't one of the two," Ramsay replied.

"Then we have it all wrong," Sophia said in dismay.

"Possibly," Ramsay replied. "I still hope my colleagues in Newcastle will find us the answer."

"You think the kidnappers are relations of the owners or something like that?"

"Or business associates," Ramsay said. "We should eat before Alastair returns and we plan our next steps."

"What can he do that we can't?" Sophia asked peevishly.

"He can question his parents, your parents, and anyone else that may have an interest in keeping you out of the way," Ramsay said. "We can't do that without giving your presence here away."

"I suppose that's true," Sophia agreed. "I still wish I'd never involved him. He makes me so angry sometimes I could scream."

Ramsay smiled. "He's very fond of you."

Sophia blushed. "Well, he has a funny way of showing it."

"We have to visit the Keswick Accommodation Kiosk," Ramsay said, to spare her blushes. "They have a place near lake Windermere that sounds ideal for us to hide out in."

"It's got to be better than feeding ducks," Sophia said, rising from her seat. "I prefer my ducks done in an orange sauce, not nibbling my fingers."

They learned the cottage had two bedrooms, a kitchen, living room, bathroom, and it was available now. *Which means it's cold, damp, and nowhere near the lake*, Ramsay thought despondently. It was, however, furnished and included bedding and towels.

"We'll take it," Ramsay said, writing the woman behind the counter a cheque. She handed them keys, extra blankets, *I knew it was cold*, dishwashing liquid, and a map, *off the beaten track confirmed*, Ramsay thought. They thanked her and dumped everything in the car.

"Now I check out of the hotel and we're ready for gracious living in the south lakes," Ramsay said.

"I don't believe 'gracious living' was mentioned, or likely to be much in evidence," Sophia told him gloomily.

"Nevertheless, it's where we're staying for the rest of the investigation."

WHEN ALASTAIR RETURNED THAT EVENING, Ramsay noticed he wasn't the same excited man he'd been when he left. Ramsay said nothing and let the talk of their investigation tomorrow bring out whatever was worrying him.

"Why can't we find that van?" Sophia asked, returning to an earlier question.

"It's well hidden," Ramsay said. "Where though, is for us to find out."

"I say we look in the Lakeland Lorries backyard," Alastair said. "It wasn't there last time, maybe it will be now."

Ramsay shrugged. "Why not," he agreed. "The offices must be closed by now and who knows what we'll find."

13

NEW SUSPECTS

LAKELAND LORRIES' offices were in darkness and so was the yard behind the house. Only the faint light from the nearby streetlamps illuminated the area.

"Will they have an alarm or a dog?" Sophia asked.

"We'll move cautiously until we know," Ramsay said. "They don't look rich enough to afford an alarm. A dog would be my best bet."

At the gate, they stopped and surveyed the shadowy space. No sounds came from the building or yard.

"A dog would have been here by now," Alastair said. "I say we go in. Any of those lockups could contain the van." Before Ramsay could urge caution, Alastair hoisted himself up onto the top of the metal gate and perched there, extending a hand to Sophia. In a moment, she was balanced on the gate beside him. Ramsay soon followed.

"I wish I was taller," Sophia grumbled, as Alastair jumped down inside the yard and helped her to the ground.

"You wouldn't if you knew how many times I bump my head on door frames and branches," Alastair replied.

When Ramsay had joined them, they began inspecting

the buildings on each side of the yard. Most were locked. They all, however, had small windows that were too high to easily see inside.

"Stand on my back," Alastair said to Sophia. "You climb up and look inside." He bent over and braced himself.

Sophia removed her shoes and climbed onto Alastair. "It's like scrumping apples when we were younger," Sophia said, giggling.

"What can you see?" Ramsay asked.

"Not a lot. The windows are dirty and covered in cobwebs. This one has barrels of something. There's no van or any other kind of vehicle." Sophia climbed down and put on her shoes.

"Next one," Ramsay said, and for the next fifteen minutes Sophia looked inside the dirty sheds.

"There's no van in any of them," Sophia said in disgust as she slipped off Alastair's back to the ground at the last shed.

"We've eliminated it from our inquiries," Ramsay said, grinning.

"At the expense of me and my clothes needing first class laundering," Sophia replied, brushing her jacket and skirt with her hands.

"The hostel has showers," Ramsay reminded her.

"If you think I'm going in any of those showers..." Sophia began.

"We'll return to my hotel, and you can use mine," Ramsay interjected, laughing. "Then we can talk again about tomorrow."

. . .

As SOPHIA SHOWERED, Ramsay and Alastair sat quietly in Ramsay's room contemplating the future. Again, Ramsay noted Alastair's grim expression.

"What's on your mind?" Ramsay asked.

"I don't want to say, certainly not when Sophia's around."

"Did you hear something at dinner that makes you suspect her or her family?" Ramsay pressed him.

Alastair shook his head. "Not her family, mine," he said bitterly. "I'm going over it in my mind, and it sounds like my parents had something to do with Sophia's abduction."

"What did you hear?" Ramsay asked.

"My dad was telling Mum that 'she got away,'" Alastair said. "That could only mean Sophia and that he was in on it, couldn't it?"

"You didn't hear more?"

Alastair replied, "Mum said, 'never mind, you'll find another way.'"

"That does sound concerning," Ramsay agreed. "You didn't hear why they were saying this? There may be context we're missing."

Alastair shook his head. "I heard Dad speaking as I returned home. I'd only just heard Mum's reply before I entered the living room and they stopped talking, but I don't see what other context can be put on it."

"It's true it's hard to see a different interpretation," Ramsay agreed. "We can't tell Sophia this, not until you've learned more. It would color her opinion of your parents for years to come."

"Agreed. It's already colored mine," Alastair said, bitterly. "I've always known Dad as an ambitious, active man who goes after and gets what he wants. I can't help feeling this would be in character for him."

"Ambitious in what way?" Ramsay asked, puzzled. *After*

all, what kind of rivalry could farmers have? The fattest pig? Fastest horse?

"He's on every committee and board around here," Alastair said, "from the local conservative party to the sheep breeders' association and everything in between. I ask him what he's aiming for, a knighthood? He says he likes to keep busy and serve the community."

"I imagine farming leaves lots of time for such things," Ramsay ventured.

Alastair laughed. "Tell that to a farmer and you'll get an earful. No, Dad has an estate manager who manages all the farm work. Dad's a driven man, but to what, I don't know. He says to build a future for our family, by which he means me and my future wife."

"An old-fashioned ambition then," Ramsay said. "A dynasty set in motion by a great founder."

Ramsay heard Sophia finishing up in the bathroom and said, "We'll say no more tonight. You listen in on your parents over the next few days and see if you learn more."

Sophia exited the bathroom, still toweling her hair dry. "What have you two been plotting behind my back?"

"We've been discussing the case and without any new ideas being formed. You're just in time to add your contribution."

"My contribution is we need to find that van because it will help us find the two kidnappers," Sophia said, flopping down on the sofa.

"I think it will be easier to spot the two men," Alastair said. "The world is full of white vans."

"The world is full of lanky fair-haired men and shorter dark-haired men," Sophia replied, snappily.

"We can keep our eyes peeled for both," Ramsay said,

heading off another spat. "But we need a breakthrough to get any further."

"Well, we won't get one sitting here," Sophia said, still cross at Alastair's rejection of her preferred plan.

"Sadly," Ramsay said, "we can't take you into pubs or we could look in every pub in town, now that people will be gathering there."

"You *can* take me into pubs," Sophia said. "I've often passed for eighteen. No one really checks."

Ramsay frowned. What Sophia said was true, unless the young person was clearly a child, few landlords or landladies bothered. Still, he was over thirty years a police officer and that had left him with a profound respect for the law.

"I'll compromise," he said at last. "I'll visit half the pubs in town, you two visit the other half. And you, Sophia, don't drink in any of them, understand?" He caught and held Sophia's gaze until she agreed.

"I'll only drink orange juice," Sophia told him.

"If we're going pub crawling, Soph," Alastair said. "Get a move on. It'll soon be closing time."

Sophia shot back into the bathroom and was out in five minutes. Her hair was still wet but at least it had shape to it now. The three left the hotel and hurried into town where the streets were busy with tourists and the pubs already loud with voices.

"I'll do every pub I find to the right along the main street, you two do all the ones you find to the left. We'll meet back here after closing time," Ramsay said. "And Sophia, this is no time to assert your independence. A low profile is what's required here."

Sophia grinned. "Yes, Grandad," she said and hurried away before Ramsay could respond.

. . .

AT CLOSING TIME, Ramsay was waiting at the meeting spot searching the streets for his two companions. It was nearer eleven o'clock before he saw them emerging from a dark side street, giggling like children. He shook his head, smiling indulgently. Parents were sometimes incredibly stupid, he decided.

"Well?" he asked, when they finally joined him.

They shook their heads in unison. "Did you?"

"I didn't," Ramsay said, severely, "and I was actually looking."

"We were too," Sophia said. "Just because we had fun doesn't mean we weren't."

Ramsay nodded, grinning. "All right," he said, "tonight was a washout. We'll start again in the morning."

"Doing what?" Alastair asked.

"For you, interviewing your parents, Sophia's parents, and anyone else who might know something," Ramsay said. "You can meet us for lunch down by the lake."

"What are *we* doing?" Sophia asked.

"Continue looking for that van and the two men," Ramsay replied. "And I'll follow up with my police colleagues."

* * *

ALASTAIR STARTED PROBING at breakfast the next morning, where his father was eating behind the morning Telegraph, while his mother nibbled on a thin slice of toast.

"What were you talking about yesterday, when I came in?" he began, looking at his mother to respond.

His father put down the newspaper at once. "What do you mean?"

"When I came in yesterday afternoon," Alastair replied,

"you were saying 'she got away' or something like that."

"Oh that," his father said. "I was buying a boat, and I thought I had the deal done, but the owner found another buyer and I lost it."

Alastair frowned. "But you said, 'got away'?"

His father laughed. "It was my joke. I'd driven a hard bargain, had the seller penned in, I thought, and couldn't sell to anyone else. But she wriggled out and sold it to someone from down south."

"We have a boat," Alastair pointed out. "Why would we want another one?"

"Oh, this one wasn't for us," his father said, airily. "It was an investment. It was a bigger boat, and I was planning to run high-quality trips on Windermere. The local boat companies are missing the high-end of the market. I thought we'd take that."

Alastair considered this. It sounded reasonable, but he'd never heard of this 'deal' since returning from university weeks ago. Had his father invented this response when he realized Alastair must have heard some of yesterday's conversation? The glances passing between his father and mother added to his suspicion.

"Are you still considering it?" Alastair asked. "Now the boat you wanted is gone, I mean?"

His father laughed. "You know me. I don't fall at the first hurdle. I'll keep my eyes open for another suitable boat and try again."

"We don't know anything about running a boat or a holiday cruise line," Alastair pointed out. "Aren't you always saying, 'don't get involved in things you don't understand?'"

"I had an eye on some people who could have set it up and run it. Don't worry, son. Your patrimony is safe in my hands."

"I'm sure it is, Dad," Alastair said, smiling. "I can rely on you."

"Cheeky devil," his father said, fondly. "What are your plans for today?"

Alastair squirmed. He'd hoped to slide out of the house without being asked that. "Well," he said, "I thought I'd go and see Soph's parents. I know they might not like the intrusion, but it's been days now and I should do something. Soph and I have been friends all our lives."

His father snorted, but before he could speak, Alastair's mother interjected, "I think that's a wonderful idea, son. These kinds of visits are always difficult, but if no one goes, they'll feel all alone."

"That's what I thought," Alastair said, relieved to have one ally. "And there may be something I could do to help."

"Staying out of their way would be the best way to help," his father said bluntly.

"And I have," Alastair said. "Only it's been days without any news, and Soph has been my best friend every summer for the past fifteen years. I must go and see them."

His father shrugged and, much to Alastair's relief, the subject was dropped.

"Dad," Alastair began, "what do you know about the Thornton's estate manager and his assistant?"

"What do you want to know about them for?" his father replied. "They won't be staying on after we get the estate."

"You said they weren't much good, but they're both local, surely?"

"Doesn't mean they're good at their job," his father said. "Prescott might make an estate manager's assistant somewhere, but he's always been a shady character. No one who knew him would hire him. As for his assistant, he's only there because decent men wouldn't work for Prescott."

"Shady in what way?" Alastair asked.

"When things go missing, Prescott will have something like it for sale soon after. And he's a fighting drunk. Lots of local places have barred him."

Alastair shook his head in disbelief at these, until now, unknown sides to local life. "And his assistant?"

"Hetherington is another such character," his father said. "They probably met on a job somewhere. Of the two, he's the worst. Been in and out of jail most of his life. Always claims it's because nobody would give him a chance. Probably why the Thorntons were happy to have him. To show their social superiority over us northerners."

"Dad!" Alastair said, shocked. "They're our friends and neighbors."

"They're part-time neighbors who 'graciously' invite us to a party once a year and that's as far as it goes."

This insight into his father's true feelings toward Sophia's family unnerved Alastair. What did his father really think of Sophia?

Rising from the breakfast table, Alastair prepared to set out for the Thorntons.

"Give them our best wishes too," his mother said as he left the house. "I phoned when we first heard, but they weren't taking calls."

Assuring his mother, he would, Alastair crossed the yard and settled himself in the Land-Rover. He'd have liked to use the vehicle's four-wheel drive to its fullest by driving across country, but he contented himself with following the road. Getting stuck in the soft, wet earth of the fells and having to be rescued wouldn't help him investigate Sophia's parents. What he'd learn from interviewing the other victims of Sophia's abduction, Alastair didn't know, but maybe they had knowledge they didn't know they had.

14

INTERVIEWING THE NEW SUSPECTS

HE'D MADE a list of questions overnight and memorized them. However, as he pulled up at the Thornton's grand portico, they were already slithering away out of mind. Undaunted, he left the vehicle and rang the bell. He was greeted by the man who acted as butler to the Thorntons when they were here. The man, John Cartwright, smiled. "Come in, Master Elliott, but wait in the hall. I'll tell them you're here. They're not seeing anyone at the moment, but they may make an exception for you."

"Thanks, Mr. Cartwright," Alastair replied. He'd known the man since childhood. They were old friends, and both knew this formal play-acting was just for the Thornton's benefit.

Alastair waited, half expecting to be told to leave. However, he was signaled to join the butler outside the living room door before being grandly announced. Alastair winked at the butler as he entered.

"Alastair," Cat Thornton greeted him, turning and holding out her hand languidly as she lay on a chaise-longue facing the window. "How nice of you to come."

"I hope you won't think this an intrusion," Alastair said, taking her hand and kissing it. This, too, was play-acting. Sophia's stepmother had always teased him about his own rather stiff, formal nature. "I didn't come earlier because I knew how upset you'd be over Sophia's disappearance."

"We were," Cat said, still without any energy or emotion, "but we're learning to cope, and it's time we had visitors to help us stop brooding."

Alastair wanted to say he didn't see any sign of her brooding but bit his tongue.

"Has there been any news?" he asked.

"None," Cat replied. "She's vanished."

"I know the police searched the country around here," Alastair continued. "Didn't they find anything?"

"Sophia's purse," Cat replied. "That's all. And she could have lost that at any time."

"I looked in the places we played when we were young," Alastair said. "I didn't find anything either."

"Like I said, vanished."

"On the radio there was a report Sophia might have returned to London. Have you heard more from that?" Alastair asked.

Cat shook her head. "The police down there are looking, but they haven't found her either. We're beginning to fear she might be dead."

Alastair tried to look horrified at this. "I hope not," he replied. "Anyway, I'm sure they'd have found her body if she was."

"Fidel says there are lots of old mine workings and other holes in the ground where her body could be hidden. He's also afraid she's dead."

"The early reports said she'd run away from home,"

Alastair continued. "That didn't sound like Sophia to me." His expression turned to one of puzzlement.

"Sophia and her father had an argument that morning and she stormed out of the house," Cat replied. "We didn't think it meant much, but when she didn't come back, we thought she must have decided to stay away to teach her father a lesson."

"And there's nothing you can think of to explain her staying away this long? I'm clutching at straws," Alastair said, with a worried grin, "as you see. She means a lot to me."

"We know how you feel about Sophia," Cat said. "We've known since you were both children."

"I want to do something to find her," Alastair said, "and I don't know what."

"We all feel that way, Alastair," Cat replied soothingly. "If I could suggest anything, I would."

"You have checked with your house in London?"

"Oh, didn't you know?" Cat exclaimed. "She phoned us from London a few days after she went missing. Assured us she was all right and everything, but she was staying away from our house in case it was being watched."

Alastair feigned astonishment. "Then why is everyone still looking?"

"Because the very next day, she left the house where she was staying and hasn't been seen again."

"But the search is still going on down there?" Alastair asked.

"The police say it is, but London's a big place with lots of places to hide. We've phoned all her friends' homes, and no one claims to have seen her. This is why we're growing so despondent. We think she fell in with the wrong people."

Alastair frowned. "If I knew anyone in London, I'd go

down and search. As it is, I can't see how that would help. I don't know people she'd go to or places she might hide."

"We can only wait and hope for the best," Cat said, nodding sadly.

"I wish..." Alastair began, before his voice trailed away.

"We wish too," Cat agreed. "We wish there'd been no argument, wish we'd prevented her leaving, wish we'd realized sooner... You can imagine all the things we wish we'd done differently, but it won't help. It's up to the police now."

"What was the argument about?" Alastair asked. "Maybe there's a clue in that."

"It was about nothing, really," Cat replied, shifting uncomfortably. "Just her dad being over-protective and Sophia not having it. They'd clashed over this many times before. That's why we weren't concerned, at first."

Alastair noted Cat's discomfort and smiled inwardly. Sophia had told him in no uncertain terms what her father wanted and how she wasn't having it. Alastair had silently cursed her father who was too tunnel-visioned to understand Sophia would always reject coercion of any kind, even the well-meaning sort.

"So, no clues there?" Alastair probed. "Was it money or friends or activities, maybe? As I said, I'm desperate for a clue that I can follow."

"It was more about her considering her future," Cat said, "now that she has finished school."

Alastair noted she was still uncomfortable, though growing closer to telling him.

Alastair smiled. "I can understand that. Her first summer of freedom from school and her dad wants her to think about a job or marriage or something."

Cat agreed quietly.

"If that was it," Alastair said, almost eagerly, "maybe we

should be looking at ports and airports. She may have set out on a pilgrimage or something like that."

"Sophia isn't religious," Cat replied, more easily now.

"Oh, I didn't mean a religious pilgrimage, more a journey long considered to a sight she'd longed to see. To find herself, if you like."

Cat almost smiled. "Unless she could go first class, Sophia wouldn't go anywhere. Believe me, she might talk a good story of not caring about wealth, but she doesn't ever try its opposite."

This made Alastair take pause. He was well-off, but Sophia was used to the movie star lifestyle. Would she want to stay here in the north, far away from the bright lights of London, Paris, Monte Carlo, Las Vegas, and Hollywood?

"Could she have taken money with her? To buy plane or ferry tickets, I mean?"

"She had nothing but her purse with her," Cat said. "We went through her clothes and belongings with the police right at the start. She had only what she needed to walk the trails, cool off, and come home."

"But she did have her bag and purse," Alastair persisted.

"Her smallest bag," Cat replied. "She couldn't have packed even a change of undies in that."

"Do you or Mr. Thornton have any theories I could follow up?"

"We think she got a ride into Keswick, pawned something, bought a train ticket for London, and hid out there with a friend," Cat said, "only staying long enough to phone us and left again. It's what happened after she left her friend's home that frightens us."

"You never received any demands for money?"

Cat shook her head. "None. If we had, she'd be home by now."

"Is there a reason someone might want her out of the way for a time?"

"What on earth do you mean?"

Alastair frowned. "I'm not exactly sure, but is there some event in your lives or Sophia's life where it might be advantageous to someone if Sophia wasn't there?"

Cat's expression was a mix of puzzlement and suspicion. "Not that I, or Fidel, know of. This was our usual family summer stay. It isn't her birthday or ours, or anything that might trigger a kidnapping."

Sensing Cat was becoming upset at all these questions, Alastair said, "I'm sorry. I came to show my concern and assure you of my and my family's best wishes, but I've let my worry get the better of me and subjected you to a third-degree interrogation."

Cat smiled. "I understand," she said. "You're feeling what we are. It's horrible not knowing."

"Is Mr. Thornton at home?"

Cat nodded. "He's in his office. Says he's on the phone to his contacts in Hollywood, sounding out opportunities."

"It must be worrying for you both," Alastair said. "Not having a regular income, I mean."

Cat laughed. "It is a worry, it's true. But we aren't the kind of people who need a regular income."

Alastair blushed, embarrassed. "I-I didn't mean that," he found himself stammering. "I just meant not being able to practice his craft, his profession."

"In the world of movies, projects come and go," Cat replied, laughing. "Sometimes you're up, sometimes you're down. It isn't like a regular job."

"I wish I could tell Mr. Thornton how sorry I am for this awful time," Alastair said. "Please tell him we're thinking about you all, and if there's anything we can do, let us know."

Cat thanked him and rang the bell for the butler to show him out. When Alastair and the butler were nearing the outer door, Alastair asked quietly, "Do you have any thoughts on where Sophia may be?"

"The police asked me that and I have to say, I don't," the butler replied.

"Oh, well. I'll see you in the Dog and Gun one of these nights," Alastair said as he left.

"Maybe," the butler said. "I'm often there."

Alastair jumped into the Land-Rover, his mind going over what he'd heard. As he drove down the drive, he decided he'd learned nothing. A deep foreboding filled his mind because, to him, his own parents seemed more likely to be the abductors than Soph's parents or anyone else in the house. Ramsay may favor the Thornton's estate manager or his helper, but his own feelings had been shaken by the peculiar conversation with his parents about a boat. He needed to learn more at his own home.

After parking the Land-Rover, Alastair went in search of his father. He ran into his father's estate manager, who was just leaving the house.

"Hello, Alastair," the man said; they'd known each other since Alastair was a child. "How did you find the Thorntons?"

"I only saw Catherine," Alastair said, still uncomfortable about addressing adults he'd known all his life by their first names. "She seemed resigned to the likelihood of bad news."

"Aye, I can understand that. A child gone missing is a terrible thing, even for a stepmother."

"By the way, Angus," Alastair said, as it looked like the

estate manager was preparing to move on, "what do you know about my father's new scheme of buying a boat?"

The man was surprised. "I've never heard of it. Best you ask your father. If it doesn't concern the land, and it doesn't sound like it does, I wouldn't be part of the planning."

"I'm about to ask him," Alastair replied, grinning. "I've only just heard of it myself."

Alastair considered his options. Having exposed his doubts about his parents, he needed to confirm or remove them. That meant investigating further. His parents had explained their conversation he'd overheard but unsatisfactorily in his mind. The estate manager had denied all knowledge of it. How to proceed?

An idea came to him at once. Where did his father learn of this boat being for sale? Local newspapers? Country magazines? Boating magazines?

Finding his father in his office, Alastair said, "Dad, I've been thinking about your idea for superior cruises on the lake, and I see where you're coming from. All those people in four- and five-star hotels around the lake with no way of enjoying it."

His father nodded. "The idea came to me one night at an event in Sharrow Bay Hotel. The bar and lounge were full of people with nothing to do except dancing, and you can't do that every day and night of your stay."

His wife glared at him. "Maybe not, dear, but once in a while wouldn't come amiss."

Alastair's father said, "We danced at the Hunt Ball only last year. That should be often enough for any rational person."

"Where did you learn about the boat?" Alastair asked, quickly. "Maybe there'll be another along soon."

"I don't quite remember," his father replied. "You know how it is, someone tells someone, who tells you."

"Wasn't it that horrible little man from Lakeland Lorries who told you?" Mrs. Elliott asked. "I'm sure it's what you told me at the time."

'Yes, that's right, my dear. It was him."

"Is that how he knew about it? They were transporting it?" Alastair asked.

"I believe so," his father replied. "From where it was docked into a warehouse down Manchester way."

"Do we use Lakeland Lorries a lot?" Alastair asked.

"Not a lot. They're a rundown, shabby outfit, but they're cheap. I had them pick up and deliver a bundle of stuff a few weeks back, and that's when the driver was telling me about the boat."

"A bundle of stuff?" Alastair asked.

"Oh, just junk from the farm to take to the municipal waste dump."

Alastair's insides were trembling as his father spoke. *Was that bundle Soph? Is that all she is to him? Would the waste people confirm a shipment if he knew the date? Would Lakeland confirm the boat move if he asked them?*

"I'll ask Lakeland Lorries tomorrow to look out for another boat," Alastair said after the pause caused by his mind reeling. "As you say, they could give us another early opportunity. Even if they aren't doing the moving, they're in the business and will likely hear if someone else is."

"Now you're beginning to sound like a businessman," his father said, approvingly. "You focus on our family, and we'll go far. Leave finding Sophia to the police; it's their job, not yours."

15

THINGS HIDDEN, REVEALED

ALASTAIR REDDENED at his father's rare praise and asked, "By the way, Dad, does this boat business mean you've given up on getting the Thornton estate?" Despite the praise, Alastair hadn't liked the way his father ruthlessly dropped Sophia from Alastair's future.

His father was suddenly alert. "Why? Did they say anything about their plans when you were over there?"

"I only saw Cat, so they didn't," Alastair replied. "But it reminded me you were anxious to get the estate up until very recently."

His father subsided back into his chair. "I still am. I'd hoped you and Sophia would marry and she'd bring the estate into the family. But that doesn't look likely now."

"You think Fidel Thornton would give her the estate as a dowry?" Alastair asked, puzzled. "Does anyone do dowries now?"

"What are you talking about, lad? The estate belongs to Sophia, not her dad."

"How do you know that?" Alastair asked.

"Sophia's mam told me. We were friends from childhood, and she told me of the provisions in her will that last summer she was here. Very ill already, she was. Heart-breaking."

"Have you seen the will?"

"Nay, lad. It's nothing to do with me," his father said. "Anyway, when it became clear you and Sophia weren't to marry, I thought I'd consider another scheme until Thornton is forced to sell."

"Forced to sell?"

"Absolutely. The estate is losing money hand over fist," his father replied. "Ever since old George Brockbank, his estate manager, died. You remember him?"

"I do," Alastair laughed. "He was always chasing Soph and me away from his precious pheasant and grouse chicks when we just wanted to play with them."

His father nodded, grinning. "He was very proud of his success with the game shoots was old George. I can't imagine he'd take kindly to a couple of scamps like you two spoiling the season."

"After Mr. Brockbank, the Thorntons had that friend take over as estate manager," Alastair said, wracking his brain for a name.

His father laughed. "His friend was some London fellow who didn't know a grouse from a pheasant, or anything else about estate management. That's when the rot set in. This present chap isn't much better, but he does have some gumption, unlike the friend."

"So, the estate is losing money?" Alastair asked.

"Aye. If he doesn't sell soon, it'll go under, and I'll get it for a song. They owe every supplier in the neighborhood, and some have even cut them off. I hear one of the big suppliers, national not local, is working on sending them into receivership."

"I'm surprised you'd want us to have the estate," Alastair said, laughing.

"We could turn it around in months. If we get it this winter, and I think we will, it'll make money next summer, you'll see."

"How will you get the birds for the shooting?" Alastair asked.

"I've already told Angus we need twice the number raised for next year. That's how confident I am."

"And if someone outbids you at the sale?"

"They'll be in a heap of trouble until they sell it to me," his father said grimly. "With that estate joined to ours, you'll be the largest landowner in the county. Marry well and we can expand even on that."

Alastair's affection for his father always took a knock when his father's ruthless business streak was nakedly displayed, and after their morning conversation, this time was no exception.

Could his father have thought holding Sophia for ransom for that estate was just being a tough negotiator? It wasn't so many centuries ago the England-Scotland border struggles had included many such instances of thuggery. His father was an old-school man, but just how old-school was he? This seemed like a time to see.

"I still hope to marry Soph," Alastair said. "I can't stop hoping she'll be found, and her father will relent on his foolish insistence that she marry me."

It was his father's turn to be puzzled. "Was he doing that?"

Alastair nodded. "Soph told me just before she disappeared. I hope she's just lying low until he's learned his lesson."

"But that means she doesn't want to marry you."

"I hope it means she doesn't want to be *forced* to marry me," Alastair replied. "And that deep down, she will realize she does still want to marry me."

"Still?"

Alastair flushed. "We married when I was about twelve and she ten. Ted Pringle, the gamekeeper's son, was the vicar. He was older than us, more mature, so it had to be him."

His father laughed. "Good luck with that. Every child that's ever lived has played that game."

"You've no idea where she is?" Alastair asked.

"Me? No. She was always your friend, not ours," his father replied. "I think she saw us as country bumpkins. Though I did think she was fond of you, even as late as last year's visit."

"She was," Alastair said, "and if her father hadn't interfered, she still would be."

"If you married, what would you do among all those London and Hollywood folks that Thornton's always boasting about?"

"I wouldn't go to London," Alastair said.

"And what if she did, and she turns out to be a gambler, the way her father and stepmother are?"

"A gambler?" Alastair cried.

"It isn't just their northern estate that's on the rocks. I hear they owe some unpleasant people a lot of money and they're pressing him for it."

"How do you know this?"

"Our Member of Parliament keeps his eyes open when he's down there in London. Thornton may not be here much, but his estate's still important to the constituency. He says Thornton's done for, if he doesn't get money soon."

Alastair found now he was eager to be off. Ramsay and

Soph needed to know this, if she didn't already. He paused. If she knew, why hadn't she told them? After all, this was a strong motive for her abduction.

"I'll let you get on, Dad," Alastair said, rising from the chair he'd taken.

"It's time you were here with me as I work, son. It will be yours to manage soon enough and you should be ready."

"I'll do that," Alastair replied. "Only I have to go out right now."

His father nodded, smiling. "All right, but don't leave it too late. By the way, why did you think I might know where Sophia was?"

His piercing gaze made Alastair jump, but he replied steadily, "I had a sudden idea that, if she'd run away, she might have gone to a local family she knew. And you know everything that goes on around here."

"No one would have sheltered her once the police appeals began," his father said. "She's not an adult, she's a child in the eyes of the law."

"I know, but I thought for the first hours or even a day, they might. And when she realized her friends would be in trouble for sheltering her, she ran away again. I thought, as you're well-informed about local doings, you might know."

"Well, if it happened, I haven't heard about it."

Alastair left as quickly as he could, taking the Land-Rover, and driving into town to find Soph and Ramsay.

* * *

CAT SIPPED her afternoon cocktail as she read the latest Vogue. She heard Fidel clumping down the stairs and approaching the Conservatory where she was enjoying the sun through its glass panes. As she had many times since marrying Fidel and spending the season up here, she wondered when they had summer. Her own childhood and younger life had been spent in California and the bracing climate of northern England had not yet begun to grow on her.

"What did Alastair want?" Fidel asked as he entered the Conservatory.

"He said he'd come to offer best wishes and ask if there was anything he could do to help? He says he's been searching at the places he and Sophia enjoyed when they were children."

"As if they're not still children," Fidel said, laughing, but his voice sounded brittle, the tension near the surface.

"They're at that awkward age," Cat agreed placidly. Fidel's concern for Sophia was too much to bear some days.

"I can't understand why she hasn't called again," Fidel said, striding around the room like a caged beast. "She said she would."

"Perhaps something scared her," Cat replied.

"Such as what?"

"Maybe someone watching the house," Cat said. "There are some seriously anxious people down there hoping to be paid soon."

"They wouldn't watch the house," Fidel objected.

"It was just an example," Cat said. "Maybe it was something completely different."

Fidel paused in mid-stride. He shook his head. "I just worry she's been kidnapped."

"Kidnapped?" Cat exclaimed. "What makes you say that?"

"She said she'd been kidnapped up here, why not down there?"

"Because the same person being kidnapped in two locations, so far apart, within a month is too incredible to be possible," Cat said. "No movie investors would put money into a script like that."

Fidel returned to pacing. "Why doesn't she phone?"

"Perhaps because she's sick of hearing what she should do and has decided to do what she wants to do," Cat said, wearily. "I'm sorry, Fidel, you brought this on yourself. You really did."

"I just want what's best for her."

Cat laughed, shaking her head. "And what's best for you."

"Isn't that what everyone wants?" Fidel said. "That things should work out best for everyone? Wouldn't it be best for you and the boys too?"

"Me? It doesn't affect the boys and me at all. I have my own family money; we'll do just fine whatever happens here."

Fidel bit his lip and returned to pacing. These unsubtle hints that he might not be in Cat's future were becoming more and more obvious. He needed to turn things around, but how?

16

INTERVIEWING A KIDNAPPER

RAMSAY AND SOPHIA arrived at their favorite lunch time café at the same time after their separate morning searches.

"Did you have any success?" Ramsay asked as he held open the door and Sophia scooted in.

"I think so," she replied, looking about for a corner table where they might talk quietly unheard. They were early, so had their choice of tables and sat as far away from the few other customers as they could. "What about you?"

"My ex-colleagues tell me the two men are likely Edward Connery and Patrick Kennedy, both local Newcastle men, but their uncle, Evan Williams, runs Lakeland Lorries in Keswick," Ramsay replied. "I don't think there's any doubt."

"I saw the shorter of the two at the Lakeland Lorries offices," Sophia said. "He may be still there now. It looked like he's working on a vehicle today."

Ramsay nodded. "Paddy Kennedy. He's a mechanic. The other is a driver."

"Then we should go right away and confront him," Sophia suggested.

"We'll wait until Alastair gets here, have lunch, and then

I'll question Kennedy in my 'Inspector' guise," Ramsay said, firmly. Kennedy would recognize him, of course, but maybe letting the man know he was police would make them less likely to attack him. The last thing they needed, however, was the men recognizing Sophia.

"He'll be gone by then," Sophia grumbled.

"Not if he's working on a vehicle," Ramsay said. "They take time to fix." Fortunately for Ramsay, their discussion was cut short by Alastair's arrival.

"What news, Alastair?" Sophia asked.

Alastair grimaced. "Nothing yet, but I've spoken to both our parents, which is a start."

Sophia's expression spoke of her disappointment. "I saw the shorter man, but Ramsay won't go and interrogate him."

Alastair turned to Ramsay, who said, "After we've shared what we learned this morning and had lunch."

Alastair laughed. "I'll second that. I'm starving."

"Men," Sophia said shortly, but she studied the menu as well.

As they ordered and ate, they quietly shared what they'd learned. Alastair quickly recounting his meetings with Cat and his father, omitting the part where he'd asked about the boat but sharing the information about Sophia's mother's will.

"A will?" Sophia cried.

A will, Ramsay thought. *That's new. Is it the solution to this riddle?*

When his two fellow sleuths had taken his revelation into their thinking and were quiet, Alastair continued, recounting more of his conversation with Cat and asking if they could see anything in Cat's words he'd missed.

Sophia said, "She's smooth and slippery, always has been. When they first married, she did things that I complained to dad about and she explained them away, making it seem like I was trying to cause trouble between them. Dad took her part over me. That's when I learned where I fitted in the family."

"It's not unusual for children of a previous marriage to create trouble," Ramsay said, gently. "Your father's response was probably just recognizing human nature is predictable."

"I'm not a statistic," Sophia said angrily. "I'm a truthful person and I was a truthful child. He should have known that."

"But you were only three years old, Soph," Alastair said. "You can't possibly remember what you said or did."

"I remember what it felt like," Sophia said, "because all the things that happened weren't at the very beginning when I was three. Lots happened since, and I'm still not believed."

"Time to move on," Ramsay said, putting an end to Sophia's teenage rant. "I'll find our man and see if I can give him a scare. We need them to do something that gives the game away." He rose to his feet, placing a ten-shilling note on the table. "This is for lunch. If there's change, give it to the waitress."

He left the café and walked quickly to the Lakeland Lorries yard where he saw the mechanic with his head under the bonnet of an old truck.

"Mr. Kennedy?" Ramsay said as he arrived at the man's side.

Kennedy jumped so suddenly his head banged on the flimsy metal of the bonnet. He stepped back, rubbing his head with his flat cap. "Who wants to know?"

"Ex-Detective Inspector Ramsay of Northumberland Police," Ramsay said, stressing the 'ex' because it was an offence to impersonate a police officer. "I'm surprised our paths never crossed." He saw the flicker of recognition in Kennedy's eyes.

"Our paths crossed not so long ago," Kennedy said.

"I meant when I was a serving police officer," Ramsay replied, smiling.

"Why would they?" Kennedy said. "I'm not a criminal."

"That's not what I've been told," Ramsay said, "but we'll let the past go by without arguing about it. The local police have been kind enough to accept my assistance in looking for the missing girl, Sophia Thornton."

"Nought to do with me," Kennedy said.

Ramsay didn't miss the way the man's face grew paler or how his voice tremored as he denied his involvement. *Not a good liar, our Mr. Kennedy.*

"It's odd then, because I saw you and Mr. Connery chasing a girl around the time she was missing."

"So what?" Kennedy said. "We walk on the fells when we have time off. There's nought much else to do round here. And we were asked to help in the capture of a loony from a mental home, not a missing kid."

"I later found a girl's handbag in that farmhouse," Ramsay said.

Kennedy shrugged. "We never go into the farmhouse. Else we'd have found it and reported it too."

"I handed it in," Ramsay said, "and now I've seen you and where you work, I can send my police colleagues your way."

"They can come," Kennedy said. "I've nothing to hide."

"Of course," Ramsay said, softly, looking about furtively, "what you say sounds like sense. Maybe I could just accept your word."

"Maybe you should," Kennedy said. "After all, what have you got?"

"Not a lot," Ramsay agreed, "but you see my dilemma? I should make them aware, yet it's so thin the link between what I found and what I saw... I don't want to cause trouble without good reason."

"I don't need the aggravation," Kennedy said, "so, if there's a way I can help you make the right decision..." He let the sentence die away.

"Maybe there is," Ramsay said. "Only, I need to think about it and do some background research." He nodded to Kennedy before saying, "It'll take me a day or so. I'll be back." He turned and walked away, hoping the man wouldn't feel it was a trap. Popular legend had it the police were all corrupt and Ramsay felt Kennedy was a man who would believe it. It was important he did, or they would still be stuck, unable to move forward.

Back at the café, Ramsay told them of the trap he'd set. When he finished, they were both unimpressed by what they heard.

"He'll never fall for it," Alastair said.

"He'd have to be stupid not to see through this," Sophia concurred.

"You'd be surprised how easily persuaded these kinds of people are when it comes to believing all cops are corrupt," Ramsay countered. "Give it a day or so and we'll know."

"You're expecting them to silence you?" Sophia asked.

Ramsay nodded. "Maybe by a bribe or maybe by violence."

"Violence?" Sophia cried.

"They probably haven't been paid yet," Ramsay said, "so I'm thinking violence will be their first choice."

"How can we counter that?" Alastair asked, puzzled.

"By keeping our eyes and ears open at all times," Ramsay said. "Starting now."

"You shouldn't have done this," Sophia said. "It's my problem, not yours."

"It's our problem," Ramsay said. "They knew about me before and wanted me hurt. All I've done is make myself visible to them at a time of my choosing. Before I did that, they could have discovered who I was and caught me unawares. Now I know. Their advantage of surprise is gone."

"I think it's still dangerous," Alastair said. "We need to stay with you all day and night to be sure you're safe."

Ramsay laughed. "Starting today, Sophia will be with me day and night in the cottage."

"I should move in too," Alastair said. "I'll bring a sleeping bag and sleep on the floor, if necessary."

"It isn't necessary," Ramsay said. "They don't know where we're staying, so it will be here in Keswick or out in the country they'll attack."

Sophia shook her head. "It's too public. They'll follow us back to the cottage, you'll see."

Ramsay considered. "You may be right, so today, I'll drive back there alone. That way, if they follow, they won't see you, Sophia."

"How do I get there?" Sophia asked.

"Alastair is too much of a gentleman to let you walk," Ramsay replied. "I'll leave early and you two follow an hour or so later. That should give them time to follow me and reconnoiter the location."

"And attack you," Alastair cried. "No chance. We'll follow very soon after."

"Suit yourselves," Ramsay said. "I thought you might want to enjoy the evening before we settle in for the night."

"How could we do that, knowing you were alone and likely being killed while we partied?" Sophia said.

Ramsay laughed. "You win. Now, you two go and don't approach me again today. You'll see my car leaving around seven, while it's still light enough to see on these narrow Lakeland roads down in the valley bottoms."

"Didn't you hear or understand what I told you earlier," Alastair cried, as they rose to leave without further discussion. He felt aggrieved they were ignoring his most important finding.

Ramsay laughed. "I grow more forgetful every day. It's retirement, it softens the brain. What did you learn?"

"My father said, Soph's real mam had made a will leaving the estate to Sophia."

"I hadn't forgotten," Ramsay said, nodding, "and we must find that will. Only, we have several irons in the fire. The trap I hope I've just set being the most pressing." He paused, frowning, then continued, "Investigating without a team of people to search down leads is more difficult than I thought and very slow work. And remind me again of what you learned about the Thornton's estate manager and assistant?" He realized, with some embarrassment, that, thinking of the will and what it might say, he'd missed a lot of Alastair's findings.

"I think you're right about them," Alastair replied. "Dad says they're both shady characters, but the assistant, a man called Hetherington, is a villain. In and out of jail, often drunk and disorderly, he sounds like just the man to do something as wild as kidnap his employer's daughter for money."

"But they didn't ask for money," Sophia exclaimed.

"Maybe because they didn't know how to manage a kidnapping," Alastair responded. "As inspector Ramsay says, it's been conducted very oddly for a traditional kidnapping."

"We need to meet our Mr. Hetherington and sound him out," Ramsay said. "Meanwhile, you two should go and don't get seen by our two adversaries."

"I say we open Dad's safe at the manse and find that will," Sophia suggested to Alastair.

"It's broad daylight, we'd be seen. Anyway, do you know the code?" Alastair asked.

Sophia shook her head. "Not to this one. Maybe you know a safecracker," she asked Ramsay.

"The ones I know blast safes open with explosives," Ramsay said, grinning. "Not the approach you need to take."

"I don't see why we shouldn't," Sophia replied. "After all, it's my family safe, and I want to get into it. Why shouldn't we blast it open?"

Ramsay laughed. "Because we don't want to be caught blowing up safes. We'd be arrested."

Sophia agreed, then added, "But you must know someone who could get into it."

"You've watched too many episodes of *The Saint*," Ramsay said. "Gentlemen safecrackers don't exist in our time. Maybe they did in the past but not now or, at least, not in this neck of the woods."

"One of the many amenities the North is short of," Sophia said mischievously.

"Hey," said Alastair, "this is my home, and we don't need any of the things you call 'amenities' up here."

This was obviously a continuance of a quarrel from times gone by and Ramsay stepped in to stop it. "Could your mother have made the will up here in the north?"

Sophia considered. "She could, I suppose, after all she was born and grew up here. She loved it."

"Then you should try the local Probate Office," Ramsay said, looking at his watch. "If you're quick, you'll have time to find the will before they close."

"It's better than wandering the streets until you leave," Sophia agreed. Then, turning to Alastair said, "We're going to the Probate Office."

Checking the street carefully before they exited the café, the two amateur sleuths left to spend the afternoon sorting through dusty old documents.

When they were gone, Ramsay ordered a currant slice, ate it, and finished his tea, all the while watching the street hoping to see Kennedy. It wasn't too long before his patience was rewarded. Kennedy and Connery emerged from the side street where the yard lay and began examining everyone they could see.

Ramsay rose, paid his bill at the counter and left the café, pretending not to notice the two men across the street. As he walked, he saw them setting out in the direction he was traveling, following him from the other side of the street. He'd give them an afternoon of exercise, he thought, smiling to himself. *I hope they like window shopping because they're going to do a lot of it today before I give them the opportunity they so much desire.*

17

A TRAP IS SET

BY SEVEN O'CLOCK, even Ramsay had had enough. He turned away from the lake, where he'd been watching the men pretend to be interested in ducks, and made his way to his car. As he entered the parking area, he saw Sophia and Alastair, the perfect courting couple, in a fond embrace that hid Sophia's face.

As he pulled out onto the lane, he saw Kennedy watching and assumed Connery had gone for a vehicle. Ramsay drove slowly along the lane, slow enough for Kennedy to keep up walking, and then, when he turned onto the main street, parked and went into a newsagent for the evening newspaper. When he came out, he saw a Lakeland Lorries van parked farther down the street. Throwing the paper onto the passenger seat, he drove off with the van following.

An hour later, at the cottage, he parked off the road and got out of his car. The van was nowhere to be seen as he made his way indoors. Hidden by a net curtain, Ramsay watched through the window. He saw the van pass slowly by and its occupants taking in the cottage, its doors and windows, its location off the road, and the surrounding low bushes, before finally making its way up the hill and back to Keswick. Other vehicles followed closely on its tail, much to Ramsay's relief. Unless the two decided to park somewhere nearby and walk back, the evening traffic would keep him safe.

Though he felt confident in his ability to defend himself against one assailant, against two he was much less sure, so he was pleased when Sophia and Alastair arrived about fifteen minutes later.

"Well?" Sophia demanded.

"They followed me, and they now know where I live," Ramsay replied. "I think we can expect something to happen overnight or early tomorrow."

"Then I'm staying," Alastair said. "We need to even the odds a little."

Ramsay nodded. "Very well, but you phone and tell your parents where you are. If nothing else, it might mean the police find our bodies quicker."

"Hah!" Alastair snorted. "When they see two of us, they'll run. They can't afford a fight. A quick kill is what they want."

Ramsay smiled. "I hope you're right. Now, what did you two learn at the Probate Office?"

"This!" Sophia said, triumphantly drawing a facsimile copy of a will from her bag. She handed it to Ramsay who quickly read the few paragraphs it contained.

"Now we have a motive," he said.

"And I'm now more than ever sure it's Cat," Sophia said. "She's the sneaky one in the family."

"Or both your parents working together," Ramsay said. "Still, at this moment, all we have is a confirmed motive for your murder, which didn't happen, and not for your abduction, which did. And we have a much more plausible amateur mastermind for the kidnapping."

"The will has to have a bearing on the case, though," Alastair said. "Otherwise, why keep it a secret all these years?"

"Was it a secret?" Ramsay asked Sophia. "I mean, did you ever ask if your mother left you anything and was told she didn't?"

Sophia frowned. "I don't think I was ever told she didn't, but it was clearly assumed so. I was never told I had money and an estate coming to me when I was twenty-one and you'd think someone would mention it, now I'm closing in on twenty-one."

"Perhaps your parents were planning to tell you nearer the time," Ramsay said, "so knowing your future wealth wouldn't lead you to make bad decisions with your life."

"Possibly, but I think it's mean," Sophia replied. "I'm not a social butterfly. I don't do the usual foolish things young people do, and I'm not stupid. That should have counted for something."

Alastair was clearly itching to say something but holding back, not jumping in. Ramsay asked, "You have something to add, Alastair?" From their earlier discussion, he knew what Alastair would say.

Alastair and Sophia stared at one another. Each had a look of impending doom in their expressions, Ramsay thought.

"My father has been told your dad is practically bank-rupt, Sophia. There's a good chance they weren't telling you because there's nothing left. Even the estate doesn't pay its way anymore."

Sophia's horrified expression changed to laughter. "You mean I'm penniless. I've just learned I have a large inheritance, including an estate, in the same moment you tell me it no longer exists?"

Alastair squirmed uncomfortably. "I don't know that. I'm only repeating what my father told me, but he's usually right about these things."

Still finding this revelation amusing, Sophia said, "Then my father was right the other day when he said I should be looking for an occupation and not wandering around in a dream all day."

"If your father has squandered your inheritance," Ramsay said, "he'll be in trouble with the law. It wasn't his money to spend."

"Fat lot of good that will do me," Sophia said bitterly.

"I mean it provides a stronger motive than just losing the money you should have when you reach the age of majority," Ramsay said. "Alastair's dad also told him of an even more pressing motive."

"Oh, good," Sophia said, dully. "It's great to be the center of such attention."

"He and your stepmother owe London casino owners money," Alastair said, quietly. "They may be pressuring them for payment."

"Everyone has debts in London," Sophia objected. "It's just the way it is. They pay at the end of the month or the quarter when their income rolls in."

"If they don't pay their gambling debts promptly," Ramsay added, "things can get ugly. You seem to have known about this, but you didn't mention it."

"Because it means nothing," Sophia cried. "As I said, Daddy would have paid when his money came in. People don't get hurt over this kind of thing. It's a game."

Ramsay shook his head, his expression grim. "I assure

you people who don't pay are frequently hurt, even killed, over precisely this. I'm sure your father knew that too."

"Then it lets him off the hook for my abduction," Sophia said, "and puts the blame on a casino owner. Daddy paying out a ransom on me wouldn't help him at all, unless the casino owners are behind the kidnapping. We must find which casino he owed the money to, and then we have the man behind all this."

"But the abductors never asked for a ransom," Ramsay reminded her.

"You said they were raising the anxiety levels by making father wait," Sophia countered. "You can't have it both ways."

"I'm just suggesting you don't get your hopes up about the outcome of our investigation," Ramsay said. "Your father has a strong motive, but that doesn't necessarily make him guilty. I can't believe any man would abduct or murder his own child for money. You must keep an open mind."

"I am," Sophia said. "Dad and Cat have the same motives and now we learn a London casino owner might have one too. And our favorite villains, Connery and Kennedy, may still have been doing this on their own initiative. Or this new man, Hetherington, may have put them up to it. After all, why not? It isn't the crime of the century. There was little planning or organization about it."

"I'm not happy about my parents either," Alastair interjected, deciding this was the time to get everything out in the open. "I can't shake off the feeling my father knew something about this."

"Would your dad have me kidnapped?" Sophia cried. "He's not the criminal sort, you know that. Anyway, why would he? It doesn't help him in any way."

Alastair's expression was a picture of mixed emotions as he tried to decide what to say. Finally, he spoke. "Many years ago, when I was too young to understand, a local farmer whose land butted up against ours ran into trouble. A government ministry built something that caused his best land to flood and become a marshland. He tried to get the government to provide relief; they wouldn't, saying it was nothing to do with their building. He tried to get the local contractor who worked on drainage issues, but the contractor was tied up on another job. He tried to get equipment from farther afield, but the price was too high. Dad offered to buy his land for a song, and he sold. Then the contractor who'd been tied up was suddenly free, and the drainage was fixed."

"What's your point?" Sophia asked.

"I was too young then, but years later I was told by someone I trust, my father had engineered the whole thing. Everything. Just to get his hands on that land."

Sophia looked horrified. "You think he had me abducted to get my father to sell the estate?"

Alastair nodded, miserably. "I can't forget that earlier event."

Sophia whistled. "A simple trade—your daughter for the estate. I really was the center of a lot of attention, and I had no idea."

"Not the kind of attention anyone would wish for," Ramsay added seriously. "Somehow, we have to sort the wheat from the chaff and find the guilty party."

"How?" Sophia and Alastair asked together.

"I hope it'll start tonight or tomorrow morning when our none-too-competent kidnappers arrive to remove me from their lives," Ramsay said. "If we go to bed and put out the lamps, maybe it will be sooner than we think. Good night." With this, he left them and went to his room.

"It looks like the only way I'm going to get any of my mum's fortune," Sophia told Alastair, as they arranged blankets on the couch for Alastair's bed, "is by marrying you. My father will have to hand over the estate then."

"We're already married," Alastair replied. "Don't you remember?"

"Of course, I do. A girl doesn't forget her first wedding, even if it wasn't entirely real."

"I'd love to make it real," Alastair said.

"And my father would love to hear you say that," Sophia replied. "You'd make his day."

"Did *you* love to hear *me* say it? That's all that counts for me."

"Don't be silly," Sophia said uncomfortably. "You're too tired to think straight. Good night." To hide her blushes, she left him to finish off his bed-making alone.

18

RAMSAY ATTACKED

THE EARLY MORNING late-summer sun shining through the thin curtains of the cottage window woke Ramsay. He reached for his watch and saw it was still very early, just after six in the morning.

Bracken, however, was already awake and came to Ramsay's bedside the moment he saw Ramsay reach for his watch.

"You're right, Bracken," Ramsay said, throwing off the covers and swinging his feet to the floor. "You and I can have a longer walk this morning and still be back for breakfast." He quickly dressed, crept past Alastair sleeping on the couch and, taking Bracken's leash from the hall table, slipped out into the cool morning air.

"You know, Bracken," Ramsay said, shivering as they set out on the trail that led to the top of Gummer's How, "it won't be long till there's frost on these hills."

Bracken didn't take any notice. There were too many fascinating scents on either side of the stony path.

From the summit, they gazed across Windermere and the fells beyond. Ramsay thought he could see Morecambe Bay and the Irish Sea when there was a break in the mist.

"We'll do Coniston after we've solved this puzzle, and before we leave for home," Ramsay said, staring now at the tall peak he could see on the farther side of the lake. "Today, we'll just walk on a bit and come back by the road," he continued.

Bracken was already tugging at the leash. Broad panoramas, however picturesque, didn't interest him at all. With Bracken leading, they walked on for some time before Ramsay took a crossing path he knew would lead them to the road. It was a steep hill but all downhill to where their cottage lay.

As they neared the road, they could hear a heavy vehicle climbing the hill, and the grinding of gears as the driver shifted down.

"People are up and about, Bracken," Ramsay said. "We need to get back or Sophia will think we've abandoned her."

They stepped out of the low bushes onto the narrow verge that ran along the roadside. Ramsay looked up the hill where the truck was just arriving at the crest before descending to the other side. He grinned at its painfully slow progress and turned his attention to the way down to the cottage, and, in doing so, he missed seeing the white van pulled up on the far side of the road that had been momentarily hidden by the truck.

With the heavy wagon gone, silence returned to the hillside, and the air was filled with birdsong.

"They're getting ready to fly south," Ramsay said, as much to himself as Bracken. "I read that just recently. I wonder if we shouldn't head south for the winter too, Bracken."

Bracken didn't care about birds, not when the scent of

sheep in the fields and rabbits in the hedgerows was so appealing.

Ramsay let Bracken pull him along, happy to be making a fast pace for he knew Sophia would be up and wondering about breakfast, something apparently she'd never learned to cook. Toast was all she knew.

"Girls learned Domestic Science when I went to school," Ramsay grumbled out loud, though he knew Bracken had no idea of his thoughts.

Bracken looked back at Ramsay, stiffened, and with a cry, bolted for the hedge as fast as he could, dragging Ramsay with him. Before he could speak, Ramsay felt a solid thump between his shoulder blades. Stumbling, he fell face first into the ditch. He cursed Bracken. Angrily Ramsay sat up in time to see a van swerve silently back onto the road and down the hill. Better still, he saw its numberplate. He hurriedly drew his notepad from his pocket and scribbled it down.

The van's engine coughed into life, and it raced away around a bend in the road.

"Thanks for that, Bracken," he said, stroking the trembling dog's head, reassuring him.

Bracken licked Ramsay's hand and face to re-assure *him*.

"You're right, my friend," Ramsay replied, patting the still concerned Bracken while struggling to his feet. "That was a narrow escape." He stood and found his legs were trembling. He'd need some time before he could feel confident walking down the steep slope.

As he waited for his nerves to settle, Ramsay considered how he could use this attack and grinned. "Finally, Bracken, we have the proof we need. Those tire prints in the mud, the side mirror that hit me and broke off, and their registration number, will settle it. I think we now have enough to get them."

He dusted himself down and practically ran to the cottage where his car could get him to the nearest telephone box, and he could start the wheels of justice moving.

THE LOCAL POLICE officer who answered the phone, however, had never heard of Inspector Ramsay and wanted to speak to his colleagues in Keswick before investigating kidnappings and attempted murders.

"Do that," Ramsay said, "but after you've come to the crime scene and gathered up the evidence still lying where it fell after they hit me."

The man agreed to meet him at the spot after Ramsay described it to him.

After Ramsay hung up the phone, he drove back to the cottage, wincing as every bump in the road sent stabbing pains up his back. At one particularly bad pothole, Ramsay winced and Bracken, sitting in the passenger seat, whined in sympathy.

Ramsay grinned. "It's thanks to you Bracken, I can feel the pain in my back. Without your quick thinking, I'd be a corpse right now." He rubbed Bracken's head and ears affectionately. "You know," he added, "saving *your* life from the farmer that day, saved *my* life today. It's funny how things work out."

He parked the car beside the cottage and made his way inside, where Sophia and Alastair were making breakfast for themselves.

Sophia asked, "What was that all about?"

Ramsay explained, and added, "This time I think we

have enough to get them finally taken into custody." He grabbed Bracken's leash and headed for the door.

"What about breakfast?" Sophia asked. "The police won't be here for half an hour or more."

"I'm going to sit where it happened to be sure no one comes back and destroys or removes the evidence."

"We'll come too," Sophia said. "If they know we're here, they may come to the cottage while you're sitting up there waiting."

"Good point," Ramsay said, "though I don't think they necessarily know you're here."

"If they've watched this place for any time last night," Alastair said. "They know."

"Fine, but you need to disappear when the police arrive," Ramsay said. "They don't need to know you're here, as well."

Sophia's guess about the time was correct. It was forty minutes before they saw the police car crest the hill. Sophia and Alastair quickly stepped onto the trail that Ramsay and Bracken had come from earlier to join the road, disappearing into the bushes. As agreed, they were heading back over the summit of Gummer's How and the return path to the cottage.

The officers were efficient, Ramsay noted approvingly. Almost as methodical as his own team had been back in Newcastle.

The officer bagging the broken mirror asked, "This hit you on your back?"

"It did," Ramsay said. "By now I can show you the bruise." He began to remove his jacket until the sergeant in charge said, "Not now, sir. We'll have the police doctor look at your back at the station."

Ramsay nodded, replacing his jacket. He didn't want to

leave Sophia alone at the cottage while he was at the station and replied, "I have my daughter and her boyfriend staying with me. We need to take them along in case the men come back."

"You think these are the people you suggested kidnapped that young woman a week or so ago?" the sergeant asked. He smiled. "I spoke to Keswick, you see."

"I didn't see the driver today, but I'm positive that was the van," Ramsay replied.

"And this daughter of yours..."

"Is by my first marriage," Ramsay lied. "Her mother and I split up years ago, and she remarried. Astrid and I have only just begun to know each other; her mother died last year; you see."

"Not the missing girl then?"

Ramsay maintained a blank expression. "Didn't she go to London?"

"So, they say. Only no one has found her down there either."

"If she knows her life is in danger, that's a strong motive to keep out of sight," Ramsay replied.

The sergeant nodded and returned to the car where his constable was placing a plaster cast of the tire tread.

"That everything?" the sergeant asked.

"Yes, sir. There isn't much beyond the tracks and the broken mirror."

"In order to make those tracks, the van had to leave the left lane, cross over the right lane, and onto the verge," Ramsay reminded them. "If my dog hadn't pulled me out of its path, I'd have been hit by the van and not just its wing mirror."

"The driver will say he lost control and didn't mean any of this to happen," the sergeant replied.

"He was coasting down the hill, engine off, until after he'd hit me," Ramsay said. "He only started the engine after."

"Again," the sergeant said. "Your word is good enough for me, but the driver will say something different."

"With the photos you've taken, the cast of the prints, the registration number I've given you, and a photo of my back, you'll have enough to charge him with a traffic offence at a minimum," Ramsay said. "And matching the cast you've just taken to the ones from the farm where the girl was held with the one the Keswick police have, there'll be enough to tie them together using the earlier evidence I provided."

After Ramsay had agreed to follow them to the station and make a formal statement, the police drove off to consult with their superiors. Ramsay and Bracken returned to the cottage where Sophia was waiting impatiently to hear what had transpired. As he cooked breakfast and fed Bracken, Ramsay recounted the conversation.

"They're not going to do anything, are they?" Sophia said dejectedly as she set the small table, while Alastair cooked bacon on the small stove.

"I think when they've spoken to the Keswick police and I've made my statement, they will," Ramsay said. "Particularly, if I suggest I might go to the local newspaper to flush out the two villains."

"Most of the morning will be gone on that," Sophia complained. "What are Alastair and I going to do?"

"Stay out of sight," Ramsay replied. "I'll drop you off before we get to Lakeside and the police station. Have a walk up a track. Look at some views. I'll be back to pick you up before you know it."

"Then what?"

"We'll go to Keswick and prevent those two leaving, if they haven't already," Ramsay replied.

"Are we going to fight them?"

"I more thought we could sabotage the van and other vehicles in the Lakeland Lorries yard," Ramsay said. "Becoming involved in a melee will get us arrested as well as them."

"So might sabotaging vehicles," Sophia reminded him.

"Not if no one knows we did it."

"Someone will know though," Alastair said, gloomily. "Someone always does."

19

DISAPPOINTING POLICE RESPONSE

WITH RAMSAY GONE, Alastair and Sophia discussed their morning plan.

"I'm not walking up any mountains," Sophia said when Alastair reminded her of Ramsay's parting words.

"Then," Alastair said, "I suggest something to help the investigation."

"What?" Sophia asked suspiciously.

"Hetherington," Alastair replied. "We find him, and I question him while you keep out of sight."

Sophia considered this and replied, "He should be out on the moors or in the woods, finding the birds right now. Daddy has shoots arranged right up until we planned to leave."

With this decided, they left Ramsay a note, drove north, and parked near the Thornton estate. Sophia led the way to the pheasant breeding huts in case Hetherington was there and, when they found he wasn't, they set off through the sparse wooded area in search of him out on the moors. From the top of a low rise, they could see he wasn't anywhere out on the treeless land.

"The lazy beggar," Sophia said indignantly. "He should be working."

"Maybe he is but indoors, the cold store or gun room, perhaps?"

"Well, I can't go in there, even in my Astrid disguise."

"I'll get your butler to tell me where he is," Alastair said, "and anything else he knows about him."

"Be quick," Sophia said. "I don't want to be standing out here for too long. Someone who knows me might see me."

"Take the car keys," Alastair said, handing them over. "I'll meet you there as soon as I can."

When he saw Sophia was heading for the car, Alastair quickly crossed the open ground and knocked on the house's kitchen door. It was opened by a maid he knew. The daughter of one of his father's tenants.

"Hello, Lizzie," Alastair said. "I came to see Mr. Cartwright. Can you find him for me and tell no one, please?"

Lizzie hurried away and returned moments later with the butler.

"What brings you here, Alastair?" Cartwright asked.

"I need to talk to you privately."

Cartwright nodded and led the way to his Butler's Pantry, closing the door behind them.

"What is it?"

"I'm looking into Sophia's disappearance, and I want to speak to Mr. Hetherington. I believe he was on the moors the day Sophia went missing. Maybe he saw something."

Cartwright snorted. "If he did, he hasn't mentioned it."

"I understand he isn't the kind of man to 'help the police with their inquiries,'" Alastair responded. "I thought he might tell me."

"Not unless money changes hands," Cartwright said, "and then he'll say whatever you want to hear."

Alastair nodded. "It's a chance I'm willing to take."

Shaking his head, Cartwright went off to find the man. He returned a few moments later with a small, seedy looking man in tow. He made the introductions, and Alastair explained why he was here.

"What's this to do with me?" Hetherington asked belligerently.

"I thought if you were on the moors that day, you might have seen something to help in the search."

"If I had, I'd have told the police," the man replied.

"I thought you might have forgotten what you saw and only realized later," Alastair suggested.

"What's it worth to you if I saw something?"

"It depends on what you saw," Alastair replied. "For information that helps find her, it might be quite a lot."

Hetherington shrugged. "Maybe I did see someone walking alone that day. But where, when, and which direction I can't remember just now."

"Would a pound help your memory?"

"It might help me remember where," Hetherington replied.

"Alastair," Cartwright said, breaking into the conversation, "remember what I told you."

Alastair nodded but asked Hetherington, "I suppose another two pounds would help you remember if this 'someone' was Sophia and which direction she was heading?"

Hetherington shook his head. "If I'd known it was the gaffer's daughter, I would have said, wouldn't I?"

"I don't know, would you?"

"Course I would," Hetherington replied. "But someone

else, I wouldn't bother cos it wasn't relevant to their inquiries, was it?"

Alastair was growing tired of this nonsense but kept his temper and said, "Three pounds if you tell me, it was a young woman and which direction she was going?"

Hetherington nodded and held out his hand. When Alastair had given him the notes, he said, "It was a young woman, and she was headed toward the old Leadbetter farm."

"Is there more you remember?"

Hetherington eyed him, as if judging how much more he could get. "Well," he said slowly, and then stopped. "Nah, it wouldn't be no more than hearsay."

"What?"

"Well," Hetherington said, dragging out the one word, "You may not want to hear. I'm doing you a kindness really by not saying."

"Would another pound overcome your kindness?"

"All right for you to sneer, young master," Hetherington said bitterly. "To folks like me a pound is a lot of money, and we can't afford to sell our little knowledge cheap."

"Very well, two pounds," Alastair said. He held out two more notes, and Hetherington snatched them eagerly.

"They do say she was kidnapped and on your father's orders, but I can't say for certain that's true." Hetherington's eyes locked on Alastair's and held.

"Thank you for the information," Alastair said, shocked that people may be saying this and trying to gauge whether Hetherington's expression was one of real honesty or fake.

"Much good will it do you," Hetherington replied, turning away and leaving.

Alastair and Cartwright stared at each other for a

moment before Cartwright said, "I don't believe what he said about your father is true."

Alastair frowned, not wanting to share his own doubts about his father. "I have to take it seriously though," he said.

"I told you he would say anything for money," Cartwright said. "Don't fall for it."

"I must," Alastair replied. He thanked Cartwright for his help and returned to the car, where Sophia was waiting impatiently.

"Well," she demanded as he dropped heavily into the driver's seat.

Alastair started the car. "The man is a rat and is happy to suggest my father as the person responsible for your abduction."

"Do you believe him?"

"Mr. Cartwright says I shouldn't, and I know he's right. Information you buy should always be suspect but..."

"What about Hetherington as the ringleader?"

"My guess is he'd do anything for money, so he's high on my list for chief suspect."

Sophia nodded. "I think so too. I can't remember much about him. I only saw him once, I think, but he struck me then as someone we shouldn't have hired."

Alastair laughed. "We can't all be film stars, but I take your point. There's something about him that suggests criminality."

"It was the way he looked at me," Sophia said. "I know how men look when they admire a girl, and this wasn't it."

"You never mentioned any of this before," Alastair reminded her.

"Why would I? It was a momentary glance from someone I'd never met and didn't see again. To be honest, because the outdoor staff are new every shooting season, I never think of them as being part of the household."

"How can we prove or disprove he's our man, though?" Alastair said. "With you out of their clutches, they aren't likely to be meeting or anything."

"They might, but we can't watch and wait," Sophia added.

"My father, on the other hand, we might be able to investigate further," Alastair said.

"If it is your father," Sophia replied, "we're in some difficulty. Your family position in society would be horrible."

Alastair nodded grimly. "Which is why we must prove it to be untrue."

"It's hard to prove innocence," Sophia replied guardedly. "There's always rumors and whispers, even if someone else has been convicted. No smoke without fire, people will say."

"We need to talk this over with Inspector Ramsay," Alastair agreed. "He needs to take the lead here. Me proclaiming my father innocent will only make the rumors worse. They'll say I was in on it too."

BY THE TIME Sophia and Alastair had returned to the cottage, Ramsay was already back and inclined to take a dim view of them not following orders. However, he reminded himself they weren't police constables and could do as they pleased.

"Did your statement get them moving?" Alastair asked Ramsay as they walked through the door.

"I think it might," Ramsay said. "They're still hesitant because they aren't comfortable between the van being at the farmhouse where you were held, Sophia, and the drivers being kidnappers."

"Can the police hold them for failing to report an accident?" Sophia asked.

"Only until a lawyer arrives and demands their release," Ramsay said. "It's disappointing, I know, but it's how the law works."

"You thought it would be different this time," Sophia said accusingly.

"I hoped by now they'd have gathered enough evidence from the farm to link the van, its drivers, and the kidnapping. They don't feel they have."

"We had similar luck," Alastair said, changing the conversation. "We tracked down Hetherington and interviewed him."

"Did he have anything to say?" Ramsay asked.

"He says the rumors are it was Alastair's dad behind the kidnapping," Sophia replied.

"He also said he did see a single woman on the moors that day heading to Leadbetter's farm."

Ramsay smiled. "Which means he knew where Sophia was being held, don't you think?"

"We hadn't thought of it that way," Alastair replied, "but I think it does."

"He would say he didn't, if questioned by the police," Sophia said gloomily. "After all, a few trails go past the old farm. It isn't a place that's off-limits."

"True," Alastair replied, "but he was angling for money, and I suspect he threw it in to whet my appetite. My guess is the place of your captivity is already out on the grapevine."

"I think so too," Ramsay said. "Nothing stays a secret long in a police station."

"We also think he's a genuinely nasty man," Sophia added.

"You weren't at the interview, were you?" Ramsay asked with mounting alarm.

"No, but I remembered seeing him in the house once and didn't like the look of him then."

"Phew," Ramsay said. "You had me worried there. So, what did you decide between these two?"

"It would be easier to follow up on my father's possible role in this than confirm it was Hetherington," Alastair replied. "Only the police could exert enough pressure on Hetherington to make him confess."

"They're not ready to grill the two we have given them," Ramsay replied, "so there's no chance with this seemingly unconnected man."

"How do we investigate Alastair's dad, though?" Sophia asked. "Alastair can ask questions, but beyond that we have nothing to go on, except the word of a man only looking for cash."

Ramsay considered before replying. "We know your father knows the Lakeland Lorries crowd, so if he is the man that set them up for this, he must have meetings or phone calls with them. I can ask for phone records through my police contacts, but you may have ways of finding out about meetings, Alastair."

"I'll ask Dad and Mum separately. If mum doesn't know what's going on they may tell different stories. And our farm records will list the work we've given the Lakeland gang. Dad's always saying I need to become more involved with running the business, and this is my start."

Sophia's brow was furrowed in thought. "I don't see how it could be your father, Alastair. He wouldn't know I was out on the moors alone that day. It must be someone with access to the house."

"I'd thought of that," Alastair said, gloomily, "but

someone in your house could have phoned my father the moment they learned where you'd gone."

"Which leads us back to Hetherington," Sophia said.

Alastair shook his head. "Mr. Cartwright and Dad go back a long way. He might well be Dad's spy in the camp."

"Now we're suspecting our butler," Sophia cried. "He's been with us since I was a girl. I won't believe it."

"I'm just using him as an example, Soph," Alastair replied. "He's my friend as well as Dad's."

"I still say Hetherington," Sophia replied.

"I agree," Ramsay said. "If Alastair's dad had been the ringleader, this would have been better planned and executed."

Ramsay paused before continuing, "I was puzzled from the start but when I heard that Hetherington, an unscrupulous petty criminal, had access to Sophia's family home and could have overheard her leaving, I think it makes sense. He heard Sophia leave, watched the direction she took, and just called his friends. They acted on the opportunity without any idea how to successfully carry out a kidnapping."

Sophia shook her head. "It can't have been that spontaneous. The door of the cellar had been prepared before."

Ramsay nodded. "I don't mean the whole kidnapping was spur of the moment, just the timing. They waited for the moment and pounced when it came."

"We'll need to prove he knows Connery and Kennedy before the police will believe us," Alastair said.

Sophia, who'd listened carefully as Ramsay was speaking, added, "I couldn't have explained it better, but how are we going to prove they're in league? They'll be careful not to meet while I'm still considered missing."

"I overheard the two Geordies talking in a pub on St.

John's Street," Ramsay said. "Maybe an evening or two spent in there might provide us what we need."

"Was it the Dog and Gun?" Alastair asked. "I'm sometimes in there with friends, whose local it is. They could look out for them."

Ramsay thought for a moment before saying, "Yes, Dog and Gun sounds right."

"Will they know what the men look like?" Sophia asked.

"They'll know Hetherington," Alastair said. "I'll describe the other two."

"To sum up," Ramsay said, "I'll follow up with my police contacts and you, Alastair, will investigate your father's possible involvement and have your pub friends look out for the kidnappers in the Dog and Gun."

Alastair agreed.

Sophia said, glaring at Alastair, "I'm going with the Inspector. While he cajoles his police people to snoop on innocent citizens, I'll wander around Keswick looking for any of the three 'innocent citizens.' If we learn their haunts, we might get lucky and catch them together."

"I think it best you stay out of sight," Ramsay said. "I won't be more than an hour."

"And I think it best I continue sleuthing," Sophia replied grandly.

Ramsay sighed but agreed, and they were soon in the car heading back to town, with Alastair following in the Land-Rover. Ramsay didn't like Sophia's plan, it seemed like recklessly putting herself in harm's way with little chance of finding anything useful.

20

A LINK IS CONFIRMED

AFTER FINISHING HIS TASKS, Ramsay, true to his word, was back at the car in less than an hour, but there was no Sophia waiting. Grinding his teeth, he returned to the main street and began searching. After walking the busy part of the street, on one side then the other, without finding her, he was left with the problem of either widening his search or returning to the car to wait. He was still debating with himself when, farther down the street, he saw a seedy character leaving a store with a package. In a rural area, where men worked on the land, a man in torn dungarees wouldn't normally attract his attention, but this one did because no sooner had the man set off, when Ramsay saw Sophia emerge from a shop on the other side of the road. He set off in hot pursuit of both.

"Astrid," Ramsay said quietly as he got closer.

At first, Sophia didn't respond, but then, remembering, she turned. "That's Hetherington," she said, pointing to the man still steadily making his way along the street.

"I'll walk in front now," Ramsay said. "You drop back in case he gets suspicious of you."

"He doesn't know I'm here," Sophia replied. "He's never looked back once."

"That doesn't mean a thing," Ramsay said. "Do as I say. Follow when he's out of sight, but you can still see me."

Sophia turned away and entered the entrance to a dress shop where she waited, peering around the door jamb until she saw Ramsay wave his arm. She ran quickly to catch up and saw Ramsay turn a corner into a side street. There, Sophia stopped and again peered around the corner. Ramsay was examining the entrance to a small pub or bar. She was beside him in a minute.

"Not a nice place," she said, grimacing.

"It looks like the kind of thieves' haunt we see in big cities," Ramsay replied. "I never expected to see one in a town like this."

"What do we do now?" Sophia asked.

"You watch and wait," Ramsay said. "He doesn't know me, so I can venture inside."

"The other two do know you," Sophia reminded him.

"I'll be careful entering," Ramsay said. "If I see him with one of them, I won't go in."

He stepped inside the small porch between an inner and outer door and carefully opened the inner one. With only a small crack opened, Ramsay could see a sliver of the clientele. He pushed further and saw the man he'd been following sitting alone, with his back to the door, at a small table with stools for three. Ramsay quietly closed the door and looked at his watch.

"It's nearly lunchtime," he said to Sophia. "We need to get hidden and watch who appears."

"We don't know which direction they'll come from," Sophia said, looking nervously at each end of the narrow street.

Ramsay remembered a coal loading place he passed and took her arm, hurrying her away. The small alcove in the grey stone, un-cemented walls, was just wide enough for two and deep enough to hide them from prying eyes. For a moment, Ramsay was taken back to those first stakeouts he'd shared with Miss Riddell.

"We can't see," Sophia complained.

"We can hear if you keep quiet."

They strained their ears and within a few minutes, they heard harsh voices entering the alley to their left. Ramsay peered around the corner of the wall and pulled back. He nodded to Sophia, who almost danced with joy.

"And you wanted me to stay at the cottage," she crowed.

"Yes, yes," said Ramsay. "But stay here this time while I confirm the three of them are meeting."

This didn't take more than a moment. He trotted quickly back and told Sophia, whose previous joy was now pure ecstasy.

"I did it. I solved the case."

Ramsay shook his head. This wasn't how policemen celebrated a breakthrough. "We need the local police to see them and then find the phone call on the day of your abduction. Then, we'll have solved the case."

"Pooh," Sophia replied with a wave of her hand. "You go and get a policeman out of the office; I'll stay here and trail the kidnappers if they leave."

Ramsay hesitated, concerned she'd show herself to the three, but decided, if he was quick enough, he'd be back before they'd finished their pie and pint, the usual fare at places of this sort.

It took some persuading to get a constable to return to the bar where the three suspects were eating, but he made it before Sophia had left the coal hole. She looked disappointed, he thought with a grin.

The constable peeked his head around the bar door, as Ramsay had done earlier, before returning to them. "You're right," he said, "they do know each other. Proving that they carried out the kidnapping is still going to be difficult."

"Then the sooner you start, the better," Ramsay said bluntly. "Starting with the phone calls from the Thornton house that day."

"Even if we show someone called the two people you say kidnapped Miss Thornton," the constable replied, stubbornly, "it's your word against theirs, at this point, and if the man I saw did make a call from the Thornton house, we have no way of knowing what it was about. I'm sure the sergeant will say it isn't enough."

"It will be a start," Ramsay said, growing more and more frustrated with the slow, pedantic progress of the local police.

"As you say, sir," the constable replied. "Now, if you and your daughter will follow me, I'll take your statements."

Seeing Sophia about to give a crushing rejoinder, Ramsay placed his finger on his lips and shook his head. Sophia sighed, but with Ramsay, followed the constable back to the station.

Leaving the station an hour later, Sophia said, "They think I kidnapped myself."

"They think Sophia Thornton is a missing person and not a kidnap victim. They think I'm playing games with them and their time."

"With luck, Alastair will have more good information and we'll get the result," Sophia said, getting into Ramsay's car.

"And I will also have the information we need when I've

spoken to Jimmy Logan and Sergeant Hardraw," Ramsay said. "They might have the phone records by now."

"Then find a phone box and call them," Sophia said bluntly. "Why didn't you ask when you were in there?"

"Hardraw wasn't there, and he'll speak freer away from the office."

As Ramsay was now familiar with the location of the phone boxes in town, it wasn't long before he was talking to Logan. "Anything?" he asked immediately after Logan picked up the handset.

"Good day to you too, Tom," Logan replied. "Will you never learn the habits of civilized people?"

"Never mind the banter, was there a phone call to the Elliott house immediately before Sophia was abducted?" Ramsay said, urgently. So much of their theories depended on Logan's answer, not to mention the mental anguish the wrong answer would cause Alastair and Sophia.

"There was no call to the house from anywhere at that time," Logan replied, sensing Ramsay wasn't in the mood for delay. "If Elliott senior was involved and was alerted that morning, it wasn't by a phone call to his house. Happy now?"

"Relieved," Ramsay replied. "My two young friends are worried sick it's Alastair's father behind it all."

"I'm not saying he isn't," Logan reminded him. "Only that, if he learned of your young friend's movements and phoned to his accomplices, it wasn't from his house."

"I understand," Ramsay said, "but realistically, that was the only way he could have known in time to capitalize on the opportunity."

"I hope this is the last I'll be hearing from you on this interfering in police business of yours," Logan said, chuckling.

"Absolutely, Jimmy. I wouldn't dream of involving you further, I know how dangerous it is for you."

"I'm glad your memory still works," Logan said. "Be sure to drop in when next you're down Manchester way."

Ramsay assured him he would, hung up and returned to the car where Sophia's anxious expression confirmed what he'd told Logan.

"No call to or from Alastair's house at the time in question," Ramsay said as he slumped in the driver's seat. His own anxiety had been more than he'd realized.

Sophia's face lit up. "I knew Mr. Elliott wasn't who we're looking for. He's always had a soft spot for me."

"Then it's Hetherington," Ramsay said.

"Or Cat," Sophia almost growled.

"Would she know Kennedy and Connery?" Ramsay asked.

"If they came to the house on business," Sophia said, "why not?"

Ramsay shook his head. "She either had to cultivate their trust before she knew there was an opportunity or persuade them on the spot that day and that meant they had to be there at the house that day."

"She's a good-looking woman and they're greedy men," Sophia replied. "It isn't impossible."

"Possibly," Ramsay replied, "but not likely." He checked his watch. "I'll try Hardraw's home. He might be there having his lunch."

Hardraw wasn't home, and he returned to the car. "We need to find Alastair," he said. "The sooner he knows his dad's in the clear, the better."

. . .

ALASTAIR, however, when he arrived that evening, had little to report. His parents continued to claim their only contact with Lakeland Lorries was having them handle small local deliveries. The boat would have been beyond Lakeland's expertise, though they did get the information about the boat from them.

He'd spent an unfruitful afternoon reading through the records of the family business without finding anything that suggested a link between Lakeland Lorries and Sophia's kidnapping. He wasn't surprised; no one as business minded as his father would leave written incriminating records lying around to be read by his son. Alastair finished by saying, "There's still one document to see and that's the phone bill for the past month. That is now my best hope for a result, either way."

"It seems to me," Sophia said, "if your father was happy for you to go through the family papers, he's sure there's nothing to see there."

Alastair nodded. "My thoughts, exactly."

Ramsay laughed. "We have some good news for you, Alastair. My colleague has been told by the Post Office there were no calls into or out of your house at the time we're interested in. Still, if your father hides the phone bill when it arrives, that will be a different story."

"That's great news," Alastair replied, his face lighting up with relief and pleasure. "And I'd already decided he wouldn't hide the phone bill, though I was still nervous. I was embarrassed by his pleasure at my finally taking an interest. It made me feel guilty. It never occurred to me how much it hurt him that I never would agree to take part."

Ramsay nodded. "People rarely understand that businessmen do what they do because they enjoy pitting their wits against the marketplace. It's rarely about money."

"Is that your considered opinion after years of being employed by the government?" Sophia asked mischievously.

"It's my considered opinion after interviewing such people over thirty-odd years," Ramsay replied. "They enjoy the risk and the game."

"Changing the subject," Sophia said. "When will the phone bill come in and we can finally put this to rest?"

"Soon," Alastair said. "The one in the files was five days after the previous month's end."

"Great," Sophia replied, gloomily. "This could go on forever. I feel it would be best if I stopped hiding, went to the police, and identified those men as my abductors."

Ramsay shook his head. "It won't work. You didn't see their faces when you were being held, and they were too far away when you were being pursued. Any competent lawyer would have them out of custody in no time and your life would be in even greater danger."

"So, what's next?" Alastair asked.

"We push them into making a mistake," Ramsay said. "It's risky, but better than waiting for your family's telephone bill to arrive."

"Sergeant Hardraw may have my house's phone records by now," Sophia said. "You should call him again, Inspector."

Ramsay smiled and said, "We must wait until he's home from work. Meanwhile, we should make sure Kennedy and Connery don't just drive away after meeting with their leader, Hetherington. If he is their leader."

"We can't watch all night," Alastair said. "Can we?"

"I think it would be best," Ramsay replied. "They must be getting anxious by now, constantly being taken in for questioning by the police."

"We'll need warmer clothes," Sophia said, eyeing her summer blouse and skirt with misgiving.

"I have an old jacket in the car," Ramsay offered.

"And I have some coveralls in mine," Alastair added, grinning. "If you go off shopping, you may miss the fun."

Sophia immediately responded with, "I wasn't going shopping."

"Sounded like it to me," Alastair replied.

"Children," Ramsay said, determinedly, "this is no time for squabbles. We'll find our villains and work out a roster for tonight. Sophia can wrap up warmer later. Let's go."

21

INVESTIGATION OVER, RAMSAY THINKS

AFTER ESTABLISHING the van wasn't in Lakeland Lorries' yard, Sophia said, "I told you they were more likely to have packed and left straight from their rooms."

Ramsay agreed, saying, "We had to be sure they weren't at work."

They walked quickly through the lanes to the guest house where the two men were staying.

"Told you so," Sophia cried, triumphantly, when they saw the van pulled up alongside the guest house gate.

"You two watch the windows and door of the guest house while I let down their tires," Ramsay said.

"I can do that," Sophia cried. "You two watch out for me."

"It might be better if I did it, Soph," Alastair said. "You wouldn't much enjoy prison."

"Pooh," Sophia said. "They don't send people to prison for letting air out of tires. It's my adventure, remember? I'm doing it."

Ramsay sighed but, with a long-suffering expression, agreed. "Very well, Alastair and I will cross the street where we can watch without it being too obvious. You keep low, so the wall hides you, and do all four tires, starting with the two on the roadside."

"Why them?"

"Because if they come out before you're finished, at least you'll have one or two done and can get away without being seen. Only if I signal it's all clear, do you go around the van and do the curbside tires," Ramsay said. "And don't start until we're across the road and have signaled it's safe."

It was Sophia's turn to sigh in exasperation as Ramsay and Alastair crossed quickly over the street. A moment later, Ramsay signaled for her to start.

Stooping down to be hidden by the wall, Sophia ran as quickly as she could to the front tire and unscrewed the valve cap. She'd blown up bicycle tires often enough to know how this worked. Pressing the valve, she waited impatiently for the air to hiss out, all the while watching the street for vehicles.

Fortunately, it was a quiet lane at the back of the terrace and no vehicles disturbed her as she moved to the rear tire and let the air out of that one too. As the hissing died away, she looked over to Ramsay. He signaled her to continue, and she slipped around the back of the van and started flattening the rear tire on that side. This was the dangerous time, Sophia now realized. She couldn't see Ramsay's signals or the guest house door for the garden wall. She had to rely on hearing the men leave the building.

However, there were no sounds from the guest house, and she continued flattening both tires. When all four were flat, she crept back to the rear of the van and ran across the road to where Ramsay was waiting.

"All done," she said, gasping. Her heart was pounding, and her breaths came in rapid succession.

Ramsay smiled. Sophia's excitement at her triumph was so extreme he thought he might have to offer first aid.

"We should walk on," Ramsay said, "in case anyone looks out and sees us."

As Sophia walked, her heart rate returned to normal, and her breathing recovered. "Where are we going?"

"There's a bus shelter down the street. It has a bench we can sit on while we wait for them to emerge."

They hadn't even reached the shelter when they heard, then saw, Connery and Kennedy at the van. The men weren't pleased to find it inoperable, that much was clear.

Ramsay was looking back when he saw the taller man eyeing them suspiciously. "We have to get out of here and fast," he said. "Run."

They ran across the road, down an alley, back to the center of town. "Where are we going?" Sophia asked.

"The cop shop," Ramsay replied. He was glad the hiking he'd done this summer meant he could talk even after running hard. "We'll be safe, and we can persuade the police to go and catch those villains."

The two men, however, had clearly decided flight was better than exacting revenge on them for they never appeared on the main street. The three sleuths were able to walk the last few yards, entering the station without hindrance.

It took some time for the officers in the station to get after the two men, even after Ramsay reminded them of his previous evidence and the information, they'd received from the Lakeside police station only an hour or so before. By the time they did head out for the guest house, with Ramsay, Sophia and Alastair following, the men were nowhere to be seen.

"Lakeland Lorries," Sophia cried. "They'll be getting a vehicle from there."

The group ran to the yard, only to see a light truck disappearing around the corner at the farther end of the street.

"Someone get back to the station and alert the highway patrol cars," Ramsay said, taking charge, forgetting he wasn't in the police anymore. They didn't seem to mind, and one constable ran off at a blistering pace for the station.

"He'll get the word out quickly enough," the remaining officer said. "He's a Fell Runner in his spare time. He could catch that lorry if we asked him to."

"So long as a car is on the trail of those two before they reach a major road," Ramsay said, "I'll consider it a job well done."

Once again, back at the station, they were asked to make a statement explaining how they came to see the two men trying to leave and what they saw the men doing before they were allowed to leave. Their statements didn't mention they'd let down the van's tires to prevent a quick escape.

"I THINK THE INVESTIGATION'S OVER," Ramsay said as they walked back to the car. "Those two will say who hired them and that will be that."

"I'm glad," Alastair replied. "I'm growing tired of all this."

"You're hopeless, Alastair," Sophia said caustically. "I've never enjoyed anything so much in my life."

"Inspector," Alastair said, "You must phone Hardraw. He told you to call at seven when we spoke to him at the station, and it's almost that now."

Ramsay frowned and seemed about to refuse before saying, "You're right. We shouldn't count our chickens on this being over. We've had so many disappointments." He led them back to the main street and the phone box he regularly used now that he had no access to a hotel phone.

Sergeant Hardraw, however, was as reluctant to hand out personal information as Logan had been. Ramsay understood the situation. He too would have been nervous in his working life. After reminding Ramsay that nothing he was about to say was official, and certainly not given out by him, Hardraw said, "There was a phone call from the Thornton house at the time you're interested in. I've checked the number the call was made to, and it was to Lakeland Lorries."

"We have them," Ramsay said, pleased to have yet another link made in the growing chain of evidence.

"Not so fast," Hardraw replied depressingly. "We don't know who made the call or why. It's suggestive, I agree, but you wouldn't have accepted this in your day."

Ramsay was forced to agree he wouldn't have done before adding, "But once you've questioned the people at each end of the call, we will have them."

Hardraw agreed that it would be a priority tomorrow, and Ramsay hung up.

"I don't know why anybody bothers with the police," Sophia said, crossly. "They seem to put obstacles and delays in the way of everything."

Ramsay laughed. "There's nothing the police like less than presenting a case in court only to have it thrown out because they didn't dot the 'i' or cross a 't.'"

"We understand, Inspector, but you've had thirty years to get used to this, we haven't," Alastair said.

The unhappy duo continued to complain as they drove back to the cottage, making Ramsay smile. To change the conversation, he suggested they feed themselves and

Bracken at the cottage before finding a quiet pub to celebrate in.

"Why not go straight to a pub and celebrate over the meal?" Sophia suggested. She was already tired of the limited menu Ramsay could cook.

"Very well," Ramsay said. "The next one we see, we'll stop."

AFTER THEY'D EATEN, Sophia made her way to the Ladies Room to powder her nose, leaving Alastair and Ramsay alone.

"If it *is* over," Ramsay said, as they watched her disappearing through the door, "maybe you could start persuading Sophia you're the one for her."

Alastair pulled a face, wryly expressing his doubts. "I'd love to, but the thing is, I'm the son of a northern landowner, a successful one, I agree, but Sophia is the daughter of a famous film producer. She's used to London society and even Hollywood, where every leading man in the movie world is looking for a young woman as beautiful as she is. We aren't a likely combination, are we?"

In his heart, Ramsay agreed, but said, "You're a decent young man and the people she meets in those places are snakes, by and large. Sophia's a sensible woman; she knows the difference."

"Hah!" Alastair responded. "You sound like my dad. He's full of those empty, feel-good, half-truths too."

"I think you're taking too dark a view of your situation," Ramsay said. "It was Sophia who wanted you along on this adventure, not me. You need to see how others see you."

"I'll tell you how others see me," Alastair replied angrily. "A year ago, I was telling friends how beautiful Sophia was.

One replied, 'it's true, she's a dish.' Another said, 'it's true—but she's a beautiful porcelain dish and you're only a shabby pewter spoon.' The old rhyme, you know. And he's right."

"They're your friends, Alastair. They're going to rag you over everything, you know that."

Alastair's expression remained grim. "Many a true word spoken in jest. Isn't that how the proverb goes?"

"Alastair," Ramsay said, almost equally angrily. "I'm not one of your young pals, so let me tell you some home truths. You're a handsome man. You have energy, initiative, a family business that's growing strongly, and you love her. The only person holding you back is you and this morbid belief you're not worthy. Snap out of it, man."

Alastair was momentarily taken aback and appeared ready to take offence. Then he grinned. "Just like my father," he said, shaking his head. "Old people today are hopelessly out of date. Cinderella doesn't marry the prince anymore; she marries the court jester because he has 'talent.'"

22

A SUSPICIOUS LEAD

As she returned to the table, Sophia asked "When the police finally have my abductors, can I come out of hiding?"

Ramsay shook his head. "Those two may have kidnapped you, but the person or people they were likely working for are still at large."

"Do you really think the police will unmask the person behind those two?" Alastair asked. "They seem completely unconcerned, to me."

"I fear they will," Ramsay replied. "It's in Connery and Kennedy's best interests to cooperate and spread the blame as widely as they can."

"You 'fear?'" Sophia asked.

Ramsay hesitated before saying, "I fear you won't like the news."

"You're sure it was someone in my family and staff?"

"No, I don't know for sure," Ramsay said, "because, while we've seen your mother's will, it doesn't entirely confirm who it is either way. Like you, I think your stepmother is the most likely, and I think that's what the police interrogation will reveal."

"I hope it is," Sophia said. "My father was always good to me until this recent urge to have me marry Alastair."

"I have to say," Alastair interjected, "when Sophia told me this, I thought it was more likely to be her dad. I'd liked him up to that moment, but I object to being involved in his schemes, especially one that involves Soph being forced into marriage."

"People change," Ramsay said. "And there are often reasons we don't know about. That said, I don't believe any father would kill his own child. It isn't in our nature."

"Are you a father?" Alastair asked, puzzled. Ramsay's family life hadn't been explained during these hectic days.

"I was," Ramsay said, "but my children and wife died in the Blitz."

"How awful," Sophia cried.

"It was, and still is," Ramsay said, "but it's why I don't believe it's your father behind this. Hetherington is still my first choice, but your stepmother is my second one. It's the stuff of nursery stories, the Wicked Stepmother."

"Maybe that's why I suspect her," Sophia said, thoughtfully, "and not my father, who was the one getting on my nerves."

"So far as we know at this time," Ramsay said, "your father was only trying to make you an advantageous marriage."

"With exactly the opposite result of what he hoped for," Alastair said, with a note of anger in his voice.

Ramsay said nothing but thought *Fidel Thornton must be a complete idiot not to have seen he was pushing them apart with his behavior. What he wanted was well on its way to happening, and he set it back for maybe years.*

Another thought came to Ramsay's mind. *What if he could see it but was desperate to have it happen quicker? Maybe*

he thought they were so close, he just needed to push them a little?
Why would he need to hurry it along? The most likely reason
was a debt to some dangerous people.

"Sophia," Ramsay said, "in London, does your father
associate with shady people? Gangster types like the Krays
or the Richardsons, I mean."

"Everybody does," Sophia said. "People know they're
awful human beings, but 'they bring a bit of spice to otherwise dull parties,' is how Cat described it, when I questioned her about a guest list."

"They were at your parent's parties?" Alastair asked,
incredulously.

"Not often," Sophia replied. "At least, I think not often. I
just happened to see a guest list when I was old enough to
understand who the people on the list were."

"I wish you'd mentioned this earlier," Ramsay said.
"We've been wracking our brains for someone nasty enough
to kidnap you and not ask for a ransom and couldn't think
of anyone. Now you tell us your parents have dealings with
some of the worst monsters in the country."

"But they're in London and the dealings my father had
with them were only party invitations," Sophia cried. "There
can't be any connection."

"What if your father has borrowed from them, or just
taken money from them on the understanding of a favor
that he can't return, now that he's out of the studio? What if
they owned a casino, he owes debts to?" Ramsay asked.

"Father's a rich man," Sophia replied. "He wouldn't need
to take money from people like that just because he's out of
work for a few months."

Ramsay thought this over. *What if he'd been living beyond*
his means for some time? What if the banks or other reputable
sources had dried up?

"Were his recent movies successful?" Ramsay asked.

"He said so, though not apparently successful enough for the studio," Sophia replied. "Not enough return on their investment was how he said they put it."

"He told you this?" Alastair asked.

Sophia shook her head. "I overheard him arguing with Cat one day."

"Was she refusing to dip into her own wealth?" Ramsay asked.

"I don't know," Sophia replied, frowning. "I overheard when I entered the room, and they stopped arguing immediately. But father and Cat wouldn't still be together if she refused to support him, would they?"

"Who knows," Ramsay said, slowly. "You may well be right. I'm just following my thoughts on this new information you just provided."

Alastair, who'd been quietly thinking while all this was being discussed, suddenly said, "I think Soph's right. Why would London gangsters act up here when the family is in London most of the year?"

"Maybe to distance themselves from the murder," Ramsay replied.

"What murder?" Sophia asked.

"Your murder," Ramsay said. "If they weren't holding you for money or the other, that can only mean you were to be disposed of."

"But if the gangsters wanted money from Soph's dad, wouldn't they have asked for a ransom?" Alastair asked.

"I suspect that if they did, it would be quietly and long after the hunt for Sophia had gone cold," Ramsay replied. "And if the family didn't pay, well, the murder was far from their territory."

Sophia shivered. "In a way, I hope you're right and father

hadn't yet received the ransom demand. Otherwise, it means he was willing to let me die rather than pay what the kidnappers asked."

Ramsay nodded sympathetically. "Until the police get the truth out of those two villains, we don't have much to go on."

"Will your brother officers tell you what they learned?" Alastair asked. "They've been pretty insistent that you stop interfering."

"Officially they can't," Ramsay agreed, "but I think if I talk to them away from the shop they will."

"And if they don't?" Sophia asked.

"Then we are once again stuck," Ramsay said, "and we'll need to find a new lead to follow."

"Are you going to tell the local police that London gangsters might be involved?" Alastair asked.

"Only if they say they haven't learned who set those two up to kidnapping."

"But those two might never tell," Sophia said. "They may expect a better reward for not telling."

"If it goes past tomorrow night," Ramsay said, "we'll tell Sergeant Hardraw all we know. It might help in their interrogation of the two thugs, if he can suggest to them who else is being questioned in the investigation. There'll be no reward for them if their backer is in jail as well."

"What do we do in the meantime?" Sophia asked.

"We wait," Ramsay said.

Alastair hesitated but then volunteered, "Tomorrow morning, I'm going to look further into what I heard my parents saying. It bothers me and I won't rest until I have an answer I can believe."

"We'll meet you for lunch at the usual café," Sophia said. "And don't worry, I'm sure you'll find a satisfactory answer."

. . .

THE FOLLOWING MORNING, before seeking out Ramsay and Sophia, Alastair walked into the Lakeland Lorries office and asked to see the boss.

"Mr. Williams isn't in yet," the receptionist said. "Can I help you?"

"Maybe," Alastair replied. "When one of your drivers was shipping something for us, he told my father about the transportation of a boat. I wonder if you could tell me when that was?"

She frowned. "I don't think I can. After all, your father wouldn't like it if we divulged his shipments to other people, would he?"

"No, I suppose not. We were hoping you might hear of a similar boat move; you see. My father has had a notion of a new business venture that needs such a boat."

"Mr. Williams will be in soon. He may be happy to share that kind of information. I really can't."

"I understand," Alastair said. "Maybe you could confirm all our shipments. It's Elliott's Farm Holdings."

"Have you anything to show you are the son of Mr. Elliott?"

Alastair laughed. "Of course." He handed her his driving license. "I'm still at university and starting out helping dad on the farm," he explained.

When she was satisfied, she returned his license and opened the battered metal filing cabinet behind her. Selecting a thin file, she handed it to him.

Alastair opened it and quickly read each order, invoice, and receipt. There was no order for the day of Soph's disappearance or anywhere close to that. The nearest was weeks before, and it didn't involve trips to the local municipal waste.

"Everything seems to be in order," Alastair said. "We

don't do as much business with you as I'd been led to believe."

"Your business moves bigger shipments than we generally carry," the receptionist said. "At least that's what I heard Mr. Williams say."

"That's probably it. I'll call back later when the boss is about. We're still on the lookout for the right boat."

The woman was perplexed. "I've never heard of us moving a boat. It would have to be a small one because we don't have trucks large enough for something like that."

"Maybe your driver was talking about a driver friend in another company," Alastair said soothingly. "You know how word gets around."

"Probably," the woman nodded. "Certainly, the drivers talk a lot. They get lonely on the road by themselves all day."

"Thank you for your help," Alastair said, "and I'll be back soon."

He exited the building just as the owner was walking up the path.

"Good morning, Mr. Williams. I came to see you."

"Oh, aye, and who might you be?"

"We met a few days ago when I came in for a quote," Alastair said, "but you probably get lots of people doing that. I'm Jim Elliott's son and he suggested I talk to you about a boat you moved recently…" He was about to explain further when the man butted in.

"What boat? We don't do boats."

"Your driver was probably talking about a move he'd heard about," Alastair continued. "The thing is, we're looking for a larger boat for a business venture Dad has in mind. He's given the job to me, letting me cut my teeth on something simple. Simple in his mind, at least."

"If our driver told you about a boat move, it was something he heard and nought to do with us," Williams said forcefully.

Alastair nodded. "Well, if you do hear of anything like that again, please let us know. There could be a finder's fee, if we buy it."

The man shrugged. "I'll tell the lads, but you'd be best going through the boat sales, rather than hearsay from drivers."

"We're doing that too," Alastair replied and left the man watching him in bemusement.

Alastair liked what he'd heard here even less than what he'd heard from his father. If there was a 'bundle of stuff,' Lakeland Lorries didn't seem to know about it.

He drove to the Municipal Waste offices. They didn't keep records of individuals dumping waste, and there was no record of Lakeland Lorries being there on any days around the time his father had suggested. Another dead end. His suspicions were now running riot, but he had nothing he could hand over to Ramsay or the police to have them investigate.

He drove to the dump itself and questioned the guard on the gate.

"That was days ago," the guard cried. "Dozens of vehicles come here daily."

"Are you familiar with Lakeland Lorries?" Alastair asked.

"Aye, but they're never here. I know them from seeing them around."

"You would remember them if you saw them here?"

"I'd say so," the guard replied, "but like I said, I don't think I've ever seen them here."

"Definitely not recently then?" Alastair prompted.

"Oh, no. Not recently."

"Have you been on holiday recently? Maybe it was when you were away?" Alastair probed.

"I'm a widower," the guard said. "I don't much take holidays. I took a day back in the spring but that's it."

Alastair nodded. "Well, thank you for this. We understood they'd brought a shipment of rubbish here for us. It seems they took it elsewhere." He returned to his car, more than ever convinced his father had made up this story on the spur of the moment when Alastair's mother had asked about the visit of a Lakeland truck and driver to the house. And now, his father was stuck with the story because Alastair's mother remembered it. *Was she also suspicious of that visit?*

23

INVESTIGATING THE NEW LINK

WITH MOST OF the morning gone, Alastair drove back into Keswick to wait for the arrival of Ramsay and Sophia at the usual meeting place. He was moodily stirring sugar into his coffee when they joined him.

"Did you learn anything?" Ramsay asked.

"I learned that my father's story was a pack of lies," Alastair said bitterly. "The only thing I think is true is that Lakeland Lorries moved a 'bundle' somewhere on my father's orders."

"A bundle?" Sophia said.

"He described it as a 'bundle of stuff' and, when I asked what, he said 'old farm equipment.' I checked with Lakeland Lorries and the Waste facility. There's no record of anything like that happening."

"Why were you asking about this bundle?" Sophia asked.

"That's how father said he learned about the boat. The Lakeland driver told him about shipping it from the harbor to a warehouse in Manchester."

"Maybe he misremembers where he heard it," Ramsay suggested. "It is some time ago."

Alastair shook his head. "Mam asked about it at the time and that's what he told her. It's frightening for me to consider, but we must tell the police and have them ask those two thugs."

"We can tell them about this and Hetherington at the same time. He, too, might make a run for it when he hears the police are questioning his co-conspirators again."

They sat in silence for a time, each considering the implications of this new lead Alastair had found.

Eventually, Sophia said, "I agree with Alastair, but how do we do this? Alastair can't be involved when we hand the information we have over to the police. His parents may not forgive him and, if we're wrong, it will be a rift that might never be healed."

Ramsay nodded. "Even if we hand over the evidence, Alastair's parents will know he had a hand in it. The information could go to the police anonymously and we watch the fall out. It's not ideal but it will have to do."

Alastair, who'd been listening and considering, interjected, "The possibility of my father being the one behind Soph's abduction horrifies me, and I'm not convinced that what we have is the truth. Still, I agree we must tell Sergeant Hardraw."

Ramsay frowned. "If it was *my* case..." he began.

"It is *our* case," Sophia interjected. "The police aren't anywhere near solving this."

"Well," Ramsay said, "I think the evidence, circumstantial though it is, warrants serious investigation, but I agree with you, Alastair. It's highly unlikely that any sane person would think kidnapping a young woman would encourage a marriage between her and their son."

"Not even if they thought a forced marriage would be better than losing a desirable piece of land?" Sophia asked.

"As I said once before, Sophia," Ramsay replied. "This is 1964, not the Dark Ages. Even heiresses get to enjoy all the world has to offer today. That's Alastair's point, his parents can't think this would be persuasive, so it's hard to believe."

"On the other hand, if they know the kidnapped girl's parents are in serious financial difficulty and this marriage could save them from a fall, would my parents see this as the 'greater good' or 'lesser of two evils'?" Alastair asked.

"If they were in financial difficulty, the forced marriage would only save Sophia's parents if it releases some money to them." Ramsay said. "Would your father give them money when he had their daughter as a hostage?"

"I'm sure Soph's parents are in financial difficulty," Alastair said. "The gossip mill says so, and it's always right. Maybe my father was prepared to offer some cash for a wedding and the estate."

"You think, with you two married, the two families would hand over the Thornton estate to you two, and your dad, Alastair, would provide funds to tide the Thorntons over until he is hired on to do a new movie?" Ramsay considered the idea skeptically.

"That's it," Alastair said. "I know what I heard didn't go that far, but I think we can assume that's how it would play out. It's the only thing that makes any sense."

"And with the estate off their hands, my parents would be in better shape financially to wait until papa got a new movie to direct," Sophia added.

"And all this hinges on you, Sophia, becoming so desperate in captivity to agree to a forced marriage," Ramsay mused. "Except, what I overheard in the pub that night suggested you were to be killed, which doesn't fit with this hypothesis."

"Our hypothesis," Alastair said, "is based on our limited knowledge and our imagination. We don't know the whole picture, so we can't yet see the whole plot. Phone Sergeant Hardraw and tell him what I've heard."

Ramsay nodded. "It may lead to unpleasantness down the road for you, Alastair. If you can live with that, I'll go to Sergeant Hardraw now, without any hiding behind the fig leaf of an 'anonymous caller.'"

"I'll take the chance," Alastair said. "Go now."

"Maybe there's an explanation we haven't yet found," Sophia added, "and Sergeant Hardraw can get the truth out of our villains."

Ramsay left them and hurried down the street to the police station.

As they watched Ramsay go, Sophia said, "Investigating is a frustrating business. This time yesterday I was sure it was Hetherington. Now, I think it might be your father, and Hetherington is just somebody I don't like."

Alastair nodded. "I know what you mean. It's getting to be that everybody I look at is the villain."

"What if we never find the person behind this?" Sophia asked.

"Or there is no person behind it, just those two incompetent idiots who acted on impulse and got in over their heads," Alastair replied.

"I could spend years in hiding before feeling safe enough to reappear," Sophia said glumly.

"You can't spend years in hiding," Alastair replied. "You don't have the paperwork to be Astrid Jackson. You couldn't get a job or a bank account or travel or get health care or anything, really."

"Things don't look good for me, do they?" Sophia said, her expression suggesting she was losing heart.

"This isn't like you, Soph," Alastair said, smiling and hugging her. "We'll find the truth, eventually. You'll see."

"What is it that couldn't wait?" Sergeant Hardraw asked when Ramsay had been shown into an Interview Room.

Ramsay explained, repeating Alastair's story and showing how it appeared to link to the case.

"It's circumstantial at best," Hardraw responded. "But I'll ask them about the visit to Elliott and see what we get. By the way, that bag you handed in had a partial print that matches Kennedy's thumb. It's not a lot, but it's all we have linking them to the alleged kidnapping right now."

"What does he say about it?"

Sergeant Hardraw laughed. "What you'd expect. When they parked at the old farm, he saw the bag. He opened it to see if there was an address or anything to say who it belonged to. It was empty, so he dropped it where he found it in case the owner came looking for it."

"What a thoughtful, upright citizen he is," Ramsay said, shaking his head. "And their sudden wish to depart after hitting me and being told not to leave the area?"

"Just going back to Newcastle for a few days," Sergeant Hardraw said. "And they didn't know they'd hit anybody. The van's engine conked out at the top of the hill. He was so focused on getting it going again, he never noticed he'd crossed the lanes and, when he did, he swerved back onto the road. They thought they'd hit a tree branch, not a person, and so didn't stop or report the accident."

"We really can't pin them down on anything, can we?"

"Only the traffic accident," Hardraw said. "They did hit a

person, and they should have stopped, whatever they thought they'd done."

"The 'bundle' they were to move for Elliott, that might unsettle them," Ramsay reminded him.

"I'll let you know later," Sergeant Hardraw replied. "As things stand, I'll be releasing them unless I get something more tangible to hold them with."

"I have another suggestion to make," Ramsay said. "There's a man called Hetherington employed at the Thorntons. I saw him talking to the two men you have in custody and so did your constable. It's possible he overheard where the girl was going that morning and contacted his two friends with a crazy plot to make a lot of money."

Hardraw shook his head. "If Miss Thornton was held in that cellar, then it wasn't an impulsive act. The door, hinges, bolt, and lock were bought from local hardware stores recently. And, don't forget, there hasn't been a ransom demand made."

"Maybe because she escaped before they could work out a safe way to get the money without being identified and caught."

"We'll check the Thornton house phone records," Hardraw said thoughtfully. "If there's anything in this idea, there would be an outgoing call soon after the girl left the house."

"My thoughts exactly," Ramsay replied. "If there was no call, then my idea isn't right."

"We'll have the phone records for that day very soon," Hardraw said. "Hopefully, before we have to release these two."

. . .

RAMSAY RETURNED to the café where Sophia and Alastair were waiting impatiently to hear how Ramsay had fared talking to Sergeant Hardraw.

Ramsay sat back at the table and replied, "He's struggling. The only thing they can charge these people with is 'leaving the scene of an accident.' They'll be released today unless Sergeant Hardraw can break one of them."

"Will what we told him help, do you think?" Alastair asked.

Ramsay shrugged. "If it gives him something to go after, maybe. A lot depends on whether he can get the phone records of your home, Sophia."

"They could be after us again tomorrow?" Sophia asked, dismayed.

"I'm afraid so," Ramsay replied sympathetically, "unless we can tie them into the kidnapping. We must identify who was paying them."

"My parents didn't mention hiring them for anything but a 'bundle of stuff,'" Alastair said, "and none of the evidence we have suggests they did."

"Which is why I was wary of us being the people to hand this to the police," Ramsay said. "If it isn't true, if your father can prove what he really meant, the police will be wary of using anything we give them in future."

"But you do agree there is enough to have the police investigate?" Sophia asked.

"I wouldn't have taken it to them if I didn't," Ramsay agreed. "And if Alastair's parents are behind it, I'm sure the link to those two thugs will be found," Ramsay said. "I'm just uneasy that we haven't found it, and the police may not either."

"What do you say, Alastair?" Sophia asked. "They're

your parents, and it was you who heard them talking in a way that set us off on this trail."

"We've handed it over to the police, so the discussion is moot," Alastair said. "I don't want to believe it either and the sooner it is investigated properly, the sooner I'll know if my parents are monsters or they're innocent of all wrongdoing and I'm a treacherous rat."

Ramsay nodded and said, "Honesty and clarity in investigations is much better than concealment, however much it hurts us."

Alastair snorted. "Easy for you to say. I feel I'm acting like one of those communist children we hear about, snitching on his parents for an attaboy from the state."

Ramsay nodded. "I understand but we must go forward. While the police follow up on this, we can continue looking for links to the kidnappers or finding some Mr. or Mrs. X who hasn't yet appeared but who has a reason for getting Sophia out of the way."

"There's nobody," Sophia cried. "I've wracked my brains. I'd know and I don't. I'm not rich or famous."

"Your mother's will says you are," Ramsay said.

"I think you put too much emphasis on wills," Sophia said. "In real life, people don't think of these things all the time."

"Not all the time and not everyone," Ramsay agreed, "but some do."

"Do you have a will?" Alastair asked.

"I have nothing to leave and no one to leave it to," Ramsay replied.

"You have a house you told me," Sophia said. "It came to me that what we have may be an old will. A new will may exist, one that leaves everything to my father."

Ramsay realized his situation was the perfect example of

Sophia's objections. He and his wife had made wills after they bought the house but hadn't changed them when the two children were born, and he hadn't changed his after all three were killed.

While Ramsay was mulling over the implications for himself and the case, Alastair threw out a new avenue to explore.

"I'm going to suggest to my father we buy a boat I saw in a sales magazine last night. I want to see how serious he is or if this is all a sham."

Sophia smiled. "If he offers to buy it, the story was real, you think?"

"Boats of the kind and size needed to ferry rich people on lake cruises aren't cheap," Alastair replied, "and dad is a careful man where money is involved. If he takes my suggestion seriously, I'll be convinced his story was true."

"And if he doesn't?" Sophia asked.

"Then I'll know it was to hide the truth and he *is* the leader in this affair."

24

RAMSAY THE BURGLAR

AFTER HE'D COME to terms with his own behavior where wills were concerned, and making a resolution to create a new one, Ramsay said, "This is all just conjecture. If there's a different will, we need to see it and figure out which is the legitimate one. How can we do that?"

"What?" Alastair asked. Then realizing Ramsay hadn't heard a word he and Sophia had just said, continued, "You weren't listening, were you?"

Ramsay grinned. "I'm sorry, I was thinking."

Alastair repeated his plan and Ramsay agreed it was worth a try, before saying," But back to my question, how do we find if there's another will?"

"By breaking into my father's safe or that of his London lawyer," Sophia replied.

"You mean the safe here?" Ramsay asked.

"No, the one in our London house."

"You have a key for the London house, don't you?" Ramsay asked.

"I do, but it's in my room at the estate."

"Then we need to get that key," Ramsay said, "and take a trip to London."

"You think we should burgle my parents' house?" Sophia asked.

"Not 'we,'" Ramsay said. "I don't want either of you two involved in any way, but someone has to get that key. Where is it exactly?"

Sophia frowned. "I'm not sure. Probably in my bag, but it may be in my coat. I can't remember."

"Well, think, while I think of who could help us."

"You're not planning to housebreak yourself then?" Alastair asked.

"I am, but I need some instructions from an expert," Ramsay replied. He considered the old lags he'd known and which one he could trust to give him honest instructions.

"My keyring is in my purse," Sophia said, at last. "And my purse is in my blue shoulder bag. It was on my dresser when I left, but it may have been put into the wardrobe by a maid."

"Now we need to get close to your house and you can point me to the right room," Ramsay said.

"This is madness," Alastair cried. "You're not a burglar. You'll be caught and all this will blow up in our faces."

"Sophia can tell me if there are alarms or dogs, whatever security measures a wealthy film producer feels they need," Ramsay said, "and I have an old burglar friend who I know has gone straight. He'll give me tips on how to get through windows and doors without breaking them."

"We don't have any security or a dog at the manse," Sophia said. "Why would we, up here?"

"People who live in London and live among wealthy people are often concerned about such things," Ramsay said. "I'm pleased to hear your parents are not."

"They're more wary in London," Sophia replied. "We live in Kensington, and it's a nice part of town, but people do get burgled. The Underground makes it so easy for robbers to get about."

Ramsay laughed. "Then let's hope we never have subway trains up here."

"It will soon be dark," Sophia said. "If I'm to show you which is the window to my room, it's best we do it at night when the curtains are drawn. By day, all the windows to the north look out over a wide lawn, and we'd be seen getting close to the house."

"Are there trees around the lawn?" Ramsay asked.

"There are some bushes, but trees don't grow out there in the marshy ground," Sophia replied.

"Inspector Ramsay has a point, Soph," Alastair said. "We don't need to get close to the house to see the window of your room."

"How do you plan to get up to the window, Inspector?" Sophia asked, not entirely pleased with Alastair taking Ramsay's side of the question.

"I'd enter through a ground floor window, or door," Ramsay said. "I'm too old to climb up ivy or drainpipes like they do in mystery books."

"If that's your plan, we do need to get close," Sophia said, "so you can see the kind of locks on the doors and catches on the windows."

"Then we should go now," Ramsay said. "I have a flash-light in the car we can use to cover the ground."

"It won't be easy at night," Alastair said. "I know, I've done it a few times in the past." He grinned at Sophia, who scowled at him in reply.

"We can drive up the track until we can see the house," Sophia said. "There's a passing place where we can park.

They won't hear us. Dad is always working with his headphones on, and Cat plays her music loud to drown the wind moaning in the chimneys. She doesn't like the manse."

THEY FOLLOWED SOPHIA'S INSTRUCTIONS, parked the car, and set out walking the last half mile to the house.

"We must get around to the back," Sophia said, "without being seen or heard."

"Are there live-in staff?" Ramsay asked.

"Yes, our housekeeper, her husband and some maids. The outdoor staff come from the farms and go home each night."

They quickly reached the house where the curtained windows showed only slivers of light at the borders. A single lamp above the garages lit the drive and gardens at the front of the house. Sophia signaled to go left around the end of the house and into the shadowy darkness there.

"My room is the window just around this corner," Sophia said, "and there's a door only a few feet farther along the wall."

After peering around the corner and seeing no one, they quietly walked to the door.

Ramsay examined the window of the room immediately below Sophia's room before moving on to the door. By the time Sophia had finished explaining there was a staircase just inside the door, Ramsay had decided he didn't need any housebreaking advice. The house relied on its remoteness for security and the door lock would be easily opened by the picklocks he'd confiscated years before from his burglar friend.

"You two go back to the car," Ramsay said. "I'll join you as soon as I have your keys, Sophia."

"They're on a key chain with one of those small troll toys," Sophia said.

"Aren't you going to wait until Soph's parents are asleep?" Alastair asked.

Ramsay shook his head. "If they're as Sophia says, loud music and headphones, now's as good a time as ever. Now go. If anything goes wrong," he added, handing the car keys to Alastair, "you leave quickly. I don't want you two involved in any way."

Alastair took the keys and nodded. "We understand." He turned and, with Sophia reluctantly following, made a beeline for the car.

When he was sure they were well away from the house and not to be seen if someone looked out of a window, Ramsay began working on the door lock. It was a standard lock of its type, and he soon had the door open.

"I blame Miss Riddell for this behavior," he murmured quietly to himself as he stepped inside. Ahead of him a dark passageway ended in a dimly lit hall at the farther side of the house. As his eyes became accustomed to the dark, he saw to his left the staircase Sophia had mentioned. Quietly closing the door, Ramsay began climbing the stairs, keeping his feet close to the side of each step, hoping to reduce the inevitable creaking old wooden stairs created. He was confident with the loudness of the music he could hear; few people would notice one more creak or groan in an old house.

Halfway up, a stair creaked loudly beneath his weight. Ramsay paused, waiting to hear if anyone had noticed. There was no change in the sounds of the house, and he continued to the landing and turned to where he knew Sophia's room should be.

The door was unlocked, and he stepped quickly into the

room and closed it behind him. He turned on a bedside lamp and switched off his torch. The bag was where Sophia had said and, in a moment, he had the keychain with its attached troll. Placing them safely in his jacket pocket, Ramsay quickly scanned the contents of the bag in case there was something Sophia might need in the future but hadn't yet thought of. Her purse had money, so he pocketed that too. Everything else, combs, handkerchiefs, and other personal items, he left and replaced the bag as he'd found it.

He was soon outside, and the door was re-locked. With luck, no one would ever know the keys were gone and warn the staff at the family's London house.

Fifteen minutes later, he was back at the car handing over keys and money to Sophia.

"No one heard you?" Alastair asked, doubtfully.

"If they did, they haven't made a fuss," Ramsay said, starting the car. "No, I think it went perfectly to plan. Thank heavens for old houses with old locks and no security."

"We don't need security up here," Alastair said, grinning. "Our only burglars are ex-policemen."

"Long may it stay that way," Ramsay replied. "The key is on that ring, isn't it Sophia?" He'd noticed her staring at the keys, and it worried him.

"Yes," Sophia said. "I was imagining how I could use it without alerting the servants and giving away my presence."

"You've already told your father you're in London, so he wouldn't be surprised," Ramsay said.

"He'll wonder why I didn't stay in our house and why I've suddenly returned," Sophia suggested.

"You were staying with friends, and you were afraid the London house might be watched," Alastair replied.

"I should have phoned them days ago," Sophia said, still

concerned. She brightened. "Much as I hate to say it, you're right. I'll just say I was frightened and leave it at that."

It was Ramsay's turn to be cautious. "And you were right to be scared. One of the two kidnappers was gone for some days. He may well have been in London and watching the house."

"Could one of them return there? Once they've been released, I mean?" Alastair asked.

"They could both go there for all we know," Ramsay said. "They've been told not to leave but that doesn't mean they won't. We'll take the train tomorrow and we'll be very careful approaching the house. Now let's all get a good night's sleep and catch the earliest London express we can."

ALASTAIR ARRIVED home and made his way directly to his room where the Boat Sales magazine was lying open at the page he wanted. There was no time like the present, he thought, as he made his way downstairs and to his father's office.

Entering, he saw his father at his desk. His usual place to be. His father looked up at him and for a moment, Alastair saw weariness in his father's eyes. It gave him a jolt; his father was always full of life and drive.

"Dad," Alastair said, "I think I've found you a boat to replace the one you lost." He handed the magazine over to his father, pointing to the vessel he was suggesting.

His father read the description quickly and nodded. "I see what you mean. It will need a lot of renovation but it's a good thought. It has that old-fashioned feel about it, I think will appeal to the customers I have in mind."

"That's what I thought," Alastair said. "Plush Victoriana, plenty of old mahogany, and uniformed staff. Plenty of room for dinner tables or space for dancing on evening cruises or it can be a sheltered sun deck for the daytime."

"You seem excited about this venture," his father said, smiling.

"I am," Alastair said, not entirely truthfully. "I love the land, of course, but sailing and the lake are where I feel happiest."

"Do you want to run with this?"

"You mean, I should lead this venture?" Alastair asked.

"Why not? You know I want you involved in the business. What better way than to cut your teeth on a project that excites you?"

This wasn't a response Alastair had expected and it left him speechless for a moment. "It's a lot of money, dad. Are you sure you want me to handle it?"

"The first job my father gave me when I was about your age was to get electricity to our buildings, and particularly the milking sheds. The cost was about the same as I expect this to be. It was one of the best investments I've made in all these years. Maybe you'll say the same about the boat and the lake cruises."

"What market research have you done?" Alastair asked.

"His father laughed. "Not enough," he said, chuckling, "but I'll give you what I've got. If you're to run it, you'll want to do more."

"I'm going back to university soon," Alastair said, thoughtfully.

"Everybody has competing priorities, lad, and we all work them out."

"You're sure?"

"Are you?"

Alastair nodded. "I'm sure. I'll do it. Thanks, dad."

His father smiled, took a slim file from a desk drawer

and handed it to Alastair. "This is it," he said. "Not a lot for you to go on, but it means you almost have a clean slate to start with."

Alastair took the file and moved to a nearby seat. "You're right," he said, opening the file and reading the single sheet of paper inside, "not a lot to go on."

"I go with my gut," his father said, "and these days I have the clout to make things work even if my gut led me wrong. I expect you to be a little more professional than that."

Alastair nodded. "I'm learning to be methodical this summer. It's frustrating."

"Where's this lesson coming from?"

"Trying to discover what's happened to Sophia," Alastair replied. "Nothing leads anywhere, I suspect everyone and no one, and getting nowhere fast."

"It's a bad business, her running off like that," his father replied. "Youngsters who do so often end up in a worse mess than what they ran away from. I hope that hasn't happened to Sophia. She's a nice lass."

Alastair studied his father's expression as he spoke and still couldn't decide. Had his father created this one sheet of scrawled notes and handed over a pretend job to make it appear he was innocent?

25

THE LONDON END

THE CARRIAGE they took on the early train, for Ramsay had made sure his two assistants were up in time, was cold. It would be some time into the journey before its heater provided warmth. They'd taken a First-Class carriage to ensure Sophia was able to keep out of sight of most passengers. Sophia had pointed out they were more likely to meet people who knew her in First-Class than if they'd traveled in Second or Third. Ramsay said it wasn't a problem because she wasn't leaving the carriage except for dire emergencies.

"Like the loo, you mean," Sophia replied, crossly.

"That's exactly what I mean," Ramsay replied unsympathetically.

"Before we talk about today," Alastair began, "I want to tell you what happened when I suggested a boat to my father last night."

"Let's hear it," Ramsay said.

Alastair recounted the meeting and asked their opinion.

"I never thought your parents involved," Sophia said, "so I think it's a genuine venture and your father has chosen well for its leader."

Alastair reddened. He wasn't used to praise from Sophia.

"I see your dilemma," Ramsay said. "Your father could have written these notes in ten minutes and had them waiting for you, should you press the inquiry further."

Alastair nodded, glumly. "I can't decide."

"Get working on it," Ramsay said. "You'll only be sure when you have enough evidence to ask your father for the money to buy the boat."

"That could be days or weeks away," Alastair pointed out. "I'd hoped for a quick confirmation, either way."

"The quicker you work," Sophia said, "the sooner you'll know."

With this decided, they passed on to their plans for the day.

THE JOURNEY PASSED without any upsets, which didn't surprise Ramsay. No other First-Class passengers had joined the train with them at Preston and the coincidence of someone who knew Sophia joining at Manchester was slim. They pulled into London at lunch time and, after a quick coffee, made their way straight to the Thornton's London home, a pleasant house in Kensington with a view of Kensington palace.

"Why are we waiting here?" Sophia asked, after they'd stood at the end of the street for twenty minutes.

"I want to be sure there's no one watching your home," Ramsay said. "Remember, for all we know, the person they're working for is here in London."

"We haven't seen anyone," Alastair replied. "I've been watching carefully."

"Then it's time to go," Ramsay said. "Remember, Sophia, you tell the staff you're staying with friends again, and you've come to the house to phone your parents. Don't let them call."

"Can Alastair come in?" Sophia asked.

"Do the staff know him?"

"I've never been here," Alastair replied.

"None of the London staff have been up north," Sophia said. "Only Cat's maid travels with us."

"Then Alastair can be the London friend you've been staying with," Ramsay said.

Ramsay watched Sophia and Alastair stroll nonchalantly to the house. Sophia paused at the door, looked about, slipped her key in the lock, and opened the door. A moment later, the door closed, and Ramsay was alone on the street. He breathed a sigh of relief that a shadowy figure hadn't appeared from a nearby hiding place and hurried off to phone the rest of the kidnapping gang.

He'd told Sophia and Alastair he would wait in a nearby Lyons Café they'd passed in the taxi on their way to the house. Now that it was time to go there, he found he couldn't move. The thought there may still be danger nearby kept him rooted to the spot. After a moment, he shook his head. He needed to phone Sergeant Hardraw because they'd left too early to call before they set out.

SOPHIA INTRODUCED Alastair to Mrs. Reynolds, the housekeeper, and gave her the fictional background they'd invented on the train journey. The housekeeper appeared to accept it all and seemed equally satisfied when Sophia said she'd ring her parents after she'd freshened her face.

"Perhaps you could have cook make us some sandwiches and cakes," Sophia said. "We'll eat in the breakfast room.

Maybe you could show Alastair where it is and where the loo is?"

"I'll look after your friend," the housekeeper replied, smiling, "and lunch will be ready as quickly as cook can manage it."

The breakfast room was next to her father's study and his safe. If he hadn't moved the 'secret' location of its key, she would have the will read and be back in the breakfast room before Mrs. Reynolds came to clear up.

Sophia set the water running in the bathroom, assured herself Mrs. Reynolds and Alastair were safely out of sight, before slipping quickly into her father's bedroom. The safe key was in its usual place. She slipped it into the pocket of her frock and returned to the bathroom.

After splashing her face with cold water and toweling it dry, she made her way to the breakfast room where Alastair gave her a quizzical look. Sophia nodded and sat at the table. They talked polite pleasantries until the cook and housekeeper entered with lunch.

"The rest of the staff are away," Mrs. Reynolds said, explaining both retainers working beyond their usual duties.

"It's very good of you both," Sophia said. "Just descending on you like this must be a nuisance."

"You can never be a nuisance, Miss Sophia," the housekeeper replied. "Now, is there anything you or the gentleman might require?"

"Nothing at all, Mrs. Reynolds," Sophia replied, smiling broadly. "We shall sit here and enjoy the meal. We can clear up after ourselves."

The two retainers' expressions showed them to be horrified at such a suggestion. "When you're finished, Miss," Mrs. Reynolds said, "ring the bell and we'll clear away." The two left the room, shaking their heads in dismay at Sophia's suggestion.

"I think you offended their professional pride," Alastair said, grinning.

"But it got what I wanted from them. They won't come back until we ring the bell. Now, let's begin. We'll give them a minute to be sure they aren't about to return with something else, then I'll read the will."

After a few minutes, with the house still silent, Sophia unlocked and entered her father's study, opened the safe, thankful her father hadn't changed the code, and sorted through the papers inside. There was no will among them. Deflated, Sophia replaced everything and locked the safe door. She quickly rifled through the desk, filing cabinets, and credenza that made up the other furniture of the room. No will was found there either. She scanned the bookshelves that lined three of the four walls, but none suggested it was the hiding place of a will. Defeated, she returned to the breakfast room and told Alastair of her failure.

Alastair frowned. "Where else might it be?"

"If I knew that," Sophia said, "we'd already be on our way."

"Could he have it with him?"

"Why would he?" Sophia asked. "He can't have imagined he'd need it during his summer sojourn in the country."

Still frowning, Alastair said, "He might if he was planning something that required your mother's money?"

"He already has any money she had," Sophia replied. "Has had since she died."

"I know," Alastair said, slowly, "it was just a thought that came into my head."

"Not a very bright one," Sophia said waspishly.

Alastair's expression was rueful. "You're right. Stupid of me."

"I'll search his bedroom," Sophia said, "when I put the key back, which should be soon."

"Go now," Alastair said, "while everyone is dozing. I can't hear a sound out there, but if someone comes, I'll say you've gone to the loo."

Sophia nodded, rose and crossed the floor to the door. She opened it and peeked out. As Alastair had said, no one was about. She slipped through the door and ran up the stairs. Once again, she turned on a tap letting a thin stream of water run down the drain. Closing the door, Sophia ran lightly across the landing to her father's bedroom.

After replacing the safe key, she began another frantic search through cupboards and drawers that showed her nothing. No will was hidden among his clothes or the photos of Cat, his sons, and one of herself as a young girl. This last she removed from its frame in the hope the will was hidden behind the photo. It wasn't. She replaced everything to how she remembered it and returned to tell Alastair of more failure.

"It's either with your family lawyers," Alastair said, "or the new will we imagined doesn't exist. After all, it's been fifteen years or so since it was needed. Everything has probably been done with it."

Sophia nodded glumly. "I think you're right. It's gone."

"We should spend some time here, so they don't think our visit was odd, and then go to our meeting place with Inspector Ramsay," Alastair said.

"I need to make that phony phone call," Sophia said. "In all the excitement, I'd forgotten about it."

"I'll ring the bell to bring one or both of your servants," Alastair said. "You make the call."

She used the phone in her father's study, speaking loudly as though it was a bad line, pretending to tell her father where she was and who was with her. When she returned to the room, the table was clear and neither the cook nor housekeeper were in the room.

"I'm sure they must have heard that," Sophia said, rejoining Alastair.

"If they didn't, they'd have to be deaf," Alastair replied. "It was like you were using a megaphone rather than a telephone."

"Then I'll tell Mrs. Reynolds we're going out to meet friends and we might be back later."

Alastair grinned. "Will we?"

"I don't know. We must see what the inspector thinks is best."

INSPECTOR RAMSAY, when they met him in the Lyons Café as planned, was as disappointed with the result of Sophia's search as Sophia was herself. They'd lost a day and the cost of three First-Class tickets and all for nothing.

"What do you think, Inspector?" Alastair asked. "Is it up north with Soph's dad, or does it not exist?"

Ramsay was thinking with such a frown on his face his two assistants thought he was angry with them. "I think," Ramsay said, slowly, "if a different will was probated, that is read and completed, and was subsequently destroyed, then a copy should be in Somerset House or in the local Probate Office where it was lodged and completed."

"Both are here in London," Sophia said, energized by this new idea. "We can go to them today, right now."

Ramsay nodded. "We'll split our forces. You two to Somerset House, and I'll find the Probate Office for the

Kensington area. I assume your parents lived in the same house?"

"They did," Sophia replied. "Alastair and I have already had lunch, so we're leaving now." She rose to her feet, leaving Alastair to hurriedly finish his tea and join her.

"Meet me at the café in Euston Station at six for the train back to the Lakes," Ramsay said. "I'll start with the café's phone book for the nearest Probate Office." He watched them scurry out of the door, Alastair striding manfully to keep up with the hurrying Sophia.

AFTER GETTING the address of the Kensington Probate Office from the phone book, Ramsay phoned Sergeant Hardraw, who was still interviewing, the desk sergeant told him. Ramsay gave the officer the number of the phone box and hung up to wait.

The phone rang and Ramsay snatched it up.

"Mr. Ramsay?" he heard Sergeant Hardraw ask.

"Yep," Ramsay replied. "Was our information any help?"

Sergeant Hardraw laughed. "Yes and no. Kennedy said the information about Elliott was wrong. Connery said they did do jobs for Mr. Elliott. Maybe even that 'bundle.' He couldn't remember for sure."

"That's a start," Ramsay said.

"Oh, we're further along than that," Sergeant Hardraw replied. "I asked Connery for his driver's logbook on the day of this shipment. It wasn't in the book. He says it's because it was a job for a friend, not paid."

"What did Kennedy say when you put this to him?"

"As you'd expect, he told a similar tale. We asked for the date of this shipment, and he struggled because he didn't know what Connery had said."

"What did Connery say the date was?" Ramsay asked.

"He wasn't sure, but the timeframe he gave was that of the abduction, so we're pressing him on what was in this bundle and where was it taken," Sergeant Hardraw replied.

"And he said?" Ramsay queried.

"At first the dump, then, when we said we'd checked, he said they sold it to a scrap metal dealer. We're checking that. Scrap yards, unfortunately, aren't good at recordkeeping."

"Their stories are beginning to crack," Ramsay said. "Have you tried the name Thornton on them?"

"They both say they did some work for him," Sergeant Hardraw replied. "Delivering dead pheasants to the main-line train was the last job."

"Can I call you later tonight when I get back north?" Ramsay asked. "You should have more by then." When that was agreed, he hung up the phone.

26

NOTHING FOUND

AT SIX O'CLOCK, Ramsay was enjoying a cup of tea and sandwich in Euston Station's Cafe, while Bracken enjoyed a plate of meat and a bowl of water from the dog-loving waitress, when Sophia and Alastair arrived. They saw him and came straight to his table.

"Did you find a will?" Sophia demanded.

"No, did you?" Ramsay replied.

"No, but they told me not all wills were stored there," Sophia said, flopping down into the chair next to Ramsay. "I'm exhausted, standing all afternoon and walking all over London. The streets may be paved in gold, like the stories say, but they're still hard to walk on."

"You should have worn more sensible shoes," Alastair said, smiling.

He was about to ask if she wanted a tea or coffee but was stopped by Sophia's indignant cry of, "How was I to know we'd be all day on our feet? I thought it was just to open a safe, read the will, and take the next train back again."

"You should have thought ahead," Alastair said.

"Nothing has gone that simply so far. Do you want a drink or anything to eat?"

"I'll get my own, thank you," Sophia replied, jumping to her feet and heading for the counter.

"Saved myself some shillings there," Alastair said to Ramsay before following Sophia.

Ramsay smiled and shook his head as he watched them bickering at the counter while a bewildered server waited for them to order.

Sophia returned with tea and a Chelsea Bun, while Alastair had coffee and a meat pie, placed on a plate with a knife and fork, which he ignored, picking up the pie and devouring it before Sophia had started her bun. She tut-tutted and shook her head.

"What?" Alastair asked. "It's been hours since we had lunch."

"You'll have indigestion," Sophia replied primly, nibbling at her bun.

Ramsay, who'd finished his sandwich, intervened. "Now we know a new will isn't at Somerset House or the Probate Office, which means there's a good chance it doesn't exist or was never read. That is to say, the items in it that haven't yet been put into place, which is odd if it gave everything to your father. After all, our information is your father has spent all your money."

"You think there isn't a forgery?" Alastair asked.

"I don't know," Ramsay admitted, "but the sensible thing for Sophia's father to do, when he realized he needed the money, was to have a new will made giving everything to him."

"How easy is it to forge a will?" Sophia asked.

"I imagine very easy if you're a movie producer with access to all sorts of skilled prop people," Ramsay replied.

"That's good news, isn't it?" Alastair asked, abandoning the bickering for a moment. "If we find a forged will, that must be a criminal offence, even if we can't prove abduction."

Ramsay nodded. "Yes, good news, if we can find a forgery."

"That means you think my father wanted to get his hands on my inheritance and tried to have me murdered. Then, when that didn't come off, forged a will to disinherit me?" Sophia asked, her expression a mixture of horror and incredulity. "I don't believe it. Anyhow, Cat has as much access to the same people as Dad has."

"We only know what the will we've seen says," Ramsay cautioned her, "but I think in this case, it would be the other way around. Forged will first, and then the more desperate measures second."

"As we've said before, would a parent really kill their child for money?" Alastair asked.

"I've known it to happen." Ramsay said. "There's a famous old case of a mother who claimed insurance on five children she'd killed over the years. That was a long time ago, of course, so who knows how true it is."

"Is this why you didn't want me to phone my parents?" Sophia asked.

Ramsay nodded. "Partly. It seemed the most logical motive, but you were so adamant you had no money, I had to look for other possible motives. I didn't know about Hetherington or these London people then."

Sophia frowned in concentration, saying, "If there isn't a forged will, then I don't think it can be my father."

"I take your point," Ramsay said. "However, we don't know if a forged will exists or not."

"And none of this explains why they didn't kill Soph

right away," Alastair said, thoughtfully.

Ramsay nodded. "I know. Maybe all this is wrong, and it really is an angry casino owner wanting his money."

"I'm still here, you know," Sophia reminded them.

"Sorry," Ramsay said. "It's hard to discuss and even harder if we were to try and say it in a way you'd be happy with."

"It's so foul an idea," Alastair said, angrily, "that I won't believe it until there's clear proof. Your parents, Soph, have always been decent to me."

"If they want me out of the way," Sophia said, "why try and force me into marrying Alastair?"

"Maybe it was you saying you *wouldn't* marry me that brought on the decision to abduct you," Alastair said quietly.

"An angry casino owner wouldn't know any of this," Sophia responded slowly, "so if it's true, it's my father and, or, his catty wife."

Ramsay interjected. "Perhaps these things are best discussed in the privacy of our carriage on the way north."

"When did they start pushing you to marry me?" Alastair whispered, ignoring Ramsay's advice.

"The moment I arrived home from school," Sophia replied, equally quietly. "They had about a month to realize I was not going to marry you before organizing the abduction."

Ramsay could see other customers in the café beginning to listen in and interjected again. "Talk this out on the train," he glanced at the wall clock, "which is only twenty minutes from leaving, so we should find our carriage. Come along." Saying this, he felt like a parent of two quarrelsome toddlers or a 'gooseberry' escorting two lovers.

· · ·

By the time the train pulled out of the station, Sophia and Alastair had worked out a sequence of times and events to show how her parents could have organized the kidnapping and Ramsay was able to say, "Now we have that settled, we need a way to look into your father's safe for an alternate will."

"We know it's easy for you to get inside the house," Alastair said, "but we need Soph to do the digging. You'll have no idea where anything is."

"I agree," Ramsay replied, "but we can't do that when Sophia's parents are at home."

"Could you get your parents to invite them to dinner one evening?" Sophia asked Alastair.

"If the Keswick police haven't questioned *them* today about the 'bundle,' I might be able to."

"They won't know you were behind the police information," Sophia said.

"Don't be daft," Alastair said. "I'm probably the only person my parents spoke to about this. Of course, they'll know."

"I'll ask Sergeant Hardraw when we talk tonight. If they haven't alerted either sets of parents, the invitation idea is worth a try," Ramsay said. "Now, while that's going on, we have some other loose ends we need answers to. Those two thugs, for example. What more can we find to break their stories?"

"By the time we're home, they'll likely have been released," Sophia said.

"Sadly, unless they've completely lost their heads and confessed, you're probably right," Ramsay said.

"Then you two are in danger again," Alastair added.

"Which is why," Ramsay said, "we should set another trap with me as bait."

"It's me they need to kill, if we're right about them," Sophia said.

"We're not using you as bait," Alastair said firmly.

"That's my decision," Sophia snapped back. "Not yours."

"I agree with Alastair," Ramsay said. "You're the most important cog in this whole plot. With you gone, everything just winds down. There's no case. You must stay alive. Sorry."

Sophia glared at both. "So, I just hide while you have all the fun."

"Not the way I have it planned," Ramsay said. "You'll be in at the kill." He grinned. "Hopefully that's their arrest and not my death."

"Tell me," Sophia said, still suspicious.

"First, I need to be sure that wicked uncle Williams hears my plan to go fell walking," Ramsay said. "Then, I go alone with you two keeping out of sight with walkie-talkies to the police, who we also must have poised to strike."

"Nowhere on the fells is there enough cover to hide Soph and me, let alone policemen," Alastair objected.

"There is on the track up Dodd Fell," Ramsay said. "I've looked at hiking it once or twice, but it hasn't the views the others have. Too dark among the trees. For a trap, though, the forest makes it perfect."

"I hadn't thought of Dodd, it's barely a fell," Alastair agreed. "How do we know they'll be there?"

"We won't until we've set the trap, which I'll do while you're working on your parents for that dinner invitation."

"And I sit at home knitting, I suppose," Sophia said, savagely. "You do recall this is *my* adventure and not yours, don't you?"

"We do," Ramsay said, smiling. "What had you in mind?"

Sophia was nonplussed. "If they're released, I'll observe the guest house where those two thugs are staying, to be sure they're still there. No sense laying a trap if the birds have flown."

Ramsay nodded. "Very well, just don't get seen by them."

"I don't like it," Alastair said. "If they see Soph before Soph sees them, she'll be taken and killed. They won't wait like they did last time."

"They won't recognize me," Sophia replied. "I'll be in my best Astrid disguise."

Alastair frowned. "See you are. I don't want to be giving the eulogy at your funeral."

"You wouldn't say anything nice anyway," Sophia said, then seeing his expression, said, "Sorry, I take that back. It was a rotten thing to say."

Alastair glowered at her, then grinned. "It was, but it might well be true, if you get yourself killed."

"I won't, I promise," Sophia replied. She looked out of the carriage window. "It will be too dark to start when we get back."

"First thing tomorrow," Ramsay replied. "I'll see you're up early. You can join Bracken and me on our walk."

"I'll make breakfast while you walk," Sophia said. "That way we won't lose time."

Ramsay, smiling, agreed that would be best.

"When can we re-group to share our progress?" Alastair asked. "It's all right for you two, together in that cottage, I'm miles away at the other end of the lakes."

"My work will be mostly on the phone and in the local police station," Ramsay said. "I'll lunch at the regular café in Keswick and, if either of you have success to report, we can meet there and then."

With that agreed, and still hours left of their journey,

they settled down into a drowsy silence, watching the landscape flash by the window and lights appearing in the homes they passed.

IT WAS the early hours when Ramsay was able to phone Sergeant Hardraw, who wasn't pleased about being woken up.

"You said later," he grumbled, "not early."

"The train was held up by track repairs," Ramsay replied. "What did you learn?"

"That those two are as bent as it's possible to be," Sergeant Hardraw replied. "But in the end, we had to let them go. We don't have enough to hold them. You need to watch your step."

"I guessed that's how it would be," Ramsay agreed. "Still, I have a plan to get you some real reasons to jail them." He outlined the trap and waited to hear Sergeant Hardraw's response.

"You're mad," Sergeant Hardraw said. "Why would they attack you again? We've not been able to pin anything on them and, now that they know we're aware of the situation, it's too big a risk for them."

"So, you couldn't provide a couple of fit constables?" Ramsay asked.

"I'm not doing anything to aid this lunatic scheme," Hardraw replied. "In fact, I'm ordering you not to do anything so foolhardy."

Understanding he would get no help from the local police, Ramsay hung up.

"I'll invite Jimmy Logan," Ramsay told a bored Bracken, yawning at his feet. "He enjoys a good scrap."

27

SETTING A NEW TRAP

Sophia was as good as her word and by the time Ramsay and Bracken returned to the cottage from their morning stroll up Gummers How, not too badly burned bacon, eggs, toast, and baked beans were waiting. He washed his hands and sat down at the small, flimsy table the cottage was equipped with.

"You missed a wonderful morning," Ramsay said. "Blue sky and clear all the way to the coast. It's never been so lovely in the whole time we've been here."

"That's only a week," Sophia reminded him.

Looking at her carefully, Ramsay said, "Your disguise is good." He nodded appreciatively.

"I learned make-up in drama classes," Sophia replied. "They were the best thing about school. I could be almost anyone I wanted to be, if I had time."

"Astrid Jackson is enough," Ramsay said, smiling. "Where are you going to start?"

"While you're with your police pals, I'll reconnoiter Lakeland Lorries. Who knows, they just might be there.

After that, the guest house and, if they're not there, garages and lock ups for their van."

As he, his mother, and father ate breakfast, Alastair said, "I did some phoning around to get a sense of who locally might use our luxury cruises, dad."

"And?"

"The answer is not too many. Maybe once, if we have a grand opening event but not much beyond that," Alastair replied.

His father nodded. "I see it very much a seasonal service. When the expensive hotels are full, there'll be people looking for something different. When the season closes down, we'd close down the service too."

"I phoned about the boat," Alastair said. "I think they'll come down in price. It's been on the market all summer."

His father was thoughtful for a moment, then said, "Like I said, a hunch. There's no way of knowing if there's a good demand for high-end lake cruises and we have to lay out a lot of money on the boat before we'll know. What's your gut saying?"

"It says it's too early to tell," Alastair replied. "I want to hire a market research company to get a better feel for the demand."

"It'll be cheaper than fixing up that boat," his father said, chuckling.

Was his father toying with him? Stringing him along? Keeping his true intentions secret while Alastair chased down a false lead? As he had no answer to those questions, he decided he'd keep an open mind until his father made a move that would confirm the truth.

* * *

WITH THE DISHES WASHED, Ramsay and Sophia left the cottage for town. Ramsay parked in a car park off the main street where he hoped his car wouldn't stand out.

"Remember," Ramsay said, as Sophia hurried off, "if you see them, you come and get me. Don't do anything foolish."

"I won't," Sophia called back, but by now she was out of his hearing.

The Lakeland Lorries office was just opening when Sophia arrived at the front door, startling the receptionist who was wedging the outer door open. Sophia didn't bother with the social niceties. "I want a quote," she said. "I'm off to university soon, and I want to know how much it might cost." This story had worked for Alastair.

"Come in, dear," the woman replied. "The boss isn't here yet, but I can give you price lists. They'll give you some idea, and you can get a better quote when you know where you're going and how much of your things you want to take."

This was the first time she'd been inside the villain's lair, or so she considered Lakeland Lorries, and she quickly scanned the whole room, noting windows, entrances and exits, the position of filing cabinets, and the receptionist's desk.

"Will the boss be long?" Sophia asked as the woman handed her the sheet Sophia recognized was given to Alastair.

"It's hard to say, miss," the woman replied. "He often does small pickups or drop-offs on his way to work."

"Then I'll come back later," Sophia said. "I have some other companies to look at."

The woman laughed. "They'll be a lot dearer than we are. You'll see."

Sophia left the office, noting how expensive it was to send loads to southern cities where she might have wanted to go to university.

Folding the price list into her bag, Sophia hurried around to the back of the building where she hoped to see the boss arrive. Ramsay's earlier advice about the lack of hiding places in the back street returned to her forcefully as she rounded the corner. Looking around, Sophia saw a bench under a tree across the street. It looked directly down the back street. Crossing the road, she took up her station and settled down to watch.

By nine o'clock, she was hungry and mentally arguing with herself over leaving to get food or staying the course. Eventually, her imagination showed her a mental picture of Ramsay saying sternly, 'Do your duty, Sophia,' and that was enough to continue the watch.

By ten o'clock, she was starving and preparing to leave when a white van pulled into the farther end of the lane. From the front, she couldn't tell if it was the van she remembered, and the distance was too far to see who was driving. In a moment, the van turned into the Lakeland Lorries yard, and she saw the van as she remembered it that day when hiding in the bushes. She leapt to her feet and ran across the road and into the lane. As she approached the entranceway, she slowed to a walk. Forcing herself to breathe normally, Sophia strolled past the entrance and looked in. The taller of the two men was just closing the van door. Seeing her passing, his head swung to see who it was. For a moment, their eyes met, and Sophia almost panicked and ran. She held her nerve and walked on and out of his sight before running for the end of the street and busier places.

Turning the corner at the main street, she stopped and peeked back. No one was following her. Not daring to pass close to the Lakeland Lorries office door and window in case she was seen, Sophia crossed the street in the opposite direction and made her way to a bus stop where people were waiting. Moments later, a bus arrived. She got on it and was soon heading back into the town center, where she hoped she'd find Ramsay.

RAMSAY SPENT an unsatisfactory morning at the police station. They were still adamantly opposed to any suggestion of him walking slowly up a mountain track where murderers might be waiting to push him off.

"Mr. Ramsay," Sergeant Hardraw told him, "If you're killed because we couldn't get to you before they push you over the edge, we'll be crucified by the press and the public. And there's no way we could be close enough to save you. We'd be spotted immediately. And your would-be murderers would walk away instead of falling for your trap, leaving us explaining to our superiors why we had so many men out on a wild goose chase."

Wishing he had an 'Inspector Ramsay' to talk to, Ramsay left the station. He needed to go higher up. The local bobbies wouldn't risk their jobs, but an ambitious senior officer might take the chance.

It took three phone calls before he was able to speak to his old colleague, and the conversation was almost as frustrating as his earlier talk with the local police.

"Tom," Logan said, "you're no longer a policeman. You can't just phone up and ask us all to organize a trap for people you only suspect of doing anything wrong."

"I know it's them," Ramsay replied. "But I want whoever is behind it."

"I repeat, you're not a policeman," Logan said. "You can

suspect who you like, we have to have a reason for laying traps for people."

"I understand," Ramsay said, "and I'm not asking you to get involved. Just tell me if there are any of our old colleagues in the Cumberland force."

Logan sighed. "Give me an hour. I'll phone around."

Ramsay thanked him, gave him the phone number, and hung up. He now had time to kill and headed for their regular meeting café. It was too early for lunch, but a cup of tea and a sandwich would fill a space inside.

He'd just sat down to eat when Sophia burst through the door and rushed to his table.

"One of them is there now," she blurted out.

Ramsay looked about. No one seemed to be interested in her or her statement, but he thought it best to suggest she sit and tell him more, only quietly.

Sophia sat. "The tall one is at Lakeland Lorries. This could be the chance for you to set your trap."

Ramsay told her of the difficulties he'd encountered. "They're not willing to risk everything on an old copper's hunch," he ended his tale.

"Then we get other people," Sophia said. "They can be on the trail, see the attack, save you, and be the witnesses the police need to make an arrest."

Ramsay shook his head. "We don't know anyone who doesn't know you, and we can't have you recognized until we have this case solved."

"We'll have solved the case when we find a forged will that says what we think it does," Sophia said. "Though I still think it's just Hetherington. If not, it must be Cat. She'd be happy to see me gone."

"She did all this without your father's knowledge?" Ramsay asked.

"Why not?" Sophia replied. "After all, I knew the safe's code and where the key was. You can be sure Cat does too. She'll know what's at stake."

Ramsay gave this some thought. Were his feelings about his own children blinding him to the possibility of Sophia's parents being involved?

"If she thought her comfortable life, and the future wealth of her sons, was at stake," Sophia continued, "she might feel justified in getting my mother's money for her family."

"Not 'justified', I think," Ramsay replied. "Though she might act decisively to secure a better future for them where your father might dither."

"She's more the sly sort than the physical one," Sophia said. "You never know what she's thinking."

"It's just something we have to keep in mind as we proceed," Ramsay said. "After all, we don't want to find ourselves so focused on one that we're then stabbed in the back by the other."

Sophia laughed. "I'm not sure either of my parents is cut out for actual physical violence. I can almost imagine them hiring thugs to do their dirty work, but I think our backs are safe, if it is my parents."

"We've seen your mother's will," Ramsay said. "Your parents have the best motive. But Hetherington is the most likely villain. We must focus on getting one of those thugs to talk."

"Thumbscrews," Sophia said, laughing. "We should have them in our family dungeon."

Ramsay laughed. "Your years up here on the Border have rubbed off on you, I see. Let's go and put some cheese in our trap."

28

TRAP IS BAITED

THERE WAS nothing to see at the offices. They reconnoitered the back where Sophia saw the man entering, but the yard was empty of people. At the front, nothing could be seen from the road, so Ramsay went inside, ordering Sophia to stay out of the view of anyone looking from the window.

"I told them I'd be back," Sophia objected. "I can go in quite innocently."

"Your disguise is good, if it's just the owner inside," Ramsay said, "but Kennedy and Connery heard you often enough over the four days you were held. They may not recognize you by sight, but the moment you speak, he'd see it was you, Sophia, and not someone called Astrid."

Sophia fumed but, in her heart, she knew he was right. "All right," she said, reluctantly, and moved farther up the street where she was hidden by a tall privet hedge.

Ramsay stepped inside and greeted the receptionist brightly, "Good morning."

"Good morning," she replied. "Can I help you?"

"I'm moving and looking for prices on furniture removals," Ramsay replied. He kept his gaze on her as she rose from her desk to get a price list from a side table. From the corner of his eyes, however, he looked for others in the office. He saw no one, but heard two men talking in low voices in the next room.

The receptionist handed him the price list, and he studied it carefully to choose a destination he could claim was where he was going.

"I'm returning home," Ramsay said, grinning. "You probably guessed I'm a Scot."

"And where is home exactly?" the woman asked.

"Glasgow, but I've bought a house in Ayr, so I'm pleased to see your routes take you there," Ramsay said.

"Oh yes, we do a lot of work between here and Scotland," she replied. "I've been to Ayr, it's a lovely town."

As she spoke, Ramsay's ears were picking up the scraping sounds of chairs from the other room. The men were preparing to move. Would they come this way?

The office door opened, though no one emerged, as Ramsay was telling the receptionist the move wasn't for another month. He continued, "I mean to get in some last fell walking before I go and while the weather holds," Ramsay said to her. "I've been too busy in my time here, and I need to see the view from the tops before I go."

"The weather isn't supposed to be good later," the receptionist said. "I've just heard the forecast on the radio."

"What did it say about tomorrow?"

"Better," she said.

"Then I'll do Dodd Fell tomorrow," Ramsay said, loudly enough for the two men who were still in the office, and still in earnest discussion, to hear. "I'll start small," Ramsay added, his nerves jangling, urging him to leave.

"That's best," the woman said. "It's a nice walk, but you

know the trees the forestry people planted have all grown and the views aren't what they used to be."

"I didn't know that. Thanks, I'll take my lunch and sit somewhere there's still a view. I presume that's at the top?" Ramsay asked, adjusting himself to see if the men were listening. They certainly seemed to have paused at the door.

"Oh, there's more than one viewpoint," the woman replied. "You'll see when you get there. Now, is there anything else?"

"No," Ramsay said. "I've taken up too much of your time as it is. Thank you for this." He waved the price list and left as quickly as he dared.

Outside, he breathed a sigh of relief and set off to find Sophia.

"Inspector," Sophia's whispered voice came to him from the privet hedge.

"You spend a lot of time hiding in bushes," Ramsay said, chuckling.

"Only since I met you," Sophia responded tartly, stepping out and brushing herself down.

Sophia shook her head vigorously, and when leaves fell from her hair, ran her fingers through it, until she felt clean. "Was it them? Were they meeting the owner?"

Ramsay frowned. "Only one. I didn't see him, but I heard the voice, and I'm fairly sure it was the tall one."

"Did you bait the trap?"

"I think so," Ramsay said. "We won't know for certain until tomorrow morning."

"What if you can't get support?"

"Then I won't go," Ramsay said, grinning. "I want to bring these two to justice, but not at the cost of my life."

"When will you know?"

Ramsay looked at his watch. "About now. We should

return to the phone box and wait for my old colleague's call."

LOGAN HAD a name and phone number, which Ramsay dutifully wrote down while Logan told him he wouldn't get the help he needed.

"That would be a pity," Ramsay said. "I've laid the bait, and I think they understood."

"Look, Tom, this is stupid. You're retired now. Leave it to the police."

"I'm hoping that's what I will do when I speak to our ex-colleague," Ramsay replied.

"What time is this to take place?"

"I told them I'm walking up Dodd Fell tomorrow morning and plan to have my lunch at the top," Ramsay replied.

"This is still stupid, Tom," Logan said, "but I'll be there. Where can we meet and coordinate?"

Ramsay gave him directions. "We can talk tomorrow if you're here by eight o'clock. Oh, and bring walkie-talkies so we can keep in touch on the mountain."

It was agreed and Ramsay hung up, smiling. Jimmy may be from a posh place like Edinburgh, but he couldn't resist the chance of a fight.

"Well?" Sophia asked. She'd had her head inside the phone box and as close as she could get to the earpiece.

"He'll be here in the morning," Ramsay said, "and he's given me the number of another old colleague who works not too far away."

"Then phone him," Sophia demanded.

Ramsay laughed. "I'm going to. I just didn't want you to burst with curiosity while I did that." He turned back to the phone and dialed the number, entering the money when he heard the call picked up.

"Yes?"

"Hello, Mike," Ramsay said. "It's me, Tom Ramsay. Long time, no see."

Mike groaned. "I hoped when Jimmy called me, he was joking."

"No joke. I need the police's help," Ramsay said.

"You can't have it," Mike retorted. "We don't promote vigilantes taking the law into their own hands."

"Pity," Ramsay said. "Jimmy's in."

"Is that true?"

"You know me, Mike," Ramsay said indignantly. "I'm as honest as the day's long."

"I get the credit for the arrests?" Mike asked, suspiciously.

"What about Jimmy?" Ramsay said.

"It's not his patch," Mike said. "Up here he's just a civic-minded citizen."

"You drive a hard bargain, Mike, but I accept. Can you be here at eight o'clock tomorrow morning?"

"Where?"

Ramsay gave him directions and thanked him.

Mike laughed. "If this goes wrong, you'll wish we'd refused to help for about one last minute as you plummet down a thousand feet to the rocks below."

"Your confidence in us all gives me great confidence, Mike. See you tomorrow." He hung up.

"He's coming too?" Sophia said.

"He is," Ramsay replied. "We'll outnumber them. Now we just need them to make their move."

"What can I do?" Sophia asked.

"Have you a camera?"

"In my bedroom, yes," Sophia said.

"Then we'll buy you a new one," Ramsay replied. "Come on."

"What about Alastair?"

"I'm assuming he's in too," Ramsay said. "We'll ask him when he joins us."

Sophia looked at her watch. "We'd better get back to the café or he'll think we're adventuring without him."

"Maybe Alastair has a camera, and we don't need to buy one."

ALASTAIR, who'd been waiting impatiently for them to arrive at the café, didn't have a camera so, after a lunch of pie and mushy peas for Ramsay, Cumberland sausage and chips for Alastair, and a salad for Sophia, who stole most of Alastair's chips, they set off to find a shop that sold cameras.

As they walked, Alastair told them of his morning and his continuing doubts about his father. Ramsay agreed it was frustrating not to be able to finally eliminate his father from the inquiry.

"I think your dad's a good man who's giving you the chance you need to prove yourself," Sophia said. "I think the question of his innocence is settled."

"I wish I could be as sure," Alastair said, ruefully. "I hear him speaking and I see his face, everything says he's delighted I've finally begun taking up the reins. But at the back of my mind a small voice says, 'why didn't anyone else know about this' and then I can't believe him."

"There'll be a moment," Ramsay said, "when you finally know."

"I wrote and sent the first request for a price on market research this morning," Alastair said. "I'll do two more tomorrow. When dad sees how much they want for the work, I think I'll see him wriggling out."

Ramsay laughed. "Well, until that happens, we carry on and here we are at a shop that sells cameras. We need one we can easily use."

It wasn't quite as simple as Ramsay had imagined. Finding one that met with Sophia's approval tested Ramsay's patience, and he silently wished Alastair luck for their future life together. Finally, they had one that Sophia was comfortable using and looked nice, whatever that meant.

"Can you set it up to take good, clear photos at midday up on the fells?" Ramsay asked the man who was serving them.

He nodded and moved the aperture and speed settings to what he assured them were optimal settings for landscapes in the Lake District's uncertain sunshine and clouds.

"Thanks," Ramsay said, taking careful note of the dials so he could be sure they hadn't shifted by morning tomorrow. "And a new roll of film for the same conditions," he added.

With the camera bought, the three left the shop. "There's nothing more to do until the morning," Sophia said. "How are we going to fill the rest of today?"

"I'm taking a boat tour of the lake," Ramsay said. "I've been here two weeks and haven't done any sightseeing at all. You two are welcome to find something less sedate, if you prefer."

They assured him a boat ride was exactly what they wanted to do. "For me," Alastair added, it's valuable market research."

"And I can practice with the camera," Sophia said.

"There are only twenty-four shots, Astrid," Ramsay said,

"and I want you taking lots of photos of what happens tomorrow, so you use only six today. Do you hear? You may not have time to change the film once things get interesting."

Sophia nodded. "I won't, but, you know, all the years we've come up here I've never been on a boat tour."

"You've been on private boats though," Alastair pointed out.

"They never toured the lake," Sophia responded. "We drank and ate at the dock, then put out to go around that island," she pointed at Derwent Island, hardly a quarter of a mile away, "and came back. I'm not sure I've even been to the south end of the lake."

Ramsay paid for three tickets, and they waited in the fleeting sunshine for the boat to return from its present tour. The receptionist's forecast looked about right, Ramsay thought, eyeing the clouds with dismay. I hope there are enough indoor seats.

"What am I to do tomorrow?" Alastair asked Ramsay. "With you three experienced bruisers, I'm not likely to be needed."

"What if one of them does a runner?" Ramsay asked.

"I can do that," Alastair said, grinning.

"We'll let the skinny one slip away and you can tackle him," Ramsay teased Alastair.

Alastair nodded, still chuckling. "Kind of you."

"You should know Alastair is a local boxing champion," Sophia said, sensing Ramsay's disbelief. "Here and at University."

"Then you're a useful man to have along," Ramsay said, smiling at Sophia's swift defense of Alastair. "You'll get your chance, don't worry."

29

TRAP IS SPRUNG

MORNING BROUGHT JIMMY LOGAN, Mike Carstairs, and Alastair to the meeting place Ramsay had chosen, even before Ramsay and Sophia arrived.

"Well met," Ramsay said as he parked and exited his car. "Quite the old gang reunion."

"Less of the old, if you please," Jimmy said. "I'm in my prime, though I wish I could say the same of Mike. He looks ready to be put out to pasture like you, Tom."

Carstairs shook Ramsay's hand. "It's been a while, Tom. It's good to see you again, though I can't say the same for old Jimmy there. He's not the man I remember." He grinned at Logan, who cursed him in reply.

Ramsay introduced Sophia and Alastair to his ex-colleagues and explained his plan. "It's very simple," he said. "I walk up the track from the parking at the bottom of Dodd Fell and you three," pointing to the men, "lie in wait along the way. Sophia will have a radio and watch the path from the summit lookout point you'll see on the map. She'll radio you when she sees our villains."

"Do you know how to use one of these?" Jimmy asked Sophia, holding out a radio.

"No, but how hard can it be?" Sophia replied, taking it from him and examining the controls.

"We need to practice before we set off," Logan said. "It looks like a long trail. For us to be where they lie in wait and at the time they attack, we need to have that radio message."

"Study the map," Ramsay said, spreading it out on his car. "Here's the path I'll be taking; it's the most popular one. Easy going all the way to the top." He used his finger to trace the route on the map.

"Here's the path you will all take." He pointed to a thin dotted trail going more directly to the summit. "It goes from there," he pointed at a narrow entranceway at the edge of the wood, "and if you're all in prime shape like you say, you'll be well ahead of me and, moving through the woods, taking up places at strategic spots."

"What strategic spots, though?" Carstairs asked.

Ramsay pointed to places marked as lookouts along the trail he was to follow. "There are four, but one of them is much too early on the trail to suit their purpose. I think you can assume it's one of these three." He tapped the map to make his point.

"Where am I watching from?" Sophia asked.

Ramsay pointed to the end of the steeper trail and said, "Here. The trees haven't been planted this high on the fell, so you should be able to watch me from the parking place all the way along the trail."

Sophia nodded. "I need to be up there before any of this starts," she said. "They could be making their way to Dodd Fell right now."

Ramsay nodded in agreement. "Before you go, you four

practice using the radios for the next few minutes and then Bracken and I will head out to my starting point."

He watched as they spread out over the parking area. Once Sophia and Alastair seemed comfortable with the radios, Ramsay said, "I'm going. You four can continue practicing your radio skills as you're climbing, and Bracken and I are driving to the start of the trail."

"Good luck, Tom," Logan said. "Keep your wits about you up there." He nodded to the mountain that rose steeply behind him.

"I don't need luck," Ramsay said, grinning. "Not when I have you folks behind me and Bracken at my side. Good hunting, I say. Now go. And be quick."

Ramsay drove slowly to the regular trail parking, slung his rucksack with his lunch in it on his back, put a leash on Bracken, locked the car, and set out. As he walked, he noted the cars already parked. No white van, but that was too much to hope for. No one was sitting in any of the vehicles, which meant everyone was ahead of him on the path.

"I hope, Bracken," Ramsay said as they began the climb, "you have your best sniffing nose on today. Any warning you can give me could be the difference between life and death."

Bracken gave him a withering look that said his nose was always at its best and continued straining at the leash.

"We must walk slowly today, Bracken. Give our team time to get in place."

Bracken understood the word slowly and relaxed. It was a dull way to proceed, but at least they were outside and heading up to the tops again where grazing sheep and ravens wheeling in the sky whetted his appetite for the chase.

Ten minutes passed without incident. At this point, the path was closely pressed in by young trees and all that could be seen was the sky above and the trail ahead. Soon they passed out from under the trees and could see down into the long valley with Bassenthwaite and Derwentwater lakes, silvery pools in the distance.

"Now we need to be on our toes, Bracken," Ramsay said, moving to the edge of the path and looking down. "It's not so steep here, but it soon will be."

They walked on with the sun rising higher in the sky and its warmth beginning to be felt. "A good day for it," Ramsay said, and Bracken nodded in reply. Ramsay removed his jacket and stuffed it in his bag before giving Bracken some water and taking a sip himself.

They approached another forested area, which Ramsay scanned to see if there was life moving among the trees. He could see nothing and Bracken's interest in a sheep, who was eyeing them with suspicion, suggested he had no inkling of danger either.

"It will be higher up," Ramsay said, "if it's going to happen." They pressed on. Ramsay wondered if his colleagues had reached the ambush spots. He wished he had a radio, but that would have been a giveaway and he'd refused the one offered by Logan.

SOPHIA REACHED the summit out of breath from the fast pace she'd kept up; she didn't want to be the one who let them all down. Approaching the edge to survey the valley laid out before her, she saw figures below and stepped back. If the men saw her, they might recognize something about her or suspect she was watching. Then she realized she wasn't thinking straight. Anyone who reached a summit always stepped forward to see the view, including with binoculars.

Slipping the binoculars from their carrying case, Sophia

looked out. The lakes sparkled in the sunshine and boats were already out, sailing on the breeze. Casually, she swept the binoculars onto the trail, starting where she was standing and then following it down. There were people coming up, the usual hikers in shorts and boots, with large backpacks carrying their tents and cooking pots.

Finally, she saw Ramsay and Bracken, already higher up than she'd expected to see them. They were nearing the area where Ramsay had suggested he'd be attacked. She began scanning the lookouts and the trees surrounding them. There were too many leaves, and she couldn't see anyone, not even Alastair, Logan, or Carstairs. Her stomach sank. Were they still making their way through the woods?

Ramsay and Bracken disappeared among more trees as they approached the first lookout and Sophia held the binoculars, the radio, and her breath as she willed the binoculars to see through the leaves. When the two re-appeared, she saw them stop, lookout over the valley and lakes, and then walk on, disappearing once again among the trees. She heaved a sigh of relief.

BRACKEN TUGGED at the leash in his hurry to get on, while he and Ramsay passed through the next forested area and out again into the sunshine. Up ahead, Ramsay could see more trees and, he knew from the map, this was where the attack, if there was to be one, would likely take place. At this look-out, the slope down to the valley was precipitous, and there'd be no trees to save him.

"This is it, Bracken," he said as they entered the wooded area. "Get your nose ready."

Bracken looked at him as if to say, 'My nose is always ready, it's yours that doesn't work.'

After a brief stop to take in the view, they continued their walk.

ONE DOWN, two to go, Sophia thought, as she waited impatiently for them to come out of the trees and approach the next lookout. This was where Alastair should be waiting, and she couldn't help hoping nothing would occur here. It would be much better that an experienced man like Logan or Carstairs be the one to go to Ramsay's assistance. She felt immediately how disloyal that was when she knew Alastair was itching to prove himself.

RAMSAY TOOK A DEEP BREATH, squared his shoulders, before saying, "This is the big one, Bracken. This one has the deepest wood cover on the uphill side and the steepest drop on the downward side. If it's going to happen, this is the most likely spot."

Bracken ignored him. The scents of the wood promised a wealth of possible tasty meals and they were much more interesting than the faint tang of humans he was noticing.

They walked on, Ramsay consciously maintaining his stride to appear unaware. His eyes though scanned the trees for signs of movement. Nothing was obvious. Leaves were fluttering but only in the breeze, which was growing in intensity as his walk took him to a higher elevation.

They lost the sun as they entered the forest and were in shadow. Ramsay's senses were now buzzing with anticipation. He felt the trembling that always came on before an arrest that would likely involve violence. He saw that even Bracken was now more alert, his ears pricked up, his hackles rising, and his eyes swiftly scanning the trees along the left of the trail.

Bracken's increased alertness communicated itself to Ramsay, who was already awake to the possible danger. They walked on steadily, just a man and his dog out for a stroll. When Bracken began to growl, Ramsay whispered, "Quiet, Bracken."

Bracken quieted, but his hackles were now fully raised, and his nose was now overwhelmed by the scent of humans. Not one, more, and they were very near but not visible, which was alarming.

SOPHIA SCANNED THE SECOND LOOKOUT, frantically searching for movement among the trees. Finally, she saw it. A brief glimpse of something that wasn't the color of the forest. She pressed the radio button and said, "It's the second lookout. Get there—quickly."

BRACKEN GROWLED AGAIN. Not softly now, loudly.

Ramsay bent down and unclipped Bracken's leash. "Stay close, Bracken. I need you here." He was pleased to see Bracken stayed. Their time together, and the training Ramsay had been giving, wasn't always successful in guiding Bracken's actions.

Ramsay began drifting toward the edge of the trail now that he could see the lookout ahead. To draw them out, he wanted to be the best target he could be. His heart, though, had a mind of its own that didn't share his decision; it was thumping in his chest.

"Stay, Bracken," he whispered again as the dog looked

ready to hare off and confront whoever was among the trees. "It'll be soon. Then you go."

He'd hardly finished speaking when two men, with bala-clavas over their faces and lengths of pipe in their hand, leapt from the woods and rushed at him. Bracken sprang instantly into attack, racing across the narrowing distance between them.

Ramsay drew the police truncheon Logan had provided and advanced toward them as well. As he and the shorter man slammed their weapons together like knights of old, Ramsay saw Alastair emerge from the trees and sprint to his aid.

Ramsay gave a swift blow to the shorter one's head with the truncheon while the man's pipe crunched into Ramsay's left shoulder. Pain seared through him, and he was glad when his opponent collapsed at his feet, though still grasping at Ramsay's ankles to bring him down too. Ramsay struggled to disentangle himself but the tall one, with Bracken gripping his left wrist and Alastair hauling at his shoulder to turn him around, barged into Ramsay, sending them all into a sprawled heap on the prone body of the shorter man.

Giving up on his effort to make this about fair play, Alas-tair punched the man hard behind the ear and he, too, collapsed, down but not yet out.

Carstairs arrived and hauled the struggling man off Ramsay, twisting an arm behind the man's back and attaching a handcuff.

Ramsay breathed a sigh of relief, which wasn't easy with the weight on top of him. Bracken began licking his face and he laughed.

"I'm pleased for you too, Bracken, but I don't need a

wash. At least not right now," Ramsay said, stroking Bracken's head.

Alastair began helping Carstairs lift the man off Ramsay, who cried, "Wait. We need Sophia and the camera before we move anything." As he was speaking, Logan arrived, gasping for breath. He'd had the farthest to run.

"He's right, lad," Carstairs said. "I need crime scene photos to support my arrest of these two."

"She's on her way," Logan said. "The moment she saw it start, she radioed and said so."

When Sophia arrived, panting from her run, Carstairs guided her in taking the pictures that a crime scene photographer would take.

Ramsay lay still as the photos were taken and Bracken lay beside his head, only occasionally nuzzling and licking his face.

"I bet you don't have this in your usual photos, Mike," Ramsay said, grinning.

"I don't, but it's a helpful addition. We have an innocent man hiking with his lovable dog being violently attacked by thugs. No jury in England will let these two thugs go free when a dog is involved."

With all the photo film used up, Carstairs finished handcuffing Connery while Logan did the same for the slowly reviving Kennedy. As they did so, both men became fully aware of their situation and were unhappy to find themselves prisoners. They were even more unhappy to find their masks being removed.

"I'm Inspector Carstairs of the Cumberland Constabulary," Carstairs told them, "and you're both under arrest for assault."

"What are you talking about, man?" Connery said. "You people assaulted us. We were walking in the woods, came out onto the path and were attacked by a dog and then him," he gestured at Ramsay, "with a truncheon. We didn't do anything but defend ourselves."

"We have witnesses and photos," Carstairs replied. "Now, get walking."

"Where to?" Kennedy demanded to know.

"Keswick police station," Carstairs replied. "Where you'll be formally charged and held until we know what this was all about."

"I've just told you what it was about," Connery said. "We came out of the woods and the dog and its owner attacked us. Maybe they were frightened. I don't know why they did it, but that's what happened. It's them you should arrest."

"We know what it's about," Logan replied, picking up the lengths of pipe using his handkerchief to protect any finger-prints. "I'm Inspector Logan of Manchester Police, and we've been watching you and your friends for some time."

"We've done nothing, and you can't prove we did," Kennedy said. "Our lawyer will soon have us out."

"Our witness statements and the photos we have will put you two away for a very long time," Carstairs replied. "Get moving or we'll have half the world here, now that the day is warming up, and we don't need everyone becoming involved."

Ramsay walked behind the rest as they headed back down the trail. His shoulder hurt badly, and he still felt shaken by the ferocity of their attack. "Were they terrified of a gangster or were they being offered so much money they just wanted to be sure this time, Bracken?" he whispered to his solicitous companion who was carefully herding him to safety.

30

WHO IS BEHIND IT ALL?

AFTER GIVING his statement as an innocent fell walker attacked by two men who had attacked him before, Ramsay, Bracken, Sophia, and Alastair once again had lunch in the usual café.

"I'm going to miss this place when it's all over," Ramsay said, looking around at the room and customers. He even recognized regular customers now.

"Are you sure this time it's the end?" Sophia asked him. "I remember you saying something similar only days ago."

Ramsay smiled. "This time, the police have something serious to hold them with. Now it's up to Carstairs to discover who's behind all this."

"Would a mastermind tell them to kill you?" Alastair asked. "After all, the only offence originally was kidnapping without any harm done."

"Our mastermind, as you call them, is desperate enough to not be caught. They're willing to consider murdering others too," Ramsay replied. "Right from that first conversation I overheard, it was clear to me the person behind this is important and frightened to be exposed."

"Which doesn't narrow it down," Sophia said. "Alastair's parents, my parents, or London casino owners all fit that description."

"Only Hetherington doesn't fit the bill," Alastair added.

"Which is why Carstairs has to get something from those two," Ramsay replied.

"Sergeant Hardraw couldn't," Alastair reminded him.

"Sergeant Hardraw is an amiable man, very suited to policing a quiet, pleasant district like this," Ramsay said. "I doubt he has much experience of interrogating people on crimes of this kind."

"And Carstairs has?" Sophia asked.

"He used to be in the Newcastle city police," Ramsay said. "He knows how these people think and what will loosen their tongues. Usually, it's just the promise of a lighter sentence for information about accomplices."

"But won't the accomplices know who betrayed them?" Sophia asked.

"It's the prisoners' dilemma," Ramsay said. "Each one can't be sure the other isn't selling them out. To get the maximum advantage, each knows they must be first to speak. With real hard cases, or political cells, it doesn't always work, but with petty crooks like Connery and Kennedy who are acting way out of their league, it should."

"Have you arranged to speak with Carstairs later today?" Alastair asked.

Ramsay nodded. "I said I'd call mid-afternoon. That way, if Carstairs needs more from us, I can provide it."

"Didn't you tell him everything we know?" Sophia said.

"I think so," Ramsay replied. "We'll see."

"What do we do until then?" Alastair asked.

"Not a lot," Ramsay replied. "Maybe a walk along the side of the lake?"

"Boring," Sophia cried. "This morning has given me a taste for direct action."

"I was afraid of that," Ramsay said, laughing. "Here's an idea to consider. With those two in custody, why not visit each of your parents? Tell them about this morning and say the men are talking. Between the surprise at seeing you, Sophia, and the news the men are talking, it may make one or the other of our suspects give themselves away."

"Yes!" Sophia cried, triumphantly. "We'll do it."

"Do I get a say?" Alastair asked, smiling.

"Of course," Sophia replied, "provided you say yes. I need you there in case things turn ugly."

"Sophia's right," Ramsay said. "You must be there, though not to fight off any physical attacks. I don't see either of the two sets of parents turning violent. You're both victims of this crime, though in different ways."

"Hetherington might," Alastair said.

"He won't be there. This is just about our parents," Sophia replied. "I can't wait to see their reactions when I walk in. Will they even recognize me? My house first."

At the house, after introducing Ramsay, Sophia's reception was everything she'd hoped for. Her father was overjoyed at her safe return, hugging her to his chest, crushing the breath out of her. Cat smiled and coolly welcomed her home.

"Where have you been?" Fidel cried, holding her at arm's length to take her changed appearance in.

"Catching my kidnappers," Sophia replied.

"They're caught?" her father asked.

Ramsay thought it time to interject. "Yes, they're in custody. My colleague, Inspector Carstairs, has been interviewing them for the past hours. It seems they're talking, so we should soon get to the bottom of this strange affair."

"So long as you're safe," Fidel said to Sophia, "I don't care about the kidnappers."

"You may know them, dad," Sophia said. "They work for Lakeland Lorries."

"How should I know them?" Fidel asked.

Cat looked puzzled; something wasn't right. "Lakeland Lorries came to the house once," she said, at last.

"You're right," Fidel cried. "I used them a week or so ago to deliver some birds to the station. I'd forgotten. With everything that's happened..." He didn't finish the sentence.

"When was that, Mr. Thornton," Ramsay asked.

"I don't know off the top of my head," Fidel said slowly. "Do you remember, Cat?"

"It was a day or so after Sophia went missing," she replied, gazing intently at him.

"The Game Book will settle it," Fidel said, brusquely, "if it's important, Inspector."

Ramsay smiled. "It may be the men who came here are the men who kidnapped your daughter. Any information about their whereabouts is of interest to the police."

"Then I'd better get it," Fidel said, letting go of Sophia and heading out the door.

"Are you well, Sophia? You look well," Cat said.

"I'm very well," Sophia replied. "I escaped from them before they could do me any harm."

"I am glad," Cat replied, in her usual languid voice. "We were so worried."

As Sophia seemed about to reply in a fashion that wouldn't be helpful, Ramsay asked, "The day you saw the Lakeland Lorries men here, did you see them load the van?"

Cat shook her head. "I leave all that sort of thing to Fidel and the estate manager," she said. "Usually, Fidel does too." Again, a puzzled expression descended on her face.

"The Game Book will explain all," Ramsay said. "Perhaps the manager was busy, and your husband stepped in."

Cat nodded. "Probably," she said.

Fidel returned to the room with a large, bulky ledger open in his hands. "Yes, here it is. We'd had a successful day with the guns and had a really good number of birds to send to Randall's in London."

He showed Ramsay the entry, with the list of who shot how many and how many were released for sale to the restaurant.

"Could you identify the two drivers who came that evening if you saw them again?" Ramsay asked.

"Maybe, but it's unlikely. One doesn't look closely at servants or tradesmen," Fidel said.

"Very true, people don't," Ramsay said. "I hear that a lot in interviews. Fortunately, for the police, the servants and tradesman *do* remember." He smiled and noted the flicker of concern on Fidel's face.

"Daddy, Alastair has something he wants to ask you," Sophia said, discreetly pushing Alastair forward.

"Sophia and I have spent a lot of time together recently and it's reminded us how much we care for each other. I would like your approval before I ask for her hand in marriage," Alastair said.

Fidel looked blankly at him and then Sophia. "But...," he began, then stopped. He gave a broad smile and said, "You have my approval, of course. I've hoped for this day for some time now."

Sophia kissed him on the cheek. "I know what you're thinking. I was being my usual contrary self, but it isn't entirely true. As Alastair said, being together in this investigation has made us see each other even better than before."

She turned and smiled at Alastair, who shook his head, grinning.

Cat said, "You haven't seen Sophia in a new light, Alastair?"

"She's been the same bossy boots she's always been," he replied, grinning. "I suppose it's been on a grander scale, so maybe there's a little truth in it."

Sophia wrapped her arm around his. "I'm not bossy," she insisted. "I just know what needs doing when others are dithering. Now, we should go and tell your parents the good news before I fall out with you and call it all off."

Outside, Ramsay said, "Let me be the first to congratulate you both. I wish you'd told me you were going to do this. I probably looked stupid standing there staring in shock."

"Nobody was looking at you," Sophia said, airily. "We decided we had to ask now because, if daddy goes to prison, he might not be so accommodating."

Ramsay laughed. "That's true. How will your parents like it, Alastair?"

"That remains to be seen. I expect dad to be overjoyed that the Thornton estate will come into the family, after all."

ALASTAIR WAS RIGHT. His father's usually grave expression was gone, and his face beamed with pleasure the moment he heard the news. Alastair's mother, too, was overjoyed. "You can't know how long Alastair has loved you, Sophia, and I'm so happy to find you love him too. I thought he'd pine away until his dying day."

"Pine away?" Sophia cried, laughing and poking Alastair's torso. "You'll never convince me of that. I've been cooking for these two lately and I've never seen anyone eat as much."

"That was only because you were the cook," Alastair said, grinning.

"How is it you're out of hiding, Sophia?" Mr. Elliott asked, feeling the conversation could descend embarrassingly into a lover's talk if not diverted.

"Inspector Ramsay can best explain," Sophia said. "Inspector?"

Ramsay sketched out the events of the past weeks and concluded with, "And this morning the two kidnappers were arrested. Inspector Carstairs, who's in charge of the case, says they're cooperating, and he expects to know the name of who was behind it before the day is out."

"Good," Alastair's father said without a trace of concern. "It'll be some moneylender, you'll see." His expression remained as happy as it had been when he heard Alastair and Sophia were to marry. Nothing could spoil his delight that his hopes for his son had come true.

Ramsay, watching Alastair's parents closely, saw no guilt or fright in either of them. Whatever Alastair had overheard, it couldn't have been anything to do with Sophia's abduction.

"Not the time or place, dad, I know" Alastair said, seeing Ramsay's penetrating gaze on his father, "but I must tell you, I've asked for quotes from market research firms. I warn you; they won't be cheap."

His father nodded, grinning. "Thought you'd tell me when I was too happy to say no, eh?"

"Not at all," Alastair said. "I thought you should hear it from me rather than being surprised."

His father laughed. "It's your inheritance you're wasting if it goes wrong. You do what you think best to make it work for us. Now, I say the good news of your engagement warrants a celebratory drink. What are you all having?"

"I'd love to but must go," Ramsay said. "I have a meeting with Inspector Carstairs at two o'clock. You two can stay and celebrate, if you wish."

"Not a chance," Sophia said. "We're like the Three Musketeers, where you go, we go."

Alastair and Ramsay exchanged a swift amused glance before Ramsay said, "Then we should leave now or Carstairs will go back to work, and we'll be in the dark."

"Well?" Alastair demanded of Ramsay, when they were returning to Keswick in Ramsay's car. "You have experience of reading people so tell me, am I wrong? Is my father innocent?"

"He's a clever man," Ramsay said, "and wouldn't give himself away in front of a crowd..."

"So, you do think he's guilty?" Alastair cried.

"No," Ramsay replied. "I just don't think I can be certain on today's short meeting, particularly under the circumstances."

Alastair growled in frustration but said no more.

"For me," Sophia said, "it's Hetherington and the other two or it's Cat."

31

A COCKNEY ACCENT

CARSTAIRS MET them outside the police station as he and Ramsay had arranged. "We'll walk and talk," he told them. "But off the main street."

When they were away from the crowds, Carstairs said, "They say they never met the man who they were working for. He contacted them by phone."

"How did he know them?" Ramsay asked.

"They don't know. Kennedy said the man had a London accent, Cockney not posh," Carstairs replied.

"Which makes it even more unlikely," Ramsay noted. "How could a Londoner know of two petty crooks like these two?"

"They do transport goods to London," Alastair reminded him. "It's on their price list."

Ramsay nodded. "Still, it's strange."

"It may have been the other way around," Sophia said. "They may have been telling a story of the great ransom opportunity while they were down there. Showing off, you know. Word got to the right people, and they were contacted."

Ramsay laughed. "If it happened that way, I imagine they weren't too thrilled by it. I can see them boasting about it, but not doing it."

"There's a lot of money involved," Carstairs said.

"That lets my dad out," Sophia replied. "He hasn't got any, or so we're told."

Carstairs smiled. "What you call a lot of money isn't what people like Connery and Kennedy call a lot of money. Anyway, there's no saying they would ever be paid in full. After all, they don't know who it is, or so they say."

"Very trusting fellows, these two," Alastair added.

"They were paid half by a stranger, with a northern accent, not London, who showed up and handed them an envelope," Carstairs said. "They've never seen him since."

"Would a London casino owner have local people at his beck and call?" Ramsay mused.

"I thought of that," Carstairs replied, "but it could have been someone from the north living down there. After all, we're just off the main London to Glasgow rail line. If he took an early morning train, he'd be here before lunch, hand over the envelope, and be back in London by nightfall."

Ramsay noticed Sophia's puzzled expression. "What is it?" he asked.

"My father does a great Cockney accent. He was an actor before he went into producing."

"Was this on film?" Alastair asked. "We might get a copy from somewhere."

Sophia shook her head. "BBC radio drama. Would they keep their old shows, do you think?"

"Why not," Carstairs said. "They likely use them over again. We can ask. I'll phone them when I return to the office."

"Can you remember what one of the shows was?" Ramsay asked.

Sophia shook her head. "I was very young, and they weren't really for children. I only got to listen because dad was in it. One show was a detective series. I remember that."

"What year?" Carstairs demanded.

Sophia considered. "I'd be about six, I think, so around 1953."

"You really think it's your dad?" Alastair asked, concerned.

"I don't, but remembering how well he spoke Cockney gives me a funny feeling. But if the men don't recognize his voice," Sophia replied. "That will surely clear his name."

"Then here's hoping the BBC keeps these shows in their library," Ramsay said cheerfully. *The opposite of course would also be true. If the two recognize the voice as Fidel Thornton's, he's done for.*

"I'll phone immediately I get back," Carstairs said. "We may have an answer this evening."

"The Wheatsheaf at nine tonight?" Ramsay suggested. "You can buy me a whisky for all the work we've done for you."

Carstairs laughed and strode off back to the station.

"How can we find the casino owner, or owners, dad owes money to?" Sophia asked.

"We'll go and ask him," Ramsay said. "After all, this is information that's out on the grapevine. It's not something we could have only received from Alastair's dad."

AT THE THORNTON HOUSE, however, Fidel wasn't immediately available, Cat told them. He'd gone into town to run some errands for the farm.

"Maybe you could help us, Mrs. Thornton," Ramsay said in what he hoped was a supportive voice.

"If I can, but if it's business, I won't be able to," Cat replied.

"My colleague, Inspector Carstairs, says the men have told him the person who hired them to kidnap Sophia had a London Cockney accent. Now, we've heard from several sources you both have gambling debts. We wondered if he, or you, could tell us which casinos you frequented and how much you owe?"

Cat frowned. "They wouldn't come up here. Those people only feel safe in their own little warrens."

"They didn't come up here, Cat," Sophia said exasperatedly. "They put out a contract."

"I see," Cat said, slowly. "It's probably best you speak to Fidel. He won't like me sharing our dirty linen with others."

"Time is of the essence, Mrs. Thornton," Ramsay cajoled. "They've placed one contract that failed, who's to say they haven't another one already in place? Sophia may be in danger without any of us knowing it."

Cat considered in her slow, methodical way. "We only ever went to one casino," she said at last. "It's the *Blue Diamond* near Hatton Gardens."

"Thank you, Cat," Sophia said, before turning to Ramsay. "We need to get this to Carstairs right away. We may have the mastermind behind this at last."

"May I use your phone?" Ramsay asked Cat.

"Of course, there's one in Fidel's office, if you want some privacy."

"I'll show you," Sophia said, taking Ramsay's arm and marching him out of the room.

Carstairs wasn't entirely pleased at being interrupted during the interviews and said so.

"Sorry, Mike," Ramsay said, "but we have something new. Fidel and Cat Thornton owe money to a casino called the *Blue Diamond* in London. A lot of money, according to rumor."

"All right," Carstairs said. "I'll have it checked."

"What did the BBC say?" Ramsay asked quickly, for it seemed Carstairs was about to hang up.

"They're searching their library. Not having the right information is a problem. They index by title, episode, date and so on. Not by vague descriptions."

"Maybe we'll have more luck with the *Blue Diamond*," Ramsay replied. "See you later, when I hope you'll have lots of answers."

Ramsay returned to the drawing room and recounted his conversation, omitting the information about the search going on at the BBC. He needn't have bothered. Sophia went straight there.

"Cat," she said. "Do you remember the radio shows dad did in the old days?"

"Not really, why?"

"I was trying to tell Inspector Ramsay earlier, thinking he would know some of them but apparently he doesn't listen to the radio."

"I listen to their light music channel," Ramsay protested. "I'm not much of a fiction reader or listener. My work life was more exciting than anything they could dream up. I didn't need to be reminded."

"Sorry," Cat said. "It was early on in our marriage, and your dad was already producing movies by then."

Sophia nodded. "I suppose so. It meant more to me because it was my dad on the radio."

"When might your husband be back, Mrs. Thornton?"

Ramsay asked. The afternoon was slipping into evening. The shops would be closing now.

"I've no idea," Cat said. "He only told me what I told you. Some errands to run."

"Maybe we can catch him tomorrow," Ramsay said. "We should go."

Outside, he ordered them to get in the car quickly.

"Why?" Sophia demanded.

"I have a horrible feeling your papa may have taken a train out of town," Ramsay said. "We may have alarmed him before we meant to."

He drove quickly back into Keswick and straight to the station. There were no vehicles parked nearby that Sophia recognized as one from the estate.

"An express train wouldn't stop here," Alastair said. "They stop at Carlisle and Penrith."

"They're in opposite directions," Ramsay groaned, "and it will be over an hour to each from here."

"If he's gone, as you think," Sophia said, "we'd best alert the police at London or Glasgow."

"Where might he go from either?" Alastair asked.

"Heathrow airport at London or Prestwick near Glasgow," Ramsay said. "It depends where he thinks he'll be safe. America would be my guess. Prestwick doesn't have many flights, and not to the USA, but if he gets from there to Iceland or Denmark, he may find a transatlantic flight."

"Then it's probably London," Sophia said.

"Only the journey to London is long enough to allow any pursuers to be ready and waiting at the station. If it's Glasgow, he may well already be off the train," Ramsay said.

"We don't know he's on a train," Alastair reminded them. "He may be at home now, eating dinner."

"I'll phone," said Sophia, searching in her purse for coins. She ran to the station and found a call box.

She returned to the car minutes later with the news he wasn't home.

"I need to tell Carstairs," Ramsay said. "He's not going to be pleased with us if it is your dad and he's out of the country by now."

"Would he really flee the country over this?" Alastair asked. "It's not like its murder or high treason."

"Maybe he can't stand the thought of any time in jail," Ramsay said. "Or maybe the casino owner really is angry enough to make an example of him. Cooped up in a jail cell, he'd be a sitting duck."

"If we're going to tell Carstairs," Alastair said, "we should do it now. He can have police waiting at each end of the line."

Ramsay nodded unhappily. Sophia's expression was ghastly. The full horror of what might happen to her father if he was caught and imprisoned had come to her from Ramsay's words.

"We have to do it, Sophia," Alastair said, gently. "If it was him, and it looks like it was, he was going to kill you. That must be punished."

Sophia nodded, unable to speak. They climbed in Ramsay's car and drove the short distance to the police station in silence. Leaving his two assistants outside to console each other, Ramsay went inside and asked for his old colleague.

Ramsay was right. When told of the disaster that may be unfolding, Carstairs wasn't pleased. "If he's away and evades justice, it will be on your head, Tom. You should have known better than alerting him while our interrogations weren't complete."

"He was more forward looking than I gave any of them credit for," Ramsay admitted. "Nevertheless, if you get a message out quickly to all ports and airports, you should catch him. And what better proof than this attempt to escape?"

"We still have to prove it to a judge and jury," Carstairs growled.

"Did the BBC find any recordings?" Ramsay asked, changing the subject quickly.

"They did," Carstairs said. "It seems some of the recordings had a list of the actors involved, and he was easy to find. Two records are on the express, stopping in Carlisle after nine tonight. I'm having them brought here the moment they're dropped off."

"We might be able to listen to them after our meeting then," Ramsay said.

"I've had a record player brought into the station, so yes, we can."

"What about the *Blue Diamond's* owner?" Ramsay asked eagerly.

"He's East European and has a heavy accent," Carstairs replied, chuckling. "I spoke to him on the phone and could hardly understand a word he said. Doesn't mean he hasn't Cockneys working for him, of course."

"Then it does look like Sophia's father," Ramsay said sadly. "It's rotten news for her. How do you live with the knowledge your own father wanted you dead for the money?"

"It's rotten, but juries aren't always reliable. If he claims he tried hard to get her to marry so he could sell the estate," Carstairs said, "they might show him some sympathy."

"I'm not sure that will be much comfort to Sophia," Ramsay said.

"I'll get the call out," Carstairs said, "and we'll talk later."

"Right." Ramsay nodded. "Oh, by the way, you must congratulate my two assistants when we meet. It turns out they like bickering with each other and they're getting married after all."

Carstairs shook his head in disbelief. "All of this..." He broke off. Words failed him.

Ramsay nodded, wryly smiling, as he and Bracken left to rejoin Sophia and Alastair in the car.

32

RINGLEADER CAUGHT

NINE O'CLOCK that evening found the three musketeers, as Sophia had styled them, waiting impatiently in the pub when they saw Carstairs arrive. Ramsay waved him over to their table.

"You're late," Ramsay said, rising to his feet. "What'll you have?"

"A pint of bitter," Carstairs said, slumping into a chair. "It's been a long day."

"For all of us," Sophia said. "Now what's the news?"

Carstairs grinned. "I'm not saying anything until Tom's back from the bar. My throat's too dry from talking all day." He suddenly brightened and said, "I hear congratulations are in order."

Alastair and Sophia looked suitably pleased and agreed they were. "Luckily, we asked dad's permission before he took off," Sophia said. "I don't want to wait years to get on with my life."

Carstairs laughed. "There are other things to do in life."

"And we can do them just as easily together," Alastair replied. "Starting with getting Sophia's estate back in order."

"You're lucky to be starting out in life with an estate," Carstairs said, grinning. "Me and my missus lived in the flat above a chip shop for the first year. It was either that or move in with one of our parents."

"Here you are, Mike," Ramsay said, handing him a pint mug.

Carstairs drained half the mug in one draught. "I needed that," he said, placing the mug down on the table.

"Now, tell us," Sophia demanded.

"Are you sure you know what you're getting into?" Carstairs teased Alastair. Then turning serious, he continued, "We arrested your father at Liverpool when he tried to buy a ticket on a tramp steamer. One of those old ones that has little in the way of modern communications. It was a good thought on his part."

"And the recordings?" Alastair asked.

"On their way from Carlisle, even as we speak. That's why I was late. I wanted to hear they'd arrived."

"What if the men don't recognize my father's voice?" Sophia asked.

"They can hear him in person tomorrow, though maybe not with a Cockney accent," Carstairs replied.

"Will it be enough?" Alastair asked.

Carstairs grinned. "Oh, yes. Our two would-be murderers are happy to help the police with their enquiries if the charge is dropped to just 'forcible confinement.' Provided they recognize his voice, and are willing to swear to it, we'll have them all locked up before summer is out."

"What about Cat?" Sophia asked.

"Do you have any evidence to suggest she was involved?" Carstairs asked, looking from Sophia to Ramsay.

"Nothing beyond knowing she wouldn't turn a hair if she was involved," Sophia said grimly.

"We can only lock up people who've done something criminal," Carstairs said, chuckling. "Else the whole country would be in jail, including the police and judges. You'd be surprised how often we would like to lock up people we don't like."

Sophia nodded. "I suppose if all the money's gone, Cat will have to earn a living. That should be justice enough."

At closing time, they walked back to the police station to await the arrival of the records. When the records arrived and the first was being played, Sophia said, "That's my dad." She blinked rapidly to quell the tears forming in her eyes. "I used to say that with such pride," she whispered, almost to herself. "Now, with such pain."

Alastair put his arms around her. Carstairs removed the disc and replaced it in its protective sleeve. "That's all we need for tonight. We're all exhausted, let's call it a day."

Outside, the three took stock. "You can't drive back to the cottage at this time and this tired," Alastair said. "Come to our house. There are lots of rooms and beds."

"If your parents are happy with us being there," Ramsay said. "I'd be happy to stay here tonight. A lot is going to happen tomorrow morning when the two crooks hear the recordings and possibly get to see Fidel Thornton in custody."

"You think that will get them talking?" Sophia asked as Alastair went to find the nearest phone box.

"I do," Ramsay said. "If he's their paymaster and if he can't pay..."

Sophia considered this. "You know," she said, "I still hope there's another explanation. We still haven't ruled out Hetherington."

"Your father trying to escape suggests he's the one who ordered it, though he may have used Hetherington as a go-between, once he'd set up the plan. Tomorrow should answer all the remaining questions."

"My parents say they'd be delighted to have you stay," Alastair told them as he returned.

"Then what are we waiting for," Ramsay said, smiling and leading the way to his car.

Morning saw all three back at Keswick police station as Carstairs was arriving to work.

"Good morning," he said, shaking his head in disbelief. "Are you going to hang around here all day?"

"If we have to," Ramsay said. "Has Fidel Thornton arrived?"

"I'm told he has," Carstairs said. "I got a call at three in the morning."

"You're as determined to hear the truth as we are then," Sophia said. "That's good."

"My job is to elicit evidence, not find the truth," Carstairs said, grinning. "The truth of the matter is for a judge and jury to decide, based on the evidence they are given, and so far as anyone can discern 'truth.'"

"We'll be happy with an arrest, trial, and conviction," Ramsay said. "For now, we just want to hear what happens when you tell those people Thornton has been arrested and they see that it is so."

"I'm starting with the recordings first," Carstairs said. "Or I would if you people would let me get into the station."

Ramsay nodded. Sophia gestured him to go in. Alastair grinned at her regal dismissive gesture and Carstairs, catching his amusement, did the same.

By mid-morning, even Ramsay was losing patience. He felt his old colleague should have more consideration for his feelings. They'd only just decided to go to the café, when Carstairs emerged.

"Well?" all three demanded.

Carstairs laughed. "Well," he said, "it's been quite a morning. Kennedy, the one who was on the phone with the man who hired them, agreed the recording sounded like the voice on the phone giving them instructions, but he wouldn't go further than that."

"And his lawyer would advise him to stick with that line," Ramsay growled.

"That's his job, Tom," Carstairs said. "Or have you forgotten already?"

"I don't like lawyers," Ramsay said grimly.

"No one does," Carstairs said, "not even the people they defend. A bit like the police, really."

"Never mind all this," Alastair said, breaking into what looked like it was going to be a long tale of woe. "What happened next? You can't have spent nearly two hours on the recording."

Carstairs nodded. "We let Connery and Kennedy see Thornton in handcuffs. They pretended not to, but they recognized him, and Thornton recognized them."

"I thought they only spoke on the phone?" Sophia said, puzzled.

"Here's where it began to go wrong for your father, Sophia," Carstairs explained. "He didn't know by sight who he'd hired to abduct you. When he contracted Lakeland Lorries to do a shipment of birds to the station, he didn't know the two men who came to pick up the birds were the two he'd hired, but Kennedy recognized your dad's voice at once."

"Even though he wasn't using a Cockney accent?" Alastair asked.

Carstairs nodded. "You can change the words and the way you say them, but the voice remains much the same. Kennedy wasn't certain, but he was pretty sure he'd just spoken to the man on the phone."

"I assume they phoned Mr. Thornton when Sophia escaped," Ramsay said.

"They did, and after some bluster, got him to understand they knew who he was and unless he handed over more money, they'd do no more for him."

"And he paid?"

"Yes, the same way. A man gave them an envelope with the cash in it. They continued their search for Sophia—" Carstairs replied.

Ramsay interjected, "And for the man and his dog who'd helped Sophia escape."

"Exactly. They've made statements, and we've charged your father for his part in the abduction, Sophia. I'm sorry, this must be hard on you."

"At this point, I think I'm numb to it all," Sophia said.

"What about Hetherington?" Alastair asked.

Carstairs shook his head. "He was probably hired to help on the estate especially for the kidnapping and murder, but he was only the go-between. Maybe your father had heard of him somehow or maybe Hetherington's past came up during the hiring process. We haven't all those small details clear yet."

"Good. If he's in prison I won't have to fire him," Sophia said, "but I will fire the estate manager who hired him. They both felt like crooks to me."

"Can we tell the two families any of this?" Ramsay asked. "I think they should be told as soon as possible. Thornton's fame will have someone leaking the news to the press if it hasn't already happened."

"I was about to ask," Carstairs said. "Maybe Sophia and Alastair could gather their remaining family members in one place and you and I, Tom, could give them the news. Today, preferably."

"I'll phone my parents now," Alastair said. "Maybe they could hold the meeting at our house."

"You'll never get Cat to leave her couch for something as trivial, in her mind, as this. It will be best if we do it at my house," Sophia said determinedly.

"All right," Alastair said. "You phone your step mum and get the times she's willing to have us there."

Carstairs led Sophia into the police station and found her a phone that had some privacy. Cat, it seemed, wasn't going anywhere today, so anytime would work for her.

Alastair's father was out and wouldn't be back until lunchtime, but his mother was happy to give two o'clock as the time. She'd have her husband there whatever his afternoon plans were.

"Then we're free to enjoy some more of these last few days of summer," Ramsay said. "I'm starting with a cup of tea. Will you two join me or have you plans to make?"

"We have lots of plans to make," Sophia said, "though I have most of them already thought out."

She glanced at Alastair, who said, "We can't leave the inspector sitting alone until two."

"Don't mind me," Ramsay said. "Bracken and I will enjoy a stroll after a snack. I thought maybe Friars Crag."

"Alastair's right though," Sophia said. "We're Musketeers and we stick together to the end."

"The end will be some weeks away at the trial," Ramsay replied. "Today is just the beginning of the end, as someone famous said."

They descended on the café and ordered their usual

snacks. When the food and tea arrived and was poured, Ramsay raised his cup and proposed a toast.

"To us, the new Three Musketeers and their faithful companion, Bracken."

"To us and Bracken," the others repeated.

Hearing his name mentioned so often, Bracken grinned from ear to ear.

"It's like the nursery rhyme," Sophia said. "*The little dog laughed to see such fun.*"

Alastair smiled with the others. He said nothing but, in his mind, he finished the rhyme, '*and the dish ran away with the spoon.*'

33

EXPLANATIONS

WHEN THE ELLIOTTS and Cat Thornton were assembled at the Thornton house, Carstairs walked them through the recent events. After Carstairs finished, Ramsay described how the 'musketeers' had helped solve the riddle.

"But how did you know about the will?" Cat asked.

"I didn't," Ramsay said, smiling, "but there being something important that was hidden from us was the only thing that made sense. And the most likely 'thing' that would be was a will. And that meant Sophia's mother's will, for no one else in this domestic drama was dead."

"Couldn't Sophia have told you?"

"I didn't know," Sophia said. "My not-so-loving father never told me. I think he must have been planning my death from the moment mum died. It isn't a happy thought."

The others looked at her with expressions ranging from incredulity to sorrow.

Cat shook her head. "That can't be true. He's had years of opportunities, if that's what he had in mind."

Ramsay coughed, discreetly. "I think we can assume he

started planning Sophia's death when the studio cancelled his contract earlier this year."

"I suppose," Cat said. "But lots of people lose their jobs and don't start planning murder. Why do you think Fidel did?"

"When we did a background check on your husband," Carstairs said, "we discovered he'd assaulted the head of the studio when they told him he was out. Police were called. The studio didn't want to press charges, but it's in the police records."

"Still, it's a bit drastic," Sophia said. "Killing your own daughter for her inheritance, I mean. Why not look for another job? That's what other people do."

"He *has* been looking," Cat protested. "Being fired at one studio makes others wary of hiring you. You don't need too many flops before you're out in the cold."

"Another thing the police learned was that your father owed money to some very unpleasant people. He became convinced, and I'm sure with good reason, they would have hurt him badly, or hurt his family if he didn't pay off his debts."

"So, he decided, if anyone was going to hurt his family, it might as well be him?" Sophia asked, skepticism in her voice.

"He probably reasoned that losing a daughter from a previous marriage advantageously would be better than losing his sons and wife from the present family," Ramsay replied. "I think he was just too scared to think straight."

"Charming man, my father," Sophia said. "I'm pleased he's going to prison and won't bother me for many years."

"Understandably," Ramsay replied.

"Sophia, dear," Cat said, her voice laced with sarcasm. "If

you'd agreed to marry Alastair, as we all could see you wanted to, none of this would have happened."

"Well," Carstairs said, stepping bravely into the middle of the explosion about to happen, "I think I should be getting back to the station. You may want to discuss the future without having a police officer as a referee." He nodded to all, shook Cat's hand, thanking her for being host to this sad event, and quickly left the room.

"I'm also an interloper," Ramsay said. "Everything you need to talk about from here on is family business."

"Cat is not my family," Sophia said, "and this house will be mine on the day I marry." She glared at Cat, willing her to argue.

Cat smiled her sly feline smile. "Have no fear, Sophia. We'll be gone long before it's officially yours. In fact, I'll be gone by next week. I hate it here. It's cold, wet, and gloomy. There's nothing to do unless you like killing things. The boys and I won't miss you or your house." She rose and stalked out of the room without looking back.

"That's the end of the sad story, Soph," Alastair said as Cat closed the door behind her. "From now on it will be all happiness."

"And we won't squabble ever again?" Sophia asked, grinning.

Alastair smiled. "I wouldn't go that far; you know how you like to quarrel."

Sophia cried, "Me? It's you..."

"We should toast your happiness, Sophia and Alastair," Ramsay said, interjecting quickly. "I think you'll get along famously together."

34

RAMSAY AWAKENING TO LIFE

BRACKEN LAY in front of the glowing coal embers while Ramsay read the morning paper in his own Newcastle home. Now it was October, wet, cold, overcast, and consequently dark, even in this early morning, and he'd almost forgotten the summer and The Lakes. Reading the outcome of the trial in the newspaper brought it all back to him. The fells, the investigation, the musketeers, and the capture of the criminals. Now Thornton, Hetherington, Kennedy, and Connery were all convicted, and Thornton most heavily sentenced of the four.

"Serves him right, Bracken," Ramsay said. "And the judge recommended no parole, which is even better."

Bracken looked up but as none of this mentioned food or a walk, he settled back down with a sigh.

"And Saturday is the wedding," Ramsay said, closing the paper, "which means you have to have a bath, Bracken."

Bracken jumped to his feet and set off for the door.

"Not right now," Ramsay called. "Later, after our afternoon walk." He looked out of the window and his face fell. "We might both need one to warm ourselves after that."

The wedding was to be an intimate, family and friends only service in Keswick Church. Ramsay didn't want to go into a church, but it was Sophia's big day, and he couldn't refuse when he'd been so pointedly invited.

"We might stay overnight, Bracken," Ramsay said. "If it's fine weather the next day we could climb Coniston, like I said we would but never got there."

That sounded more interesting, Bracken thought, and returned to the fireplace to dream of sheep and ravens and the wild moors.

Ramsay lapsed into silence. The house too was silent, so quiet he could hear the ticking of the grandfather clock in the hall. '*My grandfather's clock was too big for the shelf, so it stood ninety years on the floor.*' Ramsay murmured the old lyrics to himself. He paused. Without his police colleagues, he was like that clock, standing alone, aloof, taking no part in the world around him, watching it all pass by. He shook himself. If this case had taught him anything, it was time for him to join in. The world was changing, and his new friends were moving forward with it, now he must too.

* * *

PLEASE LEAVE A REVIEW HERE: https://www.amazon.com/review/create-review/error?ie=UTF8&channel=glance-detail&asin=BoCG3YYiNT

Just one or two sentences will suffice. We 'indie authors' really need reviews.

* * *

AND PLEASE BUY the next book in the series: Ramsay and the Smuggling Ring

EXCERPT FROM NEXT BOOK IN THE SERIES

Chapter 1: North Riding of Yorkshire, England, October 1964

It was a brisk October morning, a clear sky for once, a stiff breeze blowing in from the sea where white crests topped each wave crashing on the beach. Standing at the foot of Robin Hood's Bay's main street, retired Inspector Ramsay and his dog Bracken watched fishing boats out in the bay rising and falling as yard high waves rolled under them.

"I'm glad I'm not a fisherman," Ramsay said to Bracken who was seated beside him, the cobblestones cold and damp beneath his behind.

"The tides on its way out and the day looks fine," Ramsay said, "we'll walk to Ravenscar over there," he pointed at the Raven Hall Hotel atop the 600-feet cliffs that rose from the scar, the flat rocks that ran out from the base of the cliffs into the sea, about two or three miles away, "and we'll climb the cliffs, there's a path it says in the guide book, and have our lunch in the hotel. What do you say, Bracken."

Bracken didn't like getting sand in his paws, was afraid of

the sea and those crashing waves, and his expression in answer to Ramsay's question said so, as clearly as if he'd spoken.

"It'll be fine," Ramsay said, correctly interpreting his young dog's opinion. "You'll enjoy it, you'll see." He stepped off the cobbles and onto the flat rock and then onto the sandy beach.

Bracken dragged along behind, thoroughly disgusted until a seagull sheltering from the wind on a boulder at the foot of the cliff caught his eye. Barking, he ran at the gull who rose, shrieking obscenities, presumably, and perched on a ledge higher up the cliff, well out of Bracken's reach.

Smiling, Bracken trotted back to join Ramsay only to see drumlins scooting along the shore searching for food. He raced across the sand, scattering the birds into flight. Panting he trotted back to Ramsay who said, "I told you it would be fine." Bracken ignored this and kept his eyes scanning the beach for more dangerous birds who might harm Ramsay.

"Even the wind's dropping," Ramsay said, "and the sun feels warmer. What a day to be alive. Autumn really is the best season."

Above the cliffs, trees and bushes had taken on their yellow and gold coloring, the sky was blue, except for a band of dark cloud appearing from the west, the sea was deep blue with sparkling white crests and Ramsay's heart lifted with the joy of being alive.

"No more putting ourselves in danger," he told Bracken, whose puzzled expression rightly reprimanded Ramsay. "You're right," Ramsay said. "None of it was your idea."

A sharp squall of rain pattered on them, and Ramsay looked again at the bank of cloud now covering half the sky. He looked back at Robin Hood's Bay and then forward to

Ravenscar and frowned. They were both equally distant, only the climb up the cliffs at Ravenscar on wet rocks, mud and grass would be slow and dangerous.

"We should turn back," Ramsay told Bracken. The squall returned with even more force this time and a blustery wind drove it sideways into his face. Ramsay stopped and unslung his rucksack from his back, he'd bought it especially for this trip despite being so dismissive of all those backpacked hikers he'd seen in the Lake District. From the bag he pulled out waterproof leggings, jacket and hat, all in a shocking yellow hue. When he had those on, the rain was now steady, and Bracken was pressing against his leg for comfort. Ramsay pulled out the jacket he'd bought for Bracken and tried to put it on him. Bracken was having none of this, whether it was the matching yellow he disapproved of or just the discomfort of its elastic straps around he legs, Ramsay didn't know but it was like dressing a baby who didn't like clothes. A momentary mental image of his dressing his first born, when he had no idea what to do, sent a painful jolt through him that had him gasping for air. He persevered and finally Bracken and waterproof coat were joined in a grudging acceptance.

Now torrents of rain were blocking out the view of the beach to the north and south and the waves were once again growing, they thundered on the beach making Bracken start and shudder in growing alarm.

"There's a rock overhang," Ramsay said, pointing to the low cliffs at the top of the beach, "we'll shelter under that until this passes. Rain like this never lasts too long."

The rock overhang gave some shelter, but the blustery wind swirled plenty of rain in on them. Ramsay looked about and saw a narrow vertical crevice in the rock nearby. He edged slowly to it, trying to keep under the shelter, and peered through the gap. It was too small for either of them to get through but there was a cave behind it. He looked at the crevice in puzzlement. It wasn't a natural break in the rock; it looked more like a door.

Ramsay slid his fingers inside and investigated. It was a door. He pulled at it; the door opened further until the gap was wide enough for him to slip sideways through. Inside smelled bad and he put his handkerchief over his nose and mouth.

"Come in here, Bracken," Ramsay said, signaling Bracken to join him.

Bracken shook his head and backed away.

"Come on," Ramsay urged. "The smell will clear now the door is open." He pushed to make the gap even wider. It was heavy and the hinges stiff. "All this salt air has rusted them," Ramsay grumbled to himself, and he put all his weight to the door, and it finally swung fully open. "Now, it will be better," Ramsay told Bracken who stayed where he was, shivering.

MORE BOOKS BY THE AUTHOR

On Amazon, my books can be found at the

One Man and His Dog Cozy Mysteries page

And

Miss Riddell Cozy Mysteries series page.

And for someone who likes listening to books, *In the Beginning, There Was a Murder* is now available as an audiobook on Amazon and here on Audible and many others, including:

Kobo, Chirp, Audiobooks, Scribd, Bingebooks, Apple, StoryTel

You can find even more books here:

P.C. James Author Page: https://www.amazon.com/P.-C.-James/e/B08VTN7Z8Y

P.C. James & Kathryn Mykel: Duchess Series

P.C. James & Kathryn Mykel: Sassy Senior Sleuths Series.

Paul James Author Page: https://www.amazon.com/-/e/B01DFGG2U2

GoodReads: https://www.amazon.com/P.-C.-James/e/B08VTN7Z8Y

And for something completely different, my books by Paul James at: https://www.amazon.com/-/e/B01DFGG2U2

ABOUT THE AUTHOR

I've always loved mysteries, especially those involving Agatha Christie's Miss Marple. Perhaps because Miss Marple reminds me of my aunts when I was growing up. Having written ten Miss Riddell books growing her career as an amateur sleuth, I thought it time to tell my readers what happened to Miss Riddell's earliest helper, Inspector Ramsay.

However, this is my Bio, not Miss Riddell's or Inspector Ramsay's, so here goes with all you need to know about me: After retiring, I became a writer and when I'm not feverishly typing on my laptop, you'll find me running, cycling, walking, and taking wildlife photos wherever and whenever I can.

Both my cozy mystery series begin in northern England because that was my home growing up and that's also the home of so many great cozy mysteries. However, the series will travel throughout England, Scotland, and Wales, anywhere mysteries might occur.

Printed in Great Britain
by Amazon

42385250R00158